A MUSICLAND MYSTERY

DANCING WITH DEATH

DOLLY OGAWA-AMSK

KP PUBLISHING COMPANY

ISBN: 978-1-960001-25-2 (Paperback)
ISBN: 978-1-960001-26-9 (Ebook)

Library of Congress Control Number: Pending

Editor: Allyn Amsk
Cover Design: Osakwe Eseohe Gift
Interior Designer: Jennifer Houle
Literary Director: Sandra Slayton James

Published by:

KP Publishing Company
Publisher of Fiction, Nonfiction & Children's Books
www.kp-pub.com

Printed in the United States of America

DEDICATION

I would like to dedicate the book:
To love and the power it has in our lives.

CONTENTS

CHAPTER ONE: Coffee After Work — 1

CHAPTER TWO: Forever Changed — 17

CHAPTER THREE: Saturday, the Next Day — 20

CHAPTER FOUR: A Strange Evening — 37

CHAPTER FIVE: Sunday — 45

CHAPTER SIX: Psychics and a Warning — 59

CHAPTER SEVEN: The Accident — 64

CHAPTER EIGHT: Men Are Like Buses — 73

CHAPTER NINE: Sex and Money — 83

CHAPTER TEN: Engaged — 87

CHAPTER ELEVEN: Working Things Out — 96

CHAPTER TWELVE: Things Are Not Working Out — 100

CHAPTER THIRTEEN: Monday — 105

CHAPTER FOURTEEN: The Séance — 108

CHAPTER FIFTEEN: Bad News — 117

CHAPTER SIXTEEN: Sam Enters the Hospital — 131

CHAPTER SEVENTEEN: BAD BOYS — 139

CHAPTER EIGHTEEN: Who's Counting? — 146

CHAPTER NINETEEN: The Getaway — 157

CHAPTER TWENTY: Visiting Sam — 162

CHAPTER TWENTY-ONE: George, Mei Ling, and Everything   168

CHAPTER TWENTY-TWO: Over the Edge   182

CHAPTER TWENTY-THREE: Sam's Goodbye   188

CHAPTER TWENTY-FOUR: Ready or Not   196

CHAPTER TWENTY-FIVE: Break In   210

CHAPTER TWENTY-SIX: Do Something!   216

CHAPTER TWENTY-SEVEN: Final Farewells and New Beginnings   224

CHAPTER TWENTY-EIGHT: Moving On   230

CHAPTER ONE

COFFEE AFTER WORK

The uneasy feeling that engulfed me while I was driving to work that night wouldn't let go. I just couldn't shake it. Usually, Friday is a good night. It's the first day of the weekend and it was early. Even so, I knew that I was facing a situation that was going to be hard, and at least uncomfortable, to deal with. I was expecting something unpleasant, but who knew it would be murder?

Things began to unravel at Musicland that Friday night, when I got to the cashier's desk where Big Louie, the Latino bouncer and assistant manager, and one of the good guys, was checking everyone in, just as I got there. He stood over six foot and weighed in over 300 pounds with a heart even bigger than he was. Still, with few exceptions, no one wanted to give him a bad time. It was a well-known fact that he could take care of business, I mean kick ass, if he had to.

As I looked around the room, I didn't see Stan lurking anywhere. He was a regular and usually in early. In a moment of weakness, I had agreed to have coffee with him after work that night. Against my better judgment, I had given in to pressure when he insisted. After a week of regretting that decision, I wanted to cancel, but he was nowhere around to confront him with my change of plans.

Big Louie, handed his clipboard to our cashier, Rosie, as soon as he saw me, and before I could sign in. He motioned me over to the nearest corner of the almost empty, snack bar. Whatever was on his mind, it looked like he wanted some privacy while he informed me. It looked serious.

"What's up, Sweetie?" I saw that he looked concerned. He was the closest thing I ever had to a brother.

He put his hand on my shoulder. I knew that it had to be bad.

"Frankie, before somebody else tells you," He took a breath, "you need to know that Stan has been arrested. You know who I mean. He's that customer, that weird little guy that comes in early?"

"Wow! You're kidding, right?" The words flooded out as I processed what I heard him say and, the fact is, I believed him. "Why? What's it about?"

I wasn't ready for the next part.

"It's worse than you can imagine. They found a girl in the trunk of his car. His parents turned him in when they smelled something. From what I heard; she'd been dead a couple of days." He put his arm around my shoulder.

"Oh my god! Who was it? Who did they find?" I wanted to sit down. I had a physical reaction from my whole body. The tears welled up in my eyes. "Was she anyone we know?"

"They haven't identified her yet. When they do, I'll let you know first. I wanted you to hear it from me. I heard a rumor that you were going to have coffee with him. I won't tell anyone, but I want you to be careful." He patted my shoulder. "Go sign in and take care. Okay?"

Without saying anything more, I finished clocking in. I didn't want to dance, and I didn't want to talk to anyone. I felt shaky and scared inside. It was like the time my brakes locked on the freeway and I narrowly missed being slammed into by an 18-wheeler. I took a deep breath and squared my shoulders for whatever else the night ahead would have to offer.

"Get your ass on the line, Hollywood. What are you waiting for, a bus? In five minutes, I call tickets." Tony, the manager, our very own Elvis, impersonator, was right behind me. "If you're not checked in, and on that line, I'm docking your check, Miss." He not only dressed like his hero, but he also attempted to sing like him, thinking that it would help coax the girls into his bed. I had noticed his guitar, so I knew he was planning on entertaining us after work whether we liked it or not. He was an older than Elvis, no-talent paunchy, middle-aged bully, and someday I'll tell you what I really think about him.

"Hollywood," was a nickname that some of the other girls and a few customers called me. I hated it when Tony did, but I let it go. Even as a redhead, I was famous for my even temper. "It's always a pleasure to hear your voice and see your welcoming face," I said.

"Cut the crap and get over there with the rest of those lazy broads." He motioned to the line where some of the girls were beginning to take up, what we all hoped would be a temporary pose designed to entice some of the potential customers milling around the snack bar, and bullpen.

Tonight, Tony reminded me of a snarling dog.

"Delighted to, darling. You know that I'd do anything to make you happy." I blinked my eyelashes, crossing my eyes as he turned his back to me. I watched him as he wandered away to harass some other hapless employee. My eyes were the most Asian thing about me, and the biggest legacy of my Japanese mother.

Anyway, sarcasm was wasted on Tony. He was as he was. That night he was in a white Elvis leisure suit, tight in the middle and tastefully trimmed in gold sequins. His sideburns had needed to be trimmed or they might soon be mistaken for a beard. I wondered then what the King would think if he could see this imitation of his distinctive style.

I'm not so sure he would have been flattered.

There were other early customers, milling around. Several were stoking their courage with coffee at the snack bar, as the dancehall didn't sell booze. Others were in the bullpen watching the few dancers on the floor. The jukebox was playing, "Monday, Monday," and the glass ball in the ceiling was turning, sprinkling shards of light over the dancers on the floor and those at tables.

My friend, Annie Fannie, was out on the floor. She was in a corner, grinding and chewing gum in syncopated rhythm with the music. The technique required her to rub her pelvic bones against the customer's nether parts, which many seemed to enjoy. Some of the details escape me. I never learned to grind. In fact, I had an aversion that was totally physical. I had to admit that those who mastered the technique were assured of a steady income with or without regular customers. I overheard one of the guys refer to it as "a dry fuck."

Nice.

My name is Frankie Hollingsworth, and some people call me "Hollywood." As an aspiring actress, and I was working, in the summer of '67, at a taxi dancehall called Musicland. It was a good way to pay the rent while I waited to be discovered in the time-honored, traditional way of most Hollywood hopefuls. My shifts were from 8 p.m. to 2 a.m., which worked out great because I have the whole day for auditions and casting calls.

Musicland was located in downtown L.A., and it served no liquor, but according to the billboard over the entrance, one hundred beautiful girls were available to dance with for cash. It also had music, a seedy atmosphere reminiscent of the 1930s, and customers, including Stan, who was, before now, a regular you could set your watch by.

The taxi dancehall had a long and somewhat colorful history, including the Zoot Suit wars of WWII. The war had been between civilian hipsters, sporting Zoot Suits, and some service men. It started inside of Musicland and more than twenty-five years later, it was still a topic of conversation amongst some of the older customers given to sentimental reflections regarding the good old days.

This job was perfect for someone trying to break into the movie business who needed to pay the bills. I'd done some small bits with an actual small speaking part in a commercial. Though it was nothing spectacular, things seemed to be going in my direction, according to my always hopeful agent.

After talking to Big Louie, the hairs on my arms were still erect. I felt a chill and shuddered. It felt like what my Aunt Hilda used to call "someone walking over my grave," and it made me ill.

I didn't want to talk to anyone else. I later learned all the details about how she died. Customers and the girls working there were exchanging and mixing facts and rumors all evening.

Even later my hands were shaking enough to spill my tea.

The most chilling thought was that it could so easily have been me. I couldn't understand my fear. Why was I so terrified? I knew I was being irrational. After all, he had been caught. They knew who had murdered her and he was in jail. Wasn't that the end of it?

I had a hard time convincing myself that I was safe. It had been a close one. I couldn't get over imagining that it could have been me that was found in the trunk of his car.

The evening was young, but the momentum had begun. The mirrored ball hanging from the ceiling was turning, sparkling over the dancing couples, glittering off the sequins worn by some of the girls. The Musicland dancers were reflected in the mirrors that covered three of the walls. The fourth wall displayed a flaking tacky mural that had been there since the early 1930s. Painted hula girls with grass skirts danced in front of a few palm trees; behind the bandstand.

A few years ago, management had a dispute with the musician's union, and now the bandstand was empty unless Tony decided to treat us to his version of an Elvis tune. The music to dance by came by way of a jukebox on the side of the room.

Before that night, no one even knew Stan's last name. I found out that night that it was Purdy, Stan, or Stanley Purdy. He was a small, skinny, blond, guy with nervous twitchy habits. He once told me that he was an actor too, but I wasn't impressed. He joked about doing pornos, but I didn't believe him for one minute. He wasn't ugly, but there was something sleazy and furtive about him. He reminded me of an animal, maybe a ferret, or a weasel.

For a while he'd been coming in to dance and talk with me, for at least four days a week. Stan always came in early, when the management paid us double tickets for the first half hour. Also, he gave me his door tickets, the five free minutes the guys got with their admission price, and he even tipped a dollar or two, sometimes five dollars, which all added up.

In the dancehall, the minutes count, because each minute equals one ticket. Tickets were worth two bits apiece to the girls. Those little things were important, and important to the total ticket count by the end of the evening. We were not paid a basic wage, but by the tickets. All the money we made came from the commission on the number of tickets sold. We also counted on tips, which could be generous and sometimes strangely unlikely.

Some of those customers were pretty strange, all right. Stan was just one of the strangest. There were others that were just as weird and different as Stan. I just don't think many of them were murderers.

The Musicland never had one hundred beautiful girls to dance with as advertised. In fact, the "one hundred beautiful girls" was a running joke with us. We never had that many, and I hate to admit it, but some of us were not that beautiful. Even so, with the music, a seedy atmosphere, reminiscent of the 1930s' vibe, there some very regular customers. That included Stan, who until that evening, had been so regular, you could set your watch by his appearance. It was a job that paid well for some of us.

Several of the so-called "one hundred beautiful girls" were seated on the long couch where the line gathered. Greek Helen, the undeclared queen of the place, sat relaxed with one arm draped along the back of the couch as she studied her long scarlet nails on her other hand. Mei Ling was poised in a long pale blue silk gown, slit, on the side to the thigh, which exposed one of her legs with matching four-inch-high satin sandals. Her shoulder length hair fell forward in a long smooth line. She carefully lit a cigarette in her long ivory holder, making a ceremony of it with her tiny hands.

Choug, in a red-hot pepper of a dress, that showed a lot of cleavage, leaned forward to exchange pleasantries with someone I didn't recognize in the bullpen. That was where the customers gathered to look at the dance floor or the line, when they were not checked in with a girl. Most of the time there were a lot more men in the bullpen than there were checked in with the girls.

Annie Fannie was out on the floor grinding her little heart out.

When Mei Ling lit her cigarette, Helen gave her a look and said, "Do you mind? It's bad enough when a customer blows smoke in my face. Can't you wait till you're sitting at a table?"

"Are you speaking to me?" Mei Ling had the softest voice. I had never heard it dialed up much higher than a whisper.

Greek Helen, on the other hand, could make rafters quake when she was disturbed.

"I hope smoking hasn't destroyed your hearing. Please could you point that at someone else?" Helen was cranky already and the evening had just begun.

Mei Ling said nothing as she arched one perfect eyebrow and stubbed out her cigarette. Her back was turned before Helen could say, "Thanks," even if she'd thought of it.

There were a couple of new girls, they often started them on a Friday. There would, probably, be one or two undocumented women, that would not be coming back. They seemed to have such a high attrition rate, that even I had noticed. That said something, because I usually wasn't particularly aware of what was going on, especially with the other women in there.

They were usually from Mexico, but we also had undocumented or illegals, who came through the same channels as the Mexican girls, and not to mention, girls from other countries like Hong Kong, and even some from South America. We also had undocumented or illegals, which was a term I didn't care for. Sometimes they were the wives or girlfriends of guys who were undocumented farm workers who managed to migrate to the big city. At the time, summer of 1967, Los Angeles was very cosmopolitan. We even had our share of the "flower children," but that was another story.

I suspected their absence had something to do with Tony. I was convinced he had something going on the side. Yet, if it had anything to do with a private stable, I think that I would have heard. There were always rumors about that kind of thing. It's not that Tony wouldn't try to make a buck off some unlucky girl; I just think that I would have heard. His behavior had never been limited by any moral or ethical code that I had noticed. Immoral or illegal, I wouldn't put anything past him.

While I was clocking in, like I said, I had noticed his guitar against the wall behind the cashier. It looked like we were in for a treat, and the girls couldn't get out of there before two-thirty. He was a mean slob and a rotten singer.

It was strictly against the rules to order a Coke from the snack bar after being checked out by one of the regulars. We were supposed to dash over, and plant ourselves back on the line once we were clocked out. Even though the owner always wanted someone available, once in a while, I ignored the rule.

"Get your ass back on the line!" he would demand. It was so hard not to get emotional with the boss. The only protection from Tony was to make so damned many tickets that the owner, Sam, would be on your side in case Tony decided to give you the axe.

Tony was a piece of work. A couple of months before this, he had three new girls pregnant at one time. He was a bigger creep than any of the customers, and that's saying something.

Annie Fannie sat down next to me on the line, where we waited to be chosen. She and I were the only two of the "100 Beautiful Girls," that weren't clocked in at the moment. Like I said before, there never were one hundred beautiful girls. I think the max we ever counted was about sixty, maybe eighty, tops, on New Year's Eve. Usually, it ran between thirty and fifty on any given evening.

Tonight, Annie had something on her mind. She started laying a story on me that sounded like I should know who she was talking about. I assumed it was the body. Did she know who it was? Did they think she was from the dancehall?

"Can you imagine your parents finding something like that? They must have had a notion about him, or why would they have called the police? But still, finding that must have been a shock."

"Must have been grisly. Do they know who she was?" Before Annie had the chance to answer, she was pulled away. She made a motion and rolled her eyes as a customer clocked her in.

When I calmed down, I questioned everybody I could about the details. I really wanted to know who the victim was and, as I moved around the place, that seemed to be the main topic of conversation between girl and customer. I was busy enough dancing to just get bits and pieces of the story, hoping that it was nobody I knew. Whose body could it be?

It was hard to concentrate on being charming. It was always hard to be polite to the guys who came in there. Don't get me wrong. I had made some friends that would have been worth having anywhere. Still, I had to admit that finding out that one of them was carting dead women around in the trunk of his car, was not going to make being friendly any more pleasant. Even Annie Fannie, who almost always, knew the scoop on everyone, was surprised that it was Stan.

I thought she would never admit it.

Annie sat down next to me on the line and began talking about the arrest. Remembering where you were in a story, interrupted by dancing, takes practice.

Before she could get past the body found in the trunk I asked her, "Do you know who they found? Was it someone from here? Was she someone we knew?"

"Haven't you heard anything I've been saying? They think it might be Linda. I swear to God, I knew he was a pervert. You could tell by his eyes, but I never thought . . ." She paused, before she continued, "His parents smelled something funny about his car and they called the police. When they opened the trunk, there was the body of this cocktail waitress, that had been missing for a couple of days. Maybe a week, anyway, she'd been missing. If it's her, Linda, she used to work here."

An overwhelming dread made me feel ill. It just couldn't be her. She and I used to have so many running jokes. I missed her. She was one person who could make me laugh on my worst day. She wasn't the only other girl named Linda, either. There was Mexican Linda. She was small and vivacious, also the most religious person I ever met up there. She wasn't in that night, but I heard her husband had taken her on vacation. What if it was her? Definitely wasn't blonde Linda because someone had seen her working in a massage parlor two days ago. Then, there was Fat Linda.

My mind was going in circles.

One of the regulars, and one of the oldest living pimps, Henry made an appearance at the dance hall. He was a short Filipino with shoulder length hair that he wore in an upturned flip. Henry considered himself my friend, but I didn't feel the same way. The Zoot Suit War was especially a major part of Henry's past and some of his contemporaries who were given to reminiscing about the good old days. Most nights, he would show at 9 pm. Like Stan, you could set your watch by his appearance on most weeknights. It had to be something special to interrupt his routine; because he, like many of the regulars, had very predictable schedules.

For a man in his eighties and consistently wearing bell-bottomed pants, Henry always stood out from the crowd. His attire was extremely colorful, flashy, and current, including bell bottom pants. No one could compete with his somewhat bizarre appearance, and for the most part, no one tried to.

The Musicland depended on a group of regulars, mixed with some foreign students, and a few tourists. It was a multi-cultural, multi-racial, multi-national crowd where diversity wasn't judged, but accepted. Actually,

Musicland had a distinctly non-judgmental group of customers and hostesses. They were always colorful, and the differences were interesting.

I wanted to ask him about Stan, but Henry wasn't as communicative as he usually was. In here, he was like my personal informant. He knew everybody, their history and what they were into. "Did you hear about Stan's arrest?" I ventured. I knew that he had, everyone was talking about it and there was so much speculation.

But Henry seemed annoyed.

"I did." He was very quiet. "I heard you had a date with him tonight."

"Not exactly. He wore me down until I said that I would meet him at the Olympic coffee shop and have coffee with him. I never planned to be alone with him."

"Well, my pretty, maybe you should check with me before you ever do something like that again."

As if, I thought to myself.

Henry had been maneuvering me into his inner circle since I met him. I wasn't interested in becoming one of Henry's girls.

My mind went back in time. Things had begun to come apart earlier last week when Stan had finally pushed me until I said that I would go out with him.

My gut instinct was to avoid being alone with him, ever. Customers who came in often, were considered precious commodities. Gentlemen who came in early, and reliably were even better. Certainly, I am not stupid enough to forget how any perception of theirs, regarding my lack of interest, might affect my income.

I remembered that Stan said to me, "You don't like me enough to even have coffee with me." He had been right, but it was hardly anything I would admit to his face.

"I like you. I think you're cute." I crossed my toes which is not easy in four-inch sandals.

"Then why won't you go out with me?"

"You know I have a day job. I have to get up early." This was my standard response.

"Why not Friday? You can sleep late on Saturday."

I was fishing for a response, and I didn't answer right away; I was thinking about it.

"Just for coffee," he said. "We could go anywhere you say."

Stan was not the kind of customer that would inspire more than a cup of coffee after work from me. I wouldn't even consider coffee unless I took my own car so that I could come home (alone) when I was ready to leave. Plus, it would have to be a brightly lit place and full of people I know.

"You can go in your car." I really thought he was reading my mind. "I think you really don't like me," he said.

The man was developing a decided whine and a sneer. I really disliked sneers, whining was intolerable, but I could see that I had run out of excuses.

"Alright," I said. "I'll have coffee with you Friday, after work." This had been going on for weeks and I figured now I would have to. In the dancehall you try to never say no. The problem is that a yes could be the end of the fringies, a word we used to describe the fringe benefits that could be part of the benefits of working here.

I usually tried to tell new girls to never say yes, and never say no.

Fringies were the benefits of courtship, which go with a definite maybe, so a 'definite maybe' is usually the path to take. This only worked for a while. This song and dance went on for as long as it could as now; we had arrived at the place where if I didn't let him think that he'd had an "honest-to-god, seen-in-public, date with me," I was going to lose him as part of my steady income. So, I gave in.

"Friday night," I said, "after work. We'll go to the Olympic Coffee Shop. I'll meet you there."

That was where everyone else went. Also, I felt pretty safe with a crowd of people I knew. He would feel good about having everyone see him with me. He could say we were dating, which was an ego thing, but I didn't care. I like to think, that I knew this was against my better judgment because, when I told Stan that I would go out with him, it began to bother me. There was something about him. I couldn't explain what it was but, I didn't want to go anywhere with him.

As Friday approached, I began to think of how to get out of it.

I was nervous about going out with this guy, so I had taken special care, with my appearance, because it gives me confidence to know that I look my best. I had designed and made a high-necked, long black satin gown with a side slit. I'd found matching elbow length gloves, to pull together as much glamour as I could.

Who could you trust? I could have been having coffee with someone carting a body around in the trunk of his car. I didn't want to think about it. I learned all the details later, they were scary, but worst of all, I kept thinking that it could have been me.

Somehow, the evening continued. I looked around and I saw Ed Wong. He stayed for a couple of hours. Ed was not only one of my best customers but also a dear friend. He was a large expansive man, who dressed well, and was usually good-humored and very generous. As he got off the elevator one of the girls selected "Big Spender" on the jukebox. It was almost his theme song. I am sure that he had heard about Stan, too.

He motioned me to check in.

"Don't you think it might be about time to get out of here, Frankie? I hate to say it, but it could have been you or one of your friends." He held my chair for me at a table. "I have so much fun around this place that I sometimes forget that it might be dangerous for you." Ed Wong was obviously concerned, and it made me feel less alone. "There are other ways to make a living."

"Like what? You know that I'm trying to catch a break in acting." I was annoyed that no one, seemed to take my acting seriously. "Besides, they have him in custody. We're all safe now." I smiled my best smile. "Thanks for being concerned. Besides, what other way do you think I could I make a living?"

"There's Real Estate, for instance." The rumor was that he was a partner in one of the biggest real estate firms in the Chinatown, Elysian Park, and Echo Park areas of L.A. "Your time would be so flexible that you could still arrange to get to auditions and interviews."

"Real Estate? Right." I looked at him carefully to see if he was kidding. He wasn't. "Don't worry about me," I said. "I'm not afraid of anything or anybody." But it sounded like a hollow brag, even to my ears.

"There's a couple of new girls, hot chicks, if you want me to introduce you." Tony dropped by our table to tell Ed this little bit of news. He had no class. It wasn't as if he didn't know that Ed Wong was my customer, but he wasted no opportunity to try to pry him loose. Tony was definitely not one of my fans.

"Thanks, Tony. Maybe some other time." Ed turned to me and said, "Annie is sitting on the line by herself. Would you like to invite her to our table? We'll have some coffee before I have to go."

Ed was so sweet that he would often invite my friends to sit with us. He would buy their tickets, sometimes for a whole hour, and then tip them, too. He had even brought a couple of pizzas or some other take-out with him a few times. He could make that place seem like a party.

So, I agreed, and he invited Annie. After she clocked in, we sat there talking about Stan. I didn't mention my narrow escape. That kind of poor, judgment on my part should be kept to myself. It was bad enough that everyone was referring to him as my customer.

Later, after Ed clocked us out, I walked him to the elevator with my hand on his arm. I hated to see him go. I felt safer while he was there. He had never gotten fresh with me; I wondered about that kind of gentlemanly behavior. I even wondered if he might be gay, but I just thought he enjoyed my company, and wasn't ready to get involved.

After Ed left, the rest of the evening passed in a blur of music and people. I just couldn't get that little creep out of my mind. I went right home after work, feeling like I had survived a train wreck or some other major disaster. I had survived, but it was a close call. I could have been and probably would have been, next on Stan's list. It gave me gooseflesh.

One of the girls told me that Tony and a couple of his buddies, wanted to see me in his office. I told her, "You haven't seen me. I don't want to talk to him tonight." I counted my tickets, signed myself out, and I was gone before anyone noticed. And darn, I missed his act! How disappointing! I didn't get the chance to hear him sing. Oh well, maybe some other time.

I wanted to go home. I didn't want to talk to anyone else. What could Tony want to talk to me about? What could he offer after the news of that night? Whatever it was, it wouldn't be pleasant. I didn't want to know. He was hard to deal with on a good night, and tonight wasn't. I thought the worst was over.

I was wrong.

CHAPTER TWO

FOREVER CHANGED

That night, going home, I remember driving up the hill where I lived, noticing the palm trees silhouetted against a sky that was bright with moonlight. A bat spread its wings, sailing between two of the palms. It was a summer night so clear, so empty. Five minutes from downtown L.A. and there were no people on the street. The trees and houses outlined against the summit of the hill were like a movie set the actors had abandoned. I drove to the top of the hill where I had a view of the city. I swear I felt like the last person alive in the isolation of this corner. I parked my car in a vacant spot right next to the little walkway that went directly to my front door. The streetlight was two houses away, but my living room light, could be seen, through the drapes. The moonlight gave everything a silvery sheen, but not much light for details. It was so eerie, that I half expected another bat to come soaring out of a palm tree at me, as an owl hooted from a tree somewhere on the block, not very distant. I checked to make sure that there was no one lurking on the street.

The house that I lived in was one of four other houses tucked in a cul-de-sac, in the Elysian Heights area, above the constant roar of the freeway, which seemed to dim at the top of the hill. It was a small house, with almost no front yard; the few steps up to my front door were only a few feet away from the curb. It was street parking only.

Before I got out of my car, I always had the front door key in my hand, ready to insert in the lock. I was cautious on any night, but that night, I really didn't want to fumble for a key on the front porch. I never liked to linger on a dark, deserted street at two-thirty a.m., even if it's my own front steps.

What happened next would change the way I looked at things forever.

As I was closing the door of my car, I heard a woman sobbing. She seemed very close to me. My initial curiosity grew as I quickly scanned the area to see where the sobbing woman was. The sound was almost in my ear. It was only after I closed the car door and sprinted up the steps, that I was struck by the heavy cloud of cheap perfume I had passed through. The smell was overpowering and disgustingly sweet, and worst of all, familiar. It was like night blooming jasmine with a heavy muskiness, and maybe a touch of attar of roses. It seemed like something I should recognize, this cheap scent, but with the sobbing, to tell you the truth, it was difficult and horrifying. My search for where the sound and the smell were coming from was brief. I was far enough away from the buildings next door that it couldn't be coming from there. Those two things together, the perfume and the sobbing, finished the job of scaring the hell out of me.

I probably broke some kind of speed record for getting my key in the lock and getting inside with the door closed between us. I needed something solid between me, the mysterious sobs, and that smell. Whatever that presence was or might be, my legs were so shaky, and it felt like all of my extremities were being held together with rubber bands.

I didn't believe in ghosts. I had to be hearing things. The sobbing was horrible. If someone was playing a joke on me, or trying to scare me, it was working. I hoped that it was my imagination. Maybe if I went to sleep, I would wake up in the morning to find out that this whole evening was all some kind of nightmare. I wanted business as usual. I like living alone, but there is a difference between alone and lonely.

When that evening had been ahead of me, I thought that things were going well. I knew where I stood; I didn't believe in Santa Claus, the Tooth Fairy, or ghosts. Sometimes something happens, after that your life can never be the same. If you're lucky, you live through it, and life goes on. If you're unlucky, you're dead. I found out how close to unlucky I could get and lived to talk about it. Some of my friends were not so lucky. Not lucky at all.

CHAPTER THREE

SATURDAY, THE NEXT DAY

Later, in bed with my eyes closed, I could still hear in my mind that lonely sobbing. It was creepy and it was catching. For the first time in a long time, tears rolled down my cheeks, as I realized that I was frightened.

I admitted it to myself.

It was harder to admit that I was lonely. I had a boyfriend, Toshi. I thought about calling him, but I would have been embarrassed to have him know how scared I was of something that might be my imagination. I never wanted anyone to know how vulnerable I was. I hadn't seen him for a few days, and he had not been in but that wasn't unusual. He was a student and his schedule included things that had nothing to do with me. I didn't want him to know that I had considered having coffee with Stan. He might have thought it was more than it was.

I tried to sleep, wishing I had never heard of Stan; and wishing that I never had to go back to the Musicland. I wished that what I heard was not my friend, Linda. She didn't deserve anything like that. Nobody did. It wasn't her; I told myself.

It just couldn't be.

Most of all, I found myself wishing that a person who had touched me, and danced with me, had not been a murderer.

I just couldn't deal with all that had happened. I got out of bed to turn on the nightlight. Since it was going to be hard to sleep. My mind turned over and over on the facts. The police had caught Stan, he was in custody, and had confessed. What else was there to worry about? I had a bad feeling about the way things were going. As it turned out, I had every right; my instincts were right on.

Then, I couldn't help but wonder about where I had smelled that perfume before. Racking my brain, was proving to be fruitless because nothing made sense. I stopped thinking about it and hoped that I would never hear that sobbing noise again. What bothered me was wondering why was it so familiar? A memory danced in my mind, and I thought I remembered where I had experienced that strange scent before. I was almost sure. I just couldn't accept what I thought it was. Deep down, I think that I didn't want to know; but I did.

The next morning, it didn't seem possible that all of the things that happened the night before were real. Usually, I don't waste my time worrying about things I have no control over, but this time I woke up wishing that none of it had ever happened. I wished that I had never danced with Stan. I hoped that I would never dance with a killer again. It made my flesh crawl to remember his hand on my waist, and how uncomfortable it was to have his eyes insisting on meeting mine. I could almost feel his face leaning into my hair. It was too personal. It was too close.

That other spooky thing that had happened at my front door had to be a fluke. It had something to do with raw nerves, and an overworked imagination. It just couldn't be real. In broad daylight it seemed like I was overreacting. I was wrong to be so scared. It was nothing, I told myself, just the perfect end of a perfect evening. I know that I really knew better.

That morning I didn't hear or see or smell anything unusual, but I had phone calls from some of the girls who wanted to talk about Stan. I really didn't want to talk to anybody about it, but I listened. There had been some other women found dead, who were killed in the same way; but the police had not, so far, charged him with anything else. The rumor was that the victims had not only been killed, but also tortured and partially dismembered. It had to be one of those exaggerations that occur when people don't have all the facts. I just couldn't believe that twitchy little weasel could have done all that by himself. I didn't want to believe that he even had the strength unless he had someone else helping him or telling him.

Toshi didn't call me. Toshi, was my guy, but he hadn't come in on Friday. I wondered if he had heard about the arrest. Probably not, still, it would have been nice to hear something reassuring from him. He didn't ever spend much time calling me and I didn't mind. Though this time, it would have been nice to hear his voice.

There was only one thing that could have persuaded me to go in to work that night, and that was because it was Saturday. The rule was that if you didn't work on a weekend night, your tickets would be docked for the rest of the week.

I almost didn't care.

It sounds crazy to say it, but sometimes money isn't everything. I had other things to think about and plenty to do. Even though it seemed like a good time, to take some time off, to be by myself, I knew that I would have to face going back eventually.

It was a warm, sunny, California day. I listened to the sports news and thought about getting tickets for a home game. I lived right over the hill from Dodger Stadium. Maybe Choug, would go with me or maybe I could talk Toshi into it. They were my favorite team even though I had been in mourning after Sandy Koufax retired. Still, Drysdale was the best pitcher around. Thinking about baseball cleared my head and improved my mood. Everything, from the night before took on a distance that made it all seem a little unreal.

When I went to work that Saturday, the day after they arrested Stan, it was quiet for a weekend. A lot of the girls were off, even though it was costing them. I was early and noticed not very many regulars were there. I was early. Knowing Stan wouldn't be coming in, I got signed in, and resigned myself to a spiritless evening.

I expected Toshi would be there, since he never missed a Saturday. I went over to the line to take my place next to a few of the 100 beautiful girls, who happened to come to work.

Mei Ling was there, looking feminine and perfect. "You're looking great," I said as I settled myself on the line next to her. I envied her for being the one woman I knew who was perfect at all the details. Her hair, nails, makeup, and gown were a package that she perfected and no one else came close to matching her. "Gold is a good color on you," she nodded acknowledging the complement.

She looked distracted and I could see she had something else on her mind. "How is Sam? A couple of days ago he said he might be coming home." Mei Ling and I were the only women from the dancehall that were allowed, by him, to visit him. Sam was our boss, the owner of the Musicland. The rest of the women had strict orders to stay away.

"Sam isn't coming in," she said, "he is staying in the hospital for more tests."

The owner, Sam was a sweetie. He was a businessman who loved dancehalls so much that he bought his own. Best of all, he treated the women who worked for him fairly. That was a lot more than you could say for some of the other owners at the competing dancehalls.

Nobody complained about Tony to him, because of Sam's failing health. He'd been ill for so long, that seemed to pave the way for Tony's behavior being worse, as his boss spent less time in Musicland.

Sam was a dapper seventy, currently enjoying a crush on Mei Ling. He was engaged in a harmless, and probably sexless, flirtation with the Chinese beauty. Who could blame him? She was, far and away, the nicest, most beautiful, obviously intelligent, and tastefully dressed of all the girls. Her manner was elegant and refined. I counted both of them, my friends.

Mei Ling was quiet; we were both saddened by Sam's declining health. His hospital stays were a condition that had occurred too frequently in the last six months.

One of Sam's friends had asked Mei Ling to check in, at the hospital, so that he could find out about Sam's condition. Sam's son and the two of us were his only visitors. Before she could say anything else, someone asked Mei Ling to dance. I knew that she would fill me in on Sam's condition later.

Annie dropped her body on the bench next to me. When I tried to talk to her, she looked nervous, and distracted, and you could tell there was something on her mind that she wasn't really in the mood to share. It wasn't like her usual gum-chewing insouciant self, and it worried me.

We talked about Stan.

"I knew he was crazy. I could see it in his eyes," Annie said. She was so sure that I didn't feel like arguing about it. It wasn't the first time, and probably not the last that I would hear this from her. Whenever we would talk, I knew she was talking about Stan. She was right in a way. Stan was always a little furtive. He had seemed sane enough to me. What do I know?

The newspapers said that there was some question about whether or not he would be able to stand trial. I had read the papers too, but I didn't care what they did with him unless they decided to turn him loose.

"He used to dance with French Linda before he danced with you. Remember?" I didn't, but she was whisked away before I could ask her about French Linda.

Despite Stan's arrest, work was almost fun that night, at least some of it. Big Beverly said it for all of us, "Look at them, aren't they cute? The cream of the gutter."

Most of us felt the way Big Bev did about most of the customers. Many of them were, for the most part, and with some notable exceptions, the raggle-taggle dregs of society. Musicland was in the downtown area that bordered small industry and Skid Row. That meant that some of our guys hung out on Skid Row or were misfit businessmen.

There was also the tourist trade. There were foreign students and our best customers, the Asians. Diversity was represented in excess. I loved it. Nothing makes people more interesting than their differences.

A very small Chinese man in a well-tailored suit asked me to dance. Just as we were clocking in, Big Louie taps me on the shoulder and said, "Tony wants to see you in his office when you're available."

"It's okay. I can wait for you or dance with somebody else," my intended dance partner said. He seemed shy and embarrassed, as if he were imposing.

"Tell Tony I'm clocked in, but I'll see him after we check out." I turned to him and said, "I wouldn't miss dancing with you for the world." I smiled, but I meant it. I knew he would be nicer than Tony, and way better, company.

The man was very quiet as he steered me around the dance floor. I sensed that he wasn't keen on conversation. He could almost rest his head on my chest, and I think he was comfortable with the arrangement.

The music stopped for a moment while the record changed. He looked up at me. "I admire your volume."

"You're a chemist . . . aren't you?" I smiled and choked down the laugh.

"How did you know?" He looked nervous, as if he had made a social blunder.

"Just psychic . . . I guess."

I smiled and we took off as a waltz played, and he pushed me around the floor like a broom in his tiny little arms.

Men are wonderful, and funny. Sometimes they are just wonderfully funny.

The dance ended, we parted, and I checked out before I walked up the stairs. I knocked on Tony's office door. I hoped it wasn't going to be one of those little chases around the desk that he had subjected me to, on several occasions, when he'd been drinking.

"Come on in."

Tony was behind his desk. There were two other men in there with him. One was Henry, he considered himself a friend of mine. It wasn't reciprocated. He claimed that he spent all the money his girls made on me. I had danced with him the night before, and I remembered that he thought I should check with him before I agreed to have coffee with anyone.

As if.

The other guy was Brian, who I had seen around. He wore a beard and was hard to miss since he was chunky and towered over everyone else in the room. His hairy chest was barely covered by a loud Hawaiian shirt that seemed out of place. I thought that he was dating Big Beverly, the biker chick, who was a little different in other ways. It was rumored that he was a cop, a vice-cop. My sense of him was that he was a thug, and a bully. It occurred to me that he might be involved in something with Tony.

"Hi, guys . . . it must be something special to take me off the floor. It's pretty busy down there," I said. They all looked from me to each other.

"Did you know that the woman they found dead was someone you used to talk to?" Tony couldn't wait to let me know. He stood up, put both his hands on the desk in front of him, and leaned forward.

I dreaded what he was about to say.

"I hadn't heard. I thought they didn't know who she was." It was uncomfortably warm in there.

"She was a friend of yours . . . remember Linda? You and Linda used to talk so much that the guys were afraid to interrupt. She cost you tickets," Tony smirked.

What a creep!

I was choking up, but I didn't want any one of these three to see me cry. These were guys who prospered because of women, and they treated us like disposable paper cups. Whoever she was, even if she hadn't been my friend, it broke my heart to think of one of us being savaged by a killer.

"I told them that Stan was your regular," Henry looked a little nervous. He was an elderly Filipino with every bit of his shoulder length hair was in place. That night he had on a very high style, bell bottom suit of shamrock green, his shirt was a bright yellow. In his 80's, he was one of the ugliest guys around. I was not attracted to him, but I had always considered him harmless.

Brian began. "Let's face it, Hollywood," the big guy said. "You're up to your ass in this. You were involved with the victim and the killer. What did Stan tell you?" That guy was looming over me, in an obvious effort to intimidate.

"Who are you?" I felt I should know who the hell this jerk was. He was pushing me like a cop though I wasn't certain if he was. "What do you mean . . . how am I involved? What would Stan tell me?"

"I'm Brian. I'm the best friend you have right now. Just tell me what Stan told you. Speak up or I can really make you sorry you didn't."

He really didn't convince me that he was any friend of mine, and I didn't know what he was getting at. Maybe, they thought Stan had let me in on their secrets. It sure sounded like it to me.

"I'm hoping you can tell me, so that it doesn't become official. I'm with Hollywood Vice," he said. He leaned back and with his butt, balanced himself on the edge of the desk. He and I were the only ones standing.

So, he's Hollywood Vice. Well, that explains it.

Actually . . . it explained nothing.

"Stan wanted to date me. He was getting to be a pain in the neck, about it, so I said I'd have coffee with him," I said.

"What did he tell you about himself?"

He shifted his weight and stepped forward as if to intimidate me. I don't like guys who loom over me and try to intimidate me. Big Beverly had way too much class to be dating this jerk. He stepped forward like he was about to put his hand on my shoulder.

"The only thing that Stan ever told me about himself was that he was an actor, too. I'd have to say that I didn't believe him, not even for porno. I thought he was full of it. Can I go now?" I was anxious and wanted out of there and away from whatever they had in mind.

"Why do you say porno?" He pushed himself closer and leaned over me again. "Did he say anything about porno?"

"Well, for one thing, you're vice. Why else would you be interested unless it's about a stable? I am sure that he didn't have any women working for him. Also, I didn't believe him because he was a little weasel. I've known one or two porno people. Actually, I knew one pretty well, and he was gay, but better looking."

Brian looked at me and shook his head. He dismissed me with a shrug of his shoulders, and turned to Tony with his hands lifted in a gesture that said; what can I do?" I didn't feel that he was actually giving up, but I wanted out of there.

Tony waved me away.

"Get back to work. Wait! If you hear anything down there on the line, tell me. Ok?" He turned to Brian, who nodded a yes.

Tony trusted me to confide in him. Wow, he sure didn't get it. I'd rather be tortured by having my fingernails ripped out, one at a time, with pliers.

"Right."

Why were these guys so interested? Who cares what Stan was into? They got him.

The other little niggling question was why was Henry there? I didn't know he was a buddy, unlikely as it seems, of Tony. Why were they so interested? It seemed like there was a whole lot that I didn't know. What did any of them have to do with Stan? What did they have to do with the murder?

When I closed the door to his office behind me, I started to breathe again. Why did these guys scare me?

Poor Linda, my friend, who could always make me laugh. I tried to place her in relationship to these losers. I didn't have a clue.

Why me? All these questions and no answers.

I was so out of it that I stumbled in the hall as I almost banged my head into the door. I composed myself and put my ear against the door.

It was hard to make out who was talking.

"You think she knows anything?" I couldn't guess who said that for sure, but it sounded like Tony. They continued talking, thinking that I had hurried off to rejoin the line.

"Keep an eye on her and a couple of those broads she hangs out with. I'm checking it with Big Bev. So far, so good." That was Brian the vice-cop. "I think she knows more than she's saying."

"Don't hurt her," Henry said. "Unless she lets it slip. I don't think she knows anything. I like her."

To hell with him, I thought as I gathered myself and adjusted my dress. What was that about? "Don't hurt her?" What was I supposed to know that could worry those jerks?

I felt terror about the "don't hurt her" I scurried down the steps from Tony's office. I almost knocked one of the regulars over. He interpreted it as attention and clock me in.

I kept thinking about their questions. What about the porno?

Later, Annie and I found ourselves alone on the line. It wasn't like her to be so nervous and distracted. She was pulled away before any conversation could take place.

Along with everything else, it was beginning to bug me. Greek Helen waved goodbye to a customer and sat down next to me on the line. I enjoyed the chance to talk to the other girls as it was always so edifying.

"Did you know that the girl they found in Stan's trunk used to work here?"

"I heard that." Of course, it was the biggest topic of conversation in the dancehall and would be until some other wonderful thing happened to take their minds off it. "I thought the papers said she was a waitress."

"Don't you remember Linda?" Greek Helen looked at me closely.

"There have been several Lindas in here in the last six months. There was Blonde Linda and I know it wasn't her because one of the customers told me he saw her the other day in a massage parlor. Then there is Mexican Linda, but she wouldn't go out with Stan. She isn't that stupid." After I said this, I thought, I'm the only person I know who was stupid enough to consider going out with Stan.

"That's two. You forgot French Linda. The one who used to use that awful perfume, that sweet flower stuff? She claimed it was real French perfume. It used to make me sick to have to sit close to her on the line. It didn't seem to bother the customers. I won't forget it. Remember?"

I felt ill and - I was right.

It didn't make me feel any better knowing that. The perfume that was creeping all over my house was the reason they called her French Linda.

Those jerks had been right. I knew as much about her as anyone there. Maybe, that's why I had that connection, and why she was insisting on my seeing and hearing her. It had to be some kind of psychic thing. I felt like the tears were going to be hard to hold back for much longer.

Then, I remembered that Linda had said that she was leaving the dance hall because some of the guys, one in particular, were getting to her. She couldn't stand it anymore. I was ashamed that we lost touch, but our friendship had not expanded outside of the workplace.

"Stan must have found out where she was working, and tracked her down," I said. "What a disgusting creep. It'll be too bad if they don't give him life. I hope that he is in prison for at least ninety-nine years."

I meant it.

While we were talking, Annie sat down by us and heard part of our conversation. "I heard the news is saying that he may not be competent to stand trial. I heard that he is a raving, drooling, wreck in a straitjacket."

Annie shuddered.

Mei Ling sat down long enough to look worried. I thought it was about Sam. Earlier, when she talked about his tests, she'd looked so worried about him.

I was worried too, but she had something else on her mind.

"What did they ask you?" Mei Ling's question surprised me. "Did they ask you anything about me?"

"You mean those?" I pointed up, "No. They wanted to know what Stan told me. I thought that was strange enough. Why would they ask me about you?"

What secrets did Mei Ling have that I didn't know about?

"We need to talk."

She put her hand on my arm and brushed her lips with the other. The subject was closed.

I figured it was because the line was filling up and she didn't want to share something with everyone. She changed the subject. "Have you seen Danny? Has he been in tonight?"

I hadn't, but that was interesting, too. Danny gave me the shivers. He was young, handsome and had an entourage like a rock star. He wasn't just handsome; he was oddly compelling.

"If he comes in and you see him before I do, let me know."

"Are you interested?"

She shook her head and signaled no. I didn't ask.

When Elena joined us, she said she was worried about her friend, Lupe. I had never talked to Lupe. She didn't speak much English, for one thing.

"She's not like me, she has no husband or nothing." Elena was a nice young woman who, with her husband, came here to make a better life. He worked as a mechanic during the day, and Elena worked in the dancehall, at night, to make enough money to take care of their new American baby. I liked her.

"I worry that she is so alone, with nobody, no family, no nothing." Elena sounded as concerned as she looked.

"When did you see her the last time?" I asked. The question about Lupe reinforced my concerns about some of the women disappearing. "Did you go to the police?"

It was a stupid question. As soon as I said it, I realized just how stupid. How does an undocumented person go to the police about the disappearance of another undocumented person?

Elena didn't bother with an answer; she just gave me a weary shrug.

As luck would have it, an old friend of mine, No-Nose Harry waved from the bullpen. I was delighted to see him because it meant fifteen minutes of tickets, and I knew he would buy me a cup of tea. I enjoyed sitting at a table decorously, while he regaled me with tales of his days as a gentleman of the road. Harry had spent his childhood in an orphanage in the Midwest. He didn't know much about his family. He thought they had given him to the orphanage because of his deformity.

Most of the girls considered Harry disgusting. To them he was just a freak. His face was long, and flat, with nostril slits where his nose should have been. The girls were put off by his looks and couldn't stand to sit at a table with him and drink tea.

They found him gross. Even I will admit that he was a little hard to get used to. After all the talk of murder and disappearances, my ghostly encounters and a scary vice-cop, Brian, my friend Harry, seemed like a refreshing change.

No-Nose Harry and I were friends, that is, dancehall friends. I never saw him outside of the Musicland. He was then retired and living on Social Security, luxury by his standards. "One hundred per cent American," he would claim, as if that should entitle him to something.

Although, I have never been squeamish, to tell the truth, I found him touching, gentle, and sweet. He was celibate, but he had an ambition that involved the right woman. It was not sex and not marriage. He just wanted to find someone to give a bath to. He would pay the magnificent sum of ten dollars to anyone he could find that he approved of, he was picky, who would allow him to bath her. As far as I know, he never found her, the right and perfect person who would fill the bill. He mentioned my helping him in his quest. If I know of anyone, he would be grateful and reward me handsomely. It was much like the pursuit of the Holy Grail. There was no chance he would find her, but the contemplation of it was pleasure to him. He realized I was out of the question, but he trusted me with his fantasy, and I listened.

Harry was like everybody else I ran into that night; he had something on his mind. "I want to ask you something? You know stuff and anyway . . ." he trailed off looking embarrassed.

"I think we're friends enough to ask anything. I promise I won't tell anyone, and I won't get mad at you." I said it and I meant it.

"If you heard somethin' and it turned out to be dangerous or nasty for a friend, then you need to tell them, right?" He looked down at his cup, "I don't like to be a squealer."

"No, you're right. We need to help a friend, that's just called loyalty." I thought, what the heck?

"A couple of weeks ago, I heard Tony talkin' on the pay phone to somebody and he was telling them how they could find Linda. I think it was the same Linda. You know, the dead . . ." he paused, "girl. I think he got her killed. I don't know who he was talkin' to, but he's a bad guy, Frankie. Don't trust him. I don't want you to get hurt."

It didn't surprise me. I was beginning to feel more and more Tony had something to do with Linda, Stan, and whatever else was going one. "Thanks Harry. You are a friend, and I'm glad you told me."

The truth was that besides finding out that I was saved from being murdered at the hands of a creep but there was another thing about Stan's arrest that was affecting me—losing out on money. I had lost over a hundred tickets a week off my paycheck. That wasn't a lot, but enough to affect my payments I figured by the month, and not to mention cash tips. I could not afford to lose any more of my regulars or I would be forced to take in a roommate, male or female, what I considered a fate worse than death.

Excuse me, a fate almost worse than death.

Anyway, I was still passing a polite time of day with No-Nose, when I saw Toshi leaning against the snack bar counter having a cup of coffee while talking to the new blonde Hungarian waitress. He had not called me for the last few days, but that wasn't unusual. American women expecting to talk on the phone all the time was something he really couldn't get a handle on. It was a cultural thing I supposed.

No-Nose clocked me out as his fifteen minutes were over; and we were still friends. I was grateful for his warning, but I just didn't want him to think it was so important. It must have seemed a big deal, to a guy who was afraid of practically everybody.

I patted his shoulder and said, "Don't worry . . . I won't mention it to anyone." I felt protective about the guy who was afraid of everyone.

My Toshi was charming another woman, while I was with No-Nose. I fought the urge to jump up and slap him. I fought it. I didn't want to lose another person I could count on. I wasn't thrilled to watch Toshi make another woman smile at his cute accent.

Toshi was tall, almost six feet, solid as a rock, with a black belt in Karate. He was an engineering student at USC. I was almost getting to the point where I might be in love with him, but not too close, because I was cautious about that kind of commitment. There was my acting career to think of.

He had hinted around about sharing my little place with me, and he did seem to spend a lot of time around there, but he never dropped by without calling first. He was really a gentleman and a hunk.

It was good to see him. Now, I had something to look forward to at the end of the evening. With any luck, I wouldn't be going home alone.

When we finally sat down together at a table, he seemed a little preoccupied, like there was something on his mind. I tried a few simple but probing questions, but he didn't seem willing to share whatever it was with me, and he didn't mention Stan.

I wondered if he knew.

Finally, he said he was going to dinner with his friends, but if I wanted him to, he'd come back at the end of the evening.

If I wanted him to? What else? Of course, I wanted him to.

Something about his whole attitude made me so uneasy. I felt a sinking sensation in my stomach that was more dependable, than the time-clock punch. I wondered if he was upset with me for some reason that I couldn't fathom.

Well, the whole thing nagged at me as I hung in for the rest of what turned out to be a long evening. "A long evening" was when I danced with creep after creep who wanted to maul me on the dance floor, refusing to let me sit down or have a cup of tea or a break or anything. Nights like that are hard on my feet and my disposition. I still had the creeps from the night before. It was all compounded by the interview with the gentlemen upstairs. It wasn't a perfect evening and would get even more weird before it was over.

CHAPTER FOUR

A STRANGE EVENING

I can't tell you how happy I was to see Toshi's good-looking face come through the door at one-thirty a.m.

I was finally sitting down on the line counting my hard-earned tickets, while thinking about taking the next night off. Maybe spending a Sunday evening out with Toshi. Even if they docked my paycheck, it might be worth it. As I said before, it sounds crazy, but sometimes there are things that are more important than money. Then I noticed that instead of even looking for me, he headed straight to the snack bar counter and that damned Hungarian. What could he possibly find more interesting to talk to her about than being with me?

The nerve of the jerk.

They were engrossed with each other. Then Choug and Greek Helen both made a point of coming by to tell me that Toshi was there.

I already knew.

Then our dear manager, Tony made a beeline for me on the line.

"You want me to remind him that you're here? It looks like your customer is sticking it to you, Hollywood." He smirked in a very unpleasant way. "This time I'm on your side. This place doesn't make any money when the customers talk to the waitress." How disgustingly repulsive it felt to have Tony on my side—damn that man!

Damn everybody.

I smiled and said to leave him alone.

Finally, at one-forty, he tore himself away from Miss Goulash. When he noticed me sitting on the line, glaring at his back, he came running right over. I knew something about men, and that blonde wasn't going to get him away from me that easy.

I looked up at Toshi and turned on my most radiant smile.

"I'm sorry . . . I think I must be very late," he said. He was always polite, he looked properly contrite, and maybe a little nervous.

"I didn't notice. I was very busy." I took his hand and looked up at him adoringly. "We have time for at least one dance . . . would you please?"

I held out my other hand and he took both of mine in his.

He looked so relieved that I almost wrecked the effect by laughing. "Of course," he said. "You look very nice tonight."

Not even close. I looked and felt like a piece of shit. It felt as if my entire body had fingerprints all over it. I needed a bath and my feet hurt. I hadn't combed my hair or looked in a mirror for that whole endless evening. "It's nice of you to notice, Toshi. Thank you," I murmured in his ear.

"I heard about what happened."

"What do you mean? What did you hear?"

"I heard about the girl that used to work here. They told me that the killer liked to dance with you. I'm sorry I wasn't here to protect you."

"It's not your fault. He's been arrested so we're all safe now." Boy, I thought to myself, I hope that's true.

Sliding, into his arms, as sensuously as a tired back and aching feet would allow, trying to snuggle, was a reverse technique. It was nothing like the one I'd been using to fend off unwanted displays of affection for the earlier part of the evening. I pretended he was a good dancer. There were many wonderful things about Toshi, but his ability on the dance floor wasn't one of them. I was lucky to avoid his stepping on me. He was not light on his feet, except for Karate. But he made up for it by being sweet and sexy. It was fun. I enjoyed coming on to him, until I noticed that it was ten till two, and I still had to fill out my envelope, finish counting my tickets, and get my wrap.

I wanted out of that place no later than five minutes after two. The management always asked the guys to leave first, and then the little dears would wait for us downstairs by the elevator and walk us to our cars.

As the first girl off the elevator, I was just in time to see Toshi standing there, with the Hungarian's back disappearing out the revolving front door. A coincidence? Well, maybe it was. I really didn't like it, not one bit.

I fixed my face into a warm open smile.

"Would you like to go out to eat something?" Toshi looked a little nervous.

"No, unless you're hungry, I thought we might open a bottle of champagne, and have some cold fried chicken I have in my refrigerator. I thought we could just be together. Maybe spend a day together tomorrow."

"That sounds very nice. I'm sorry I'm busy."

I was tempted to ask, who with, but I pulled myself together. The hell with him, I thought, he's as transparent as glass.

"Are you busy tomorrow or tonight?"

He looked at me closely to see if there was anything behind my expression. "Tomorrow; tonight, I planned to spend with you. Unless you're tired," he added.

What a cute accent he has, I was tired. I felt like I had just finished swimming the English Channel, but I was planning a last-ditch effort, to get his mind off that Hungarian.

"Never too tired to be with you," I smiled seductively, I hoped. I was jealous, and I wanted to hide it. "Why don't you just follow me in your car?"

When I got out of my car, I was relieved to hear no sobbing. There were pleasant green smells, but no cloying sweet flowers.

Wasn't long before we were inside the house, opened the bubbly, and he popped on the TV to watch an old cowboy movie. I took that opportunity to take a much-needed shower.

Then I put on my black lace nightie, that looked good with my red hair, and with a little makeup and the right perfume, I knew this guy would be a pushover.

I came in for a bedtime glass with him, and he looked wonderful. Why can't he be happy with me? Why does he have to fool around? Why couldn't he be loyal for just a little while longer?

But that was the basic problem, because if he started to get serious, then he might want to get married or something. Then I would have to think of my career.

I studied his face while the movie flickered on the screen. I liked his face. It was strong, and square-jawed. I noticed that his eyes turned down at the corners, giving him a kind, almost sad look. He saw me watching him and smiled at me with all of those perfect white teeth. I felt a surge of hatred for my rival. He's mine, I thought, you can't have him without a fight.

The movie finished, I turned it off, then, I took his hand and pulled him toward the bedroom. I liked everything about him. I could get crazy right this minute thinking about the smell, and the texture of his skin. He was gentle, but the energy between us was exciting. I was quickly hovering on the edge of an out of body experience, brought on by the most exquisite pleasure; when I realized that we were not alone.

It began with that heavy floral scent of perfume.

Then I heard a sob catch in an invisible throat.

"Did you hear something?" he said. He stopped moving his hand on my thigh. "It's so cold in here."

"Maybe a car," I didn't want him to stop. I didn't want it to be what I was afraid it might be.

"Your house smells like flower perfume. Do you have some in the room?"

"Nothing like this. Maybe it's a neighbor's garden." I couldn't think of anything else. I couldn't imagine how to explain. "You can smell my perfume on the dresser. I only use one kind."

"I know," he said. "And I don't think it's from a garden."

The overpowering smell was covering us like a blanket. I was very aware that there was an unseen presence in the room. Who or what I didn't care; I couldn't imagine a ghost voyeur.

But it was ruining the mood.

It's kind of kinky voyeurism now that I think back about it, but at the time, I was annoyed, and more frightened than I cared to admit. When I finally admitted to myself that it was her, I felt she was enjoying herself, and that it wasn't going to be that easy to get rid of her. I couldn't say anything out loud, or Toshi might be disturbed to find himself in bed with two women, one of which could no longer be counted among the living.

I tried to forget about her by concentrating on baseball. Sex is a lot like baseball. For instance, I had my first home run before he even got to bat, and before we ever smelled the flowers. I think I racked up about six RBI's that night. I swear I lost count, by the time he headed for the showers; we had gone into extra innings.

By the time he fell asleep, I had decided to give up my career, have babies, and follow him around coaxing him into bed every chance I got for the rest of my life. Who needs a career? Who cares about a ghostly presence in the middle of the best sex ever? My entire body felt like it was tingling and glowing. I wanted to stay in that bed, melting in his arms.

By that time, the smell had disappeared, and the cold feeling had left the room. I had almost forgotten about what I was beginning to accept as a female presence. Was this presence something to be afraid of? Was it Linda? Was this what it felt like to be haunted? Before all this happened, I would have said, that there was no such thing as ghosts. I had nothing to compare it to, and no one I felt I could share it with. I couldn't tell Toshi. I didn't think he would believe me, or even take me seriously. I don't like being laughed at. I am not crazy, and I'm not a fool.

But the sobbing, connected to that overpowering scent of cheap floral perfume, was inside my house now. Worse, it was familiar. I knew that it really was someone I had known and liked. I had a bad feeling because I knew that it really was French Linda, and she was still around.

Was she having some fun in messing with me? At least she knew how to get my attention. I wanted to cry.

Part of me was curious, but underneath the curiosity, there was another part of me. In there where I was really alone, I was frightened. I could admit the fear to myself. I didn't like it. I knew that it was something I wasn't going to get used to. Oh Linda, please. What can I do?

That night despite my nerves, I fell asleep. It was, as far as I remember a dreamless sleep until something pulled me awake. I was suddenly wide-awake, in the way that a sound or a noise can alert you to a possible danger. I waited to hear something.

Then, I smelled that overpowering scent again, but in my own bedroom, and I was paralyzed with fear. I really felt like I couldn't move or scream, like a "deer-in-the-headlights" moment. It was that damned perfume. I used to joke with her about it, but she was convinced it was wonderful. Then as my eyes grew more accustomed to the dark, I noticed a shadow. The figure seemed to be by my bedroom window. As I squinted, it seemed to look like a woman as she stood there with her face in her hands. I could barely hear her muffled sobs. Reminded me of a fight with our fearless leader, Tony, and after it was all said and done, Linda was crying at her locker, and this sounded like she did then.

What could she want? Did she want something from me? Linda, my friend French Linda. I had heard that she had gone to work for Henry, the pimp. I had heard that she was one of his girls, as a matter of fact, he told me that, but I didn't believe him. I think that it was his sales tool "if she's working for me and you like her, don't you think it might be a good idea?"

I remembered she didn't leave to go with Henry.

There was that shape in the room that seemed to me like a woman standing there with her face in her hands. I sat up in bed trying not to disturb Toshi. "Linda, is that you? Are you the one they found in Stan's trunk?" At that moment, as I whispered to her, that shadow presence disappeared. I swear that she just evaporated like smoke. Then the sobbing stopped.

There was no going back to sleep as I lay next to Toshi, thinking about the times Linda and I had spent talking and laughing on the line. We had been friends. I felt stupid that I couldn't even remember her last name. I felt guilty and ashamed for my lack of concern. As far as I knew it had been six months since I saw her and neither one of us had tried to be in touch.

We said we would, but the truth is, that for whatever reason, we didn't.

I was still restless and unable to sleep as I wondered what I could do about being haunted, and I wasn't sure that Toshi could or would understand. Actually, I was pretty sure that if I were him and had a choice, I would find it less than appealing. I lay there afraid of what could come next, with my mind racing.

Finally, sleep came after of an imaginary conversation with Linda regarding my need for privacy. It had been a long, strange evening. I could admit fear to myself, but I didn't like it. I was sure that I was living a nightmare that was real.

Then, I had an idea. I relaxed and floated off to sleep after making that decision. I would call and make an appointment with Adriana and Seji, my psychic friends. I don't remember dreaming.

CHAPTER FIVE

SUNDAY

The next morning, Toshi was gone before I woke up. He'd left me fifty dollars in an envelope with a note that explained everything. The money was to pay me back for some things of his that I had taken to the cleaners and picked up for him. I checked to make sure that he'd taken those things with him. He had. The note said that his friend was having a farewell party before he, the friend, went back to Japan. The note said that the party would probably last all evening. Toshi said that he would see me on Monday.

That was okay, I thought, maybe I'll work tonight, it's Sunday, then I could surprise him by taking Monday off.

At the dancehall, the week started on Friday, and if you missed a weekend night, they docked your pay. No use complaining, it was standard procedure, no exceptions. Still, I could afford to take a Monday off. He was worth it, and it would be nice to have some time alone with him.

There were two used champagne glasses on the table by the bed, so I got up and I took them to the kitchen to be washed. I fiddled around in the kitchen and got hungry. I went to the refrigerator for some eggs. I saw there was still some champagne in there, a little flat, but great mixed with orange juice. I made some breakfast, enjoyed my mimosa, and rinsed my dishes in the sink. It was about noontime when I decided to take a leisurely bath before getting dressed. Then, I spent some time straightening everything up, my mind replaying every lovemaking moment with him. I really felt better because after the preceding night I felt, for sure, that he was still mine.

There was an uncomfortable feeling around me that I couldn't get rid of. I really should have felt wonderful, because after the preceding night, I felt like our relationship was solid. It didn't matter. I had an uneasy feeling that left gooseflesh over my entire body about what else, or who else, had been a witness to our evening together. That other invasion of my privacy, cast a cold and scented shadow that gave me the shivers just thinking about it.

I was glad that I hadn't let him in on the presence of Linda. She, the disembodied one, the sob, the smell, and the chill.

The nerve!

And if it really was Linda, what did she want? And even better questions occurred to me; why me? Communication with her had been pretty one-sided, so far.

It wasn't Toshi's fault that there had been anything wrong with the night before. Well, there was the waitress, but maybe that was something I'd blown out of proportion because he hadn't seemed distracted with me.

I remembered that I had decided to call Adriana. If anyone could tell me what was going on, it would be her. Tomorrow, or today, if they can fit me in. I went and sat down on my couch, picked up the receiver, and dialed Adriana and Seji, my psychic, hippy friends, but I didn't reach them, and her phone wasn't taking messages. I'd have to try again before I left for work or wait until Monday. I could always get someone on Monday.

I wanted some answers. Was it the same Linda who used to make me laugh so hard on the line? I remembered one time that she plopped down next to me and leaned closer to whisper that she had overheard one of our more eccentric dancers and customer conversing on the floor. Her sense of humor was infectious.

I remembered one time when Linda had whispered behind her hand, "Vinnie is dancing with the new girl."

"No kidding," I said.

"They were on the floor by me," Linda said.

"Ok."

She continued, "he said, Why the big change? You said you wouldn't, that you didn't like it. You said you didn't like me, and I could forget it."

Then my funny friend Linda said that the girl he was dancing with said, "You're wrong, I do like you! I like you. I like you. I really like you. I need the money!"

I don't know if Linda was telling the truth, but it was hilarious, and it sounded like it could be true. She was also good at imitating accents. Lonesome George, his accent was one of her favorites. He was a regular who was devoted to me. My friend had been incorrigible, but funny. She could make me laugh on the worst night. It made a lump in my throat just thinking about her. To think of her as gone, except for her perfume and an impure interest in my love life, was awful.

Sunday night, I stepped into work looking okay, but I had things on my mind. I checked the date on the time clock and looked around before I put my purse in my locker upstairs and then came down to sign my name on the time sheet. That night I was number forty-two, a depressing number to me. Any number over thirty, I find depressing, it's psychological. Number forty-two of the one hundred beautiful girls; more or less, expected to come to work that night.

Right.

I sat next to Annie Fannie, it was unusual for her to be sitting on the line, but there weren't any customers yet, except for a couple of old codgers, who were leaning against the snack bar, drinking their cups of hot cocoa. Annie made pretty good money, but she always looked "down-at-the-heels." She was wearing a black dress that had seen better days.

"With all the money you make, you ought to treat yourself to a new dress once in a while. I like this one, but it's beginning to look like it's held together with safety pins." Somebody had to tell her. I don't usually criticize my fellow dance hall girls.

She giggled. "Do you remember when I got a new dress and wore it in here? It was about two months ago."

"Honestly, I don't."

"Well, I did and boy — did I find out something. My tickets were terrible. These guys like me if I look like I'm in bad shape. If I dress up, I guess it looks like I don't need anything, so they get stingy with me."

"You mean you have to look shabby to be successful?" That sounded strange enough to be true.

"Absolutely necessary. I don't dare buy a new dress for up here anywhere but a thrift shop."

"It figures." Of course, in the dancehall it made sense.

We laughed, but it's not funny. Some of the girls have to go to such extremes to find out what it is that draws men to their particular type. With Annie Fannie, it's her "down-and-out, round-heeled look." I dress in long gowns and most with high necklines. If I showed up some night in a nun's habit, I would probably make a bundle. In order to cater to the fantasies of the men who came in there, the women affected everything from as little as the law allowed, to those, like me, who dress more demurely by dance hall standards.

I have a wardrobe of evening clothes that most female impersonators would salivate over. My guys like side slits, sequins, beaded, push-up bras, and mandarin necklines. As far as I know, those in the briefer costumes make the same or less as those, like Annie, who have found their most appealing image and stick to it.

I didn't get to sit next to Annie for long because the next thing I knew, someone came up behind me and tapped me on the shoulder.

A live one, I thought. I turned around and screamed.

The guy was a dead ringer for the movie version of Count Dracula. With a charming middle eastern European accent he said, "Would you like to dance with me?"

I noticed that damned Tony over in the corner, watching me, and I could hardly refuse. I stood up, took a card with my number on it and stamped it in the time clock. I put it back on the rack and turned to my partner who was at least six inches shorter than me, which put his teeth uncomfortably close to my neck. I noticed as we danced around the floor that he was a very stiff formal dancer from the old school. I could just picture him in white gloves and a black cape.

Finally, he introduced himself, "Voltan." I thought it was a charming name, one that you don't hear often, especially not here.

"Would you like to join me for breakfast?"

"Yours or mine?" I'm so clever; he didn't get it. I could tell by his face the irony was lost on him of course.

I begged off with a sick headache and I glanced at the clock on the wall behind him, it was only nine o'clock.

We bid each other adieu, and off he went. I thought to myself that it was shaping up to be a fun evening.

After he clocked me out, I was back sitting on the line for five minutes, resting my feet, before Lonesome George came in. Just the right touch for just the right night, I thought. He was painfully, passionately, and miserably in love with me. That was good for business, but hard on the nervous system.

I hadn't seen him for a couple of weeks. The word was that he had been out of town on family business. No one in the dancehall hardly talked about these things. We knew exactly as much as a customer wanted us to know. With George, and his mysterious comings and goings, I had less than normal curiosity. I dealt with him on a minute-by-minute basis.

George was hovering by the time clock while motioning me to check in. He was so composed and such a natty dresser! I was always impressed by his appearance. I wondered what old movie inspired the cigarette holder he was sporting that night. There he stood, at least six feet tall, maybe a hundred and ten pounds, crooked teeth, and sartorial splendor. He was wearing a brown tweed twenty-year-old suit that was too short in the sleeves and trousers and a David Niven style scarf around his neck. He had white and brown saddle shoes and argyle socks that showed between his pant leg and shoes. He was Chinese, though, from an island that had its own dialect, so that even other Chinese couldn't understand at least half of what he was trying to say. He also had a debonair way of waving his cigarette with two fingers, so reminiscent of Bette Davis. I tried not to laugh. He loved me.

"Hi, George."

He motioned me up with a gesture towards a table. I sat down, and when the waitress came, I ordered tea. He held up two fingers at her, signaling without speaking. Then, he reached over to hold my hand.

I didn't pull away, but I knew, it was going to be one of those evenings.

I watched tears form in his eyes and drip down his cheeks. "You don wanna marry me. I give you everything, and you don wanna do nothing for me."

"I can't marry you. Please George, don't do that. I can't stand to see you cry. I'm not trying to hurt you. I don't want to make you unhappy. You're very nice, there are lots of girls who might want to marry you."

"I just wan' you."

Shit, here we go again, I thought. I can insult him or hurt him, but I can't take this night after night. His uncle owns a large gambling parlor in Chinatown and George has enough money to set up camp in here if he wants to, but I can't stand it.

"I don't think that I should dance with you anymore, George. I'm making you unhappy and I'm sorry, but I'm not going to marry you. That's it!"

I started to stand up to go check out.

"No, no don go, just wanna dance, no talking. Okay?"

I turned to him, he stood up, and we made our way to the floor. We danced while the jukebox played a mournful, old country-western tune about a lonesome whippoorwill that somehow found its way back to popular attention. The lyric, "I'm so lonesome I could die," seemed so appropriate. George depressed me because he was so depressed, and he was so lonesome. I thought he was really sweet and generous, but I was going to have to be firm, and get him to dance with somebody else. Of course, then I would lose all those tickets and at least fifty dollars and more a week in tips.

Wow, at that point I decided to reconsider, for the moment, anyway.

"If you'd like to, I'll have coffee with you after work George. Just promise you won't talk about getting married."

He smiled so joyously at my offer, that I really felt ashamed of myself. I was being a rotten, gold-digging-dance hall girl.

Shit.

He danced with me till midnight, and then he bought an extra hundred tickets, and tipped me fifty dollars. He said he would be back before two, but he had business to take care of and he left.

Then, I found myself back sitting on the line again. Little Annie Fannie was sitting there also, looking bedraggled, but cheerful. My friend Annie was a small blonde girl, the best sport in the whole place. I never heard her complain. Besides being a dedicated grinder, she was also one of the top five moneymakers up there.

It wasn't hard to imagine that it must be hard work to rub these creeps off, by giving them body massages with your pelvis, in time to the music. I couldn't do it, but the girls who could, were assured of making a living.

If you could call that a living.

Still, it was hard to be judgmental, when I earned my money convincing sad souls like Lonesome George that I was in love with them for an hour.

Maybe grinding, was a bit more honest.

When I looked up, there was Henry, in to give me a hard time and a run down on his evening. He always complained that he spent most of the money his girls made on indifferent women in the dancehall, like me. Indifferent to him, I mean.

I was still wondering about his connection to those other people that I had that brief encounter with last night. Tonight, I thought I would try to make some discreet inquiries regarding our fearless leader, Tony. If anyone knew anything, it would be Henry. I also remembered that he had suggested that they not hurt me, unless they unless they had to.

What the hell was that all about?

Henry didn't want to dance, he wanted to gossip, so we sat at a table way at the back and ordered tea. He had a sandwich, which that darned Hungarian brought to the table.

Then I saw Toshi walk in the front door and right over to the snack bar. He had his back to me, but the waitress tipped her head toward our table and I knew that she was telling him that I was working.

That son of a bitch leaned over, whispered in her ear, and walked out without even glancing in my direction.

What a jerk! After the night we shared, how could he possibly look at another woman?

I was so furious, so hurt that I could hardly remain sitting at the table with Henry. If he noticed, he didn't interrupt his story.

"She was working for me, you know. That's why she quit in here."

I didn't respond to that because my mind was still thrashing Toshi.

"As much money as I spend on you. You could at least listen, my pretty."

"You're right. I'm sorry. Who?"

"Linda, that girl that got killed. She was working for me."

"Bullshit, I used to talk to her. She wouldn't do anything that stupid." I shouldn't have said that, and I knew I'd hurt his feelings.

"What's so stupid about working for me? She made more money on her back than she was making on her feet up here. She didn't have to work so hard. She made it lying down."

"I don't believe you. Why would the papers call her a waitress? How is it that she was alone with that creep, Stan?"

"She quit. Then she was on her own. If she'd stayed with me, nothing like this could have happened to her. I take care of my girls." He leaned back in his chair adjusting the large lapels of his well-tailored suite. I especially admired the orange bell bottom pants.

It was the wrong time for this; I wasn't in the mood to listen to his crap. A sudden stab of pain reminded me of the sobbing presence. If any of what he was saying was true, it only made it worse. I had seen more than one woman slide down the tubes after they started working there. Some women were prey to any mean, dumb, hustler who chanced to cross their path. Not me, I'm not a victim and I'm not going to be one. I'm a survivor and I intend to keep that status.

I asked Henry to check me out, pleading a headache.

I could see he was offended by me and if I didn't get a little more diplomatic, I was going to lose all my steady customers, and then I would be sitting on the line, like those sad-eyed undocumented ladies, alone.

The ones that were left, of the many who worked there for a few weeks and then were never seen again.

Maybe that was what Elena was concerned about, her friend Lupe was missing. Was there a connection between the dancehall and their evaporation? Could their disappearances have anything to do with working at the Musicland?

I was annoyed with myself because I had lost my patience; before I could find out anything about Tony's scam. I was beginning to think of it that way. Tony had something going on, and I was determined to find out what it was.

Why did Brian want to keep an eye on me? What could Vice have to do with finding the body of a woman who used to work here? I don't remember that he had known her, at least when she was still working here.

While I was checking out with Henry, there was a buzz around the snack bar near the entrance elevators. It was Danny, the guy that Mei Ling had asked me about, and he was surrounded by a crowd, as always. There were a group of guys from two or three to as many as eight or nine on any given night surrounding prince charming.

I looked around to see if Mei Ling had noticed that he was here. She was on the dance floor. Then, she turned around and preceded her customer off the floor. It was very odd, not at all like her usual manners. Mei Ling moved to the checkout and hardly seemed to notice anyone. It was as if she were in a trance moving steadily away from Danny.

Annie was back on the line. She looked thin and like she needed a lot of TLCS, including some hot chicken soup. A lot of the guys really loved her. Almost any of them would have been happy to take her away from all this, but she had her principles. Though she even earned her tips, with little side extras downstairs in the TV room, no one could say she ever took advantage of a man. She was supporting the child she'd had about two years ago, because the father had a wife. She didn't want to bother him with anything. She made me crazy just talking to her, but I liked her. I liked her even though we didn't see eye to eye about men.

"You look tired Annie. Are you okay? It looks like you made good tickets tonight." She was carrying a wad all right.

"All on my feet. I couldn't coax anybody down to the TV room. How are you doing?"

"I'll live, but I may never walk again. Have you ever danced with Lonesome George?"

"Oh sure, but I shocked him. He wasn't prepared to handle my kind of dancing."

The picture of romantic George backing away from a friendly, Annie Fannie advance was hilarious. Good ol'e George, he wanted the real thing.

"Poor George . . . I guess when you dance all night every night like that, you do it automatically."

"Yeah," she grinned. "You should see how people react at a party, especially if they don't know where I work."

By this time, it was a quarter to two and those last fifteen minutes I spent in the bathroom. Wasn't long before Tony followed me in to get me to go back on the line. He pounded on the stall; that I had locked myself into, and insulted me, but I ignored him. I smoked a cigarette while I sat on the john to count my tickets.

"You're not fooling me, Hollywood. Get out on the line! I am calling tickets. Come on out of there. I know you are in there, Frankie. You've got two minutes to pull up your pantyhose and get your ass on the line."

Tony pounded on the door one more time before he left.

That dumb bastard was determined to give me some trouble, mainly because I didn't want to sleep with him, and I had made it perfectly clear that it was a permanent decision.

With almost five hundred tickets a night, what could they do to me? I went to my locker to write everything down in my little book before I filled in my envelope to turn in with my tickets.

I gathered my things and started to leave when I saw that George was by the elevator. When he saw me, he signaled that he would see me downstairs.

At one minute of two I was ready and he was waiting at the gate.

George wanted to go to Chinatown, to celebrate, but I didn't care to. I asked him to drive, but I asked him to go past the Olympic Coffee Shop, and sure enough—there was Toshi's car parked right out there in front.

I knew he had a date after work with that waitress.

I didn't want to see him. I don't like to make a scene like that, especially when I throw them. I could really be a bitch, and it has usually embarrassed me later.

We got to Chinatown, exited the car, and walked inside a Chinese restaurant. George treated me to a lavish feast, that I was too upset to enjoy. Of course, he pledged his undying love for me, but I wasn't engaging with him, even as he held my hand. He talked about all the money he'd saved toward a home for his future family. The man wanted to buy a house and have children.

He was crazy.

I could see what an obsession marriage had become to him. He said he was getting older. He said that everyone in his family had married when they were younger than he. George was afraid that there was something wrong with him because no one wanted him. He finally said, "Even beggars have wives."

I considered that insulting, but he made me feel pity, even when I was in such a rage. Why can't we love the ones who are so eager to love us? I thought of myself enduring the latest betrayal. Here was George, who would probably love me forever. He would probably be a very sweet husband, if I gave him even half a chance. Then there was Toshi my handsome lover, who was the big strong guy, which I had even considered a permanent relationship with. The same Toshi who could make wonderful love to me, expect me to run errands for him, then sleep with someone else the next night. Why should I love someone like that, who didn't even appreciate me?

It wasn't fair.

Tears of self-pity started coming. George was upset because he thought it was his fault. He was also happy because he thought I was expressing some feeling for him.

I couldn't tell him how sorry I was for myself, or how angry.

Poor George, I finally understood what it was like to care about somebody who didn't give a damn about you.

We finished up and I was ready to leave. We left, got in his car, and he drove us back to the parking lot where he walked me to my car. Our eyes met in the dawn light, and I allowed him to kiss me, even with his crooked teeth.

I knew better, but he was handy.

I shouldn't have encouraged him so much, but at the time I took advantage of his feelings for me. I even had a small premonition that I would live to regret giving him this much encouragement.

As we parted, said our goodbyes, and I hopped in my car, and I drove home; I was filled with so much emotions as I thought about it all—George, Linda, Toshi, Tony, Brian, and Ling, that I began to sob in the car. Through the tears, I managed to make it home safely.

By the time my key was in the lock, I was hiccupping, and blowing my swollen nose. Drowning in self-pity, while struggling with my embarrassment, at my own vulnerability. I couldn't let go of the awful feeling that I had in some way deserved to be dumped. I really let go after I drank some champagne. which turned out to be the whole bottle.

I could smell the familiar floral scent. The living room was cold, and I knew she was there, but I was wrapped up in my own pain.

I wanted Toshi but I hated Toshi.

I picked myself up from the couch and walked into the bedroom. I stood in front of my closet and glared at his clothes. I was full of emotions as I threw his stuff all over while I ranted. I was so angry and there was no one I could tell. I kicked things, I cried, and I ranted. I felt so sorry for myself. I hated him. I said it out loud, "I wish he were dead. I hated men. I raged until I collapsed onto my bed and fell asleep.

Sometime during the night, I heard someone sobbing. It was oddly comforting to feel her presence.

No one heard me except her. How could I know how scary it would be to have a vengeful ghost on my team?

What happened next was my fault. I didn't want it or expect it, but I can't deny that I had something to do with it.

CHAPTER SIX

PSYCHICS AND A WARNING

I decided to take Monday night off. I knew who to talk to about being haunted. I was going to see Adriana and Teji, my hippy friends. I could consult Adriana, the Earth Mother psychic, who belonged to a church that held séances and exorcisms with her ever-present boyfriend and sidekick, Teji. Maybe Adriana would have an idea about how to get this mess under control.

If I could just convince my no longer living friend, to stay out of my bedroom, I would consider that progress. At least she could be more discreet. She didn't have to get in bed with me especially when Toshi and I were making love. That didn't seem like very spiritual behavior for someone who had passed over. I thought that a person lost interest in that kind of thing once they had no more body or flesh. Linda seemed to be the exception to the rule.

Also, there was the nagging question of what she wanted or expected from me. They had her killer. What else was on her mind?

I finally reached Adriana. I had called Sunday, but she hadn't been there. I had left a message, but she didn't confirm. This time she was there, and she said that she could see me in an official kind of way around two. It was noon, so I had to pull myself together to get there on time.

After I got in the car and began to drive, I began to reminisce about us. Adriana and I were friends from the beginning of my life in L.A." She had rented me a room after she read my palm. She told me that I would be a professional dancer. I was surprised, because I had come to tinsel town to be an actress. I had never even taken a tap-dancing class. When I landed a job at the Musicland, it had been a very good laugh between us. I moved from her house, to my own small, rented home, as soon as I had enough money to accomplish that feat.

Adriana's house was lovely, old, full of antiques, cats, and strange characters all waiting around for something to happen. She had an interesting collection of hippy paraphernalia.

As I knocked on the door, using the brass hand attached for that purpose, I remembered to dodge the wind chimes, which were clinking next to a Macramé plant holder, hanging from the porch roof. There was enough of a breeze to make her front porch a little hazardous. The door swung open, and there stood Adriana.

"Frankie You're looking great. Come in."

She hugged me in her ample arms, while she pulled me into a large room with wooden floors, and large articles of furniture. Some things were covered with madras spreads, some decorated with cats, and everything covered with dust. There was a pungent background odor of pot, cat box, and a large glass pipe on the table. There were pictures of unicorns, mandalas, and pentacles. On the table there was a crystal ball, a deck of tarot cards, a brass incense pot with joss sticks unlit, and several cats.

Adriana had a rolled scarf tied around her head allowing her long black hair to hang loosely down her back. Her clothes consisted of layers of blouse, vest, skirts, scarves, chains, charms, bracelets, and bare feet. Adriana was a hippie and didn't try to hide it.

"I've missed you, Frankie. You're so caught up in your new scene, you never call me anymore. Can I get you anything?"

I wondered to myself as to what anything could mean. "Nothing, thanks. You look like you're getting very professional here. Look at all this stuff! I didn't know you could read a crystal ball." The place had always been full of furniture, cats, and people. Now, the artifacts were overtaking whatever space was left.

"I can't. The crystal ball was just for show, but now Teji is trying it out. Tell me what you need. Maybe I can help." She sat down in a rocking chair at the table, petting a gray cat that had immediately sought her lap.

"Where's Teji? I always expect to see him when I see you."

"He's consulting or sleeping." She grinned. "Not that much difference."

We shared a chuckle on that. One of the best things about Adriana was her talent, for not taking herself too seriously.

It didn't take long. I told her everything except Linda's name and Stan's. I told her that I felt haunted. My experiences with the sobbing, the smell, and the presence in my bedroom, that were all related, as honestly and without embroidery as I could manage. I told her that I couldn't seem to figure out what to do about it.

She listened, nodding as if I wasn't telling her anything outside the realm of her experience. She acted like this was the kind of stuff she dealt with every day, and for all I knew, it was.

"You smell something when she is there? Would you say it's a distinctive odor? Would you recognize it in another context?"

"You bet! I think that I would know it anywhere. I knew someone who wore that perfume. I'm pretty sure of that."

"Let me do a little reading for you. Just put your purse down anywhere."

I put it on the floor between my ankles, not trusting anybody who might walk through, physically or spiritually. I leaned toward her, so that she could hold my hand, without disturbing the cat, after she cut the cards and shuffled.

I cut the cards, and then cut them again. She spread the cards in a pattern on the table before us like some exotic feast.

"Okay . . . I see a black queen . . . I see a knave . . . you are the wise fool."

"Thanks, a lot."

"You are surrounded by different kinds of treachery."

I wanted her to tell me something I didn't know.

"There is a big problem . . . a mystery. You must find the answers before any more women suffer." She looked surprised. "More women could die. You are in danger. Others close to you are also in danger. Someone you would never suspect is a threat to your life. He is not who you think he is. There is a dark undercurrent, a conspiracy of evil. The flower scent of evil is a warning. She is warning you. More people will die."

I was stunned. I was here to solve the mystery. Was she talking about something else? How did any of this connect? I was flummoxed by what I had just heard. What did it have to do with French Linda? They had arrested Stan. He had confessed and it was case closed. A conspiracy of evil was pretty heavy duty. What dark undercurrent? What else was there to know? More than that, who might die?

"I want you to hold a séance with me and Teji." I felt comfortable with her asking since they were partners and soul mates. "Can you get some people who knew her to be at your house one evening?"

Adriana seemed to know what she was talking about. She got up from the table and paced around. "You are in the middle of more than just a murder, Frankie. I think there is a lot more to this. I also think that you should be quiet about even suspecting that there is anything else going on. Somebody you know, somebody close to you is heavily involved. How about it? Who can you trust?"

What a good question. I really had to give it some thought.

After I did, I wondered how many of that short list I could get to my house on the same night to participate in something so arcane.

Think about it.

"I'll try. I'll let you know. What night is good for you? It has to be during the week. Nobody will give up a weekend night. It has to be on a Monday or Tuesday."

"Fine. Just let me know." Adriana began to bustle around getting us some tea.

She shortly returned with a tray. "Oh, I can't make it this week. How about Tuesday, next week? Tomorrow, I have some friends coming from San Francisco and it will be kind of a spiritual gathering, but they will be leaving next Monday." She put her hand on my shoulder. "Don't wait too long. This is serious stuff. If you want to have it next week, let me know as soon as you can work it out."

I remembered that this wasn't just a friendly visit, so I put some cash under the glass pipe. Then I spent another half hour enjoying her company and her cats. On the way home my mind replayed what she'd told me. I hoped that this time she was wrong about some things.

The trouble was that she had always been so right on.

CHAPTER SEVEN

THE ACCIDENT

Monday night was uneventful, unless I counted several calls that I didn't answer. I didn't really want to talk to anyone, so I unplugged the phone from the wall to take a needed a break. It was worse because I added more concerns after talking to Adriana. It was a champagne and TV night.

Monday, after I saw Adriana, I spent the whole day planning the speech I wanted to deliver to Toshi. I wanted to include all the things that I would say to that no-good two-timer. He didn't call. The flower scent lingered close to me that evening. It was drizzling Monday night and Tuesday. It was chilly, so I put a log on the fire and watched TV. It is funny how southern California weather can be—June was sometimes chilly in L.A. but then in December it was sometimes hot. It was a tribute to all the men that I met up there that my most pleasant evenings off, were spent alone, sewing, reading the sports page, or watching TV in my own living room.

Tuesday morning found me hung over, and depressed, the weather was damp, and rainy all day, which suited my mood. I stayed in, the sport page beckoned, and then I found myself trying to get into a mystery novel

I'd been nibbling at, for at least a month. I also did a little sewing. I liked to sew since I designed the clothes that I wore to work at the Musicland albeit they weren't the kind of clothes that I could ever wear anywhere else unless I landed a job as a saloon singer. I hadn't heard about what happened until I got to work that night.

I felt better by Tuesday night. It occurred to me that if I took my friend Ed Wong up on his offer to sponsor me in real estate school, I might have to improve my day wardrobe to include more business appropriate attire.

I finished my work, got dressed, and headed to the car. I didn't like to be late, so I put the pedal to the metal and off to Musicland I went.

The day was damp and depressed, the rain suited my mood. I went to work that night, several customers said that they had called me to see if I would be in. I wasn't answering the phone; so, I wasn't expected by some.

Toshi had said that he would see me there. I had spent the whole day planning the speech, and all the things that I would say to that no-good two-timer. I hadn't heard anything from him on my night off, but it could have been because I unplugged my phone Monday evening and never thought of plugging it back in on Tuesday.

I didn't hear about what happened until I went to work on Tuesday. Usually, the crowd is not very exciting, but those of us who worked full time were usually there. I was prepared for a slow evening. I was wrong.

That night I had checked in my card on the time clock then I looked around, before I put my purse in my locker upstairs, and came down to sign my name on the time sheet. There were only fifty of the one hundred beautiful girls who didn't all manage to all show up on Tuesday night. Once, on New Year's Eve there had been 86, but that was unusual.

When I got to Musicland I scanned the room, and everyone was buzzing about something and the Hungarian waitress was replaced with the skinny brown-haired girl, Betty, who usually filled in for her on her nights off.

I was just clocked in, and on the dance floor with somebody I didn't know, when I happened to glance at the coffee bar. There was a commotion there with two of L.A.'s finest talking to Big Louie. Tony joined the group; and then I saw the men only go up and into his office.

By the time I clocked out, the room was a-buzz. Annie rushed to me, eager to tell me all about the two latest events. "They found another body. They think she worked here. And did you hear what happened to Toshi and the Hungarian waitress? You know, what's her name?" Annie was eager to tell me all about the two latest events. "Toshi was in an accident!"

"What are you talking about? What about Toshi? What about the body? Where did they find it? What's going on for God's sake?" I felt my normal life slipping away. How much could happen in less than a week?

"Annie, you said they found another body. Whose body? Do they know who?"

"I think she was one of those illegals that worked here for a while and then, poof! Haven't you noticed? They just seem to disappear. I didn't get the name."

She didn't have a chance to say more because a customer interrupted motioning her to clock in.

Then Elena sat down on the line, and I was distracted. She was sobbing and her tears covered her face.

"What's up? Is there anything I can do?" I was still shaken from the news of the accident when Elena told me something that left me really shaken.

"They found Lupe. They found her body in Echo Park. They matched her fingerprints to the license."

She began sobbing and I put my arm around her.

I knew she'd been missing, but as an illegal, how did Lupe get a license? Everyone who worked for a dancehall had to have a license and a good record with the law. How did she die?

"Is that why the cops are here?" I was trying to put it all together. How many of the women would be found? There were several that nobody had ever seen again. Were they all dead?

"Yes. I think they are asking Tony some stuff. She was hurt, and she was alone. They hurt her and took her blood. She didn't have nobody."

Elena started sobbing again, before I pulled her up off the couch and steered her upstairs. Nobody can work in that condition.

The accident explained why Miss Hungary wasn't there. I wondered if Toshi was badly injured. I had thought that Toshi would probably have waited to come in and dance with somebody else. That's the way those brave and true human beings, the customers, usually handled, the end of an affair.

I didn't have to wait long. Helen of Troy was waiting to tell me all about it.

"Don't you ever read anything besides the sports page? You mean you didn't hear what happened to Toshi and the waitress? You know . . . what's her name?"

"What are you talking about?" I hated Toshi, for that matter, both of them, but I didn't like to hear that something had happened to either of them.

"They were in an accident. I guess he was driving her home and the freeway was wet. There was a big pileup when his car went out of control. It was a big screw-up, about sixteen cars were involved."

"Is he alright? Was anyone hurt? I felt a little tightening of the skin at the back of my neck. The accident had happened when I had been so upset.

"Well, he's in the hospital, and so is she. A lot of people were injured, but nobody was killed. It was one of those freak freeway messes."

"How bad is it? Is he critical? What about her?"

"I guess we'll get the details later. Are you going to try to see him?"

"No." It was very strange, but I smelled something—just a hint of something familiar.

"I figured you would not be really happy with him. Well, I warned you about dating customers." Helen had a smirk was depressing, but it was the truth, and I had no real defense.

It wasn't bad enough that he was hurt or that I had lost his love, there was something else that nagged at me. It was creepy. I had an uneasy feeling; I couldn't put my finger on it.

Helen was checked in by one of her regulars, before I could tell her about the séance and ask her to be part of it. I really didn't know how she would respond.

It wasn't just that he was hurt or that I'd lost someone that I had real feelings for. There was something else that nagged at me, a certain uneasy feeling, but the accident seemed almost too coincidental. I knew that I had nothing to do with it, but it was so strange. It was as if my anger had caused it. That wasn't possible. Anger doesn't cause accidents to happen miles from where the person who is angry is sleeping.

Does it?

I thought that Annie would help me out. She would make fun of a séance, but I thought that she would do it because I was her friend. I had a week to convince her, and a couple of others.

I wondered who I could approach about the séance. There were three women on the line, including my friend Choug, that dark, fiery beauty, who was the most vivacious, and the most fun of anybody who worked there. She was decked out in her favorite red dress with a flower tucked behind her ear. Choug delighted in playing tricks on Tony, which endeared her to me. Though he suspected her and me, but he never caught either of us at it. She played games with the customers too.

Big Bev was sitting beside her. I didn't want to talk to her yet. I'd been trying to avoid her since I found out that her boyfriend, Brian, was the vice cop buddy of Tony, and somehow interested in whatever Stan had been up to. Then there was the religious cult that she had joined. They had something to do with spaceships. Bev traveled, a lot, in space.

Sometimes, after she missed work, she Bev would come in the next night to tell me about her adventures on Venus, or wherever. She always missed work on a full moon, and I speculated to myself about how significant that might be. Sometimes I tried to avoid her, but she liked to confide in me. Even so, she could be a possibility for the séance. Maybe, it wouldn't seem too bizarre for her tastes. Besides all that, she had known Linda.

It was a toss-up. She had problems. For one thing, the FBI was forever bugging her house, her car, and for all I know, her bra was wired for sound. She was, in spite of all this, likeable enough, just a little weird. I thought I could swear her to secrecy. The thing was, could she keep it away from Brian? I really didn't trust him. It wasn't just trust; the truth was that I was afraid of him and his threats. He had an attitude and the body language of a bully.

I sat down next to Annie Fannie. It was unusual for her to be sitting on the line, but there weren't any customers yet, except for the same couple of old codgers, who were leaning against the snack bar, drinking their evening cups of hot cocoa. They were regulars at the snack bar.

I broached the subject of the séance, Annie laughed at me, as I expected her to, but it sounded interesting, she said. So, we decided to make it for next Tuesday. Because of the weekend rules, a lot of women took Monday or Tuesday off.

That made two of us, but then Beverly overheard "Could I be part of this? I'd like to come. Could I bring a friend?"

Would it be all right if she brought a friend? It turned out to be, what sounded like Mirratz, a Venusian pal.

"Sure," I said. "The more the merrier." That made three or four of us and that was all we needed, but it would be better to have at least two more in case somebody didn't show up. Greek Helen would be sarcastic, but unless she had something else planned, she might submit to a séance for a friend, so I decided to ask her, anyway.

I didn't get to sit next to Annie and Bev for long because the next thing I knew, someone came up behind me and tapped me on the shoulder. It was Voltan, the dead ringer, and I use the word dead wisely, for Dracula.

I spent about a half hour with him and then begged off with that useful headache. It was only nine o'clock, but what a fun evening it was shaping up to be.

I still hadn't had a chance to ask Greek Helen about the séance. I had a feeling that the whole idea might antagonize her. She was the best educated and the least whimsical woman in the place.

When I saw her, I motioned to her to follow me up the stairs to the lockers, and the john. I told her about it.

"You are kidding! You want me to come to a séance because of a smell that you think is the essence, the ghost, of the now deceased French Linda?" She raised her eyebrows and rolled her big brown eyes.

"In a nutshell."

Look, I know it sounds a little strange." I was embarrassed for myself.

"A lot stranger than a little," she interrupted before she opened her locker and took out an atomizer and squirted her throat and hair while she was thinking.

"Who else have you invited?"

I told her. I also told her that I was going to invite Choug, because she used to know French Linda too.

"Great," she said, with a decided lack of enthusiasm. "All my favorite people. Annie Fannie, the grinder, Beverly from outer space, and Choug, the gangster. A great bunch. You know that they all love me, too."

I felt a little impatient with Greek Helen. Maybe, she was socially more acceptable than some of us, but she worked at the Musicland, too.

"Excuse me, but don't they call you Greek Helen around here? I know that you consider yourself a cut above the rest of us, but I thought you worked here, too. What makes you so judgmental? What did we do to you?" My face was getting hot with anger. "Nobody says anything about you."

"Take it easy," she said. "Don't get your knickers in a twist. I didn't mean it like that. It is just so nutty. Okay, I'll do it." She put down her perfume atomizer, to pick up a photo she had in her locker. "I do remember French Linda. Maybe, this will be an interesting way to show my respect. Hell, what do I know?"

She put her stuff away, and then kicked the locker shut. Suddenly, I was reminded of high school, "Look forget what I said about Annie, Beverly and Choug," she said. "You'd better get back to the line before Tony notices you're up here." I'll ask Choug for you. Next Tuesday, right? You'd better remind me. Anyway, you know Choug will do it, I'm pretty sure."

I hugged her. I could feel a slight resistance, but I didn't care. She was a born grouch, but not a total bitch.

How I got through the rest of the night is a blur in my memory. There was too much happening to take it all in. I needed help to sort through this. I felt dazed but somehow, I got through the evening. At a quarter to two, I hid in the john, to count my tickets.

One of the girls told me that Tony was looking for me. I was ready to slide out the window and go down the fire escape to avoid talking to him.

Luckily, I didn't have to. By the time I got downstairs, he was occupied with Big Bev's boyfriend Brian, and Henry. They didn't seem to notice me as I handed my ticket-filled envelope to Big Louie.

I walked straight out to my car in the parking lot, safe, in the middle of a group of women, with my head down.

CHAPTER EIGHT

MEN ARE LIKE BUSES

Both the interior and exterior of the Musicland was, a tacky, dismal dump that could depress anybody. It hadn't been painted in at least thirty years, and the dance floor hadn't been sanded in so many years, that the splinters were potentially lethal if you had the misfortune to slip and fall.

I knew a tall girl who, when offered twenty bucks to take off her shoes and dance with a customer, refused the money. She said it would cost her more in doctor bills, and not to mention the pain. Don't feel too sorry for the poor little man, because when they danced, he discovered that her tits were at eye level, and he spent the rest of the evening enjoying the proximity of the view.

Now, that I think of it, I'm pretty sure she got the twenty anyway. I love happy endings.

When I sat down on the line, Choug was there. I wanted to know if she'd heard anything about French Linda after she quit working at the hall. I told her that I felt guilty because I hadn't made much of an effort to stay in touch with her.

"She left here more than a couple of months ago, right?"

"Are you still rehashing that?" I caught Choug off-guard. "Yeah, but don't feel bad. She moved and didn't give anybody her number. She had mine and yours, she could have called." Choug had the same feeling, "Hell, maybe she was just getting settled into her new job, and everything. You know how it is."

I told her about Henry, and what he'd said about Linda working for him.

Helen had just joined us, and she chimed in. "Oh, I don't think so. Linda told me that she hated Henry, and that he wasn't to be trusted. She thought that he and Tony were friends." Helen seemed definite about that. It was reinforced by what I'd seen and overheard.

Choug said, "If she had, I'd have heard. I've got connections on the street." She did. All five of her brothers were in a gang. If you needed to hear about something going on, she could probably, find out.

I made a note to see if she could find out what kind of racket Tony and Brian, the Vice cop, were in. She might be able to pick up something.

"I wonder how Stan had found her, that little creep? What a jerk! God, when I think about dancing with him every night," Choug said.

I felt a shudder, pass through my body. The thought that No-Nose had been right, and Tony had given her away to Stan was scary.

"I wouldn't be surprised if Tony, told him where she was working. She had to give a former job reference. Maybe he made sure that Stan knew. Or she could have been spotted by one of our finest."

Helen could be right about that. She was saying what I was beginning to be sure of. I didn't want to give No-Nose away as one of my sources of information. He was turning out to be valuable, and it was just between him and me.

Choug said, "It's scary. Do any of you guys get the idea something is going on up here? Like there is a scam, that we don't know about?"

"I wish I knew. Why don't you use your connections and see if you can find out anything? If you hear something, I'd sure like to know." I didn't like feeling vulnerable. I didn't like the idea that we could be dancing with any more potential killers. "It creeps me out," I said. "What if some other guy gets the idea that we're easy targets?"

"I know. Shit, we call them creeps, but who expects these creeps to be murderers?" Helen said. "If this keeps up, I might have to go back to office work."

Greek Helen was beautiful on a large scale; her eyes, lips and body were all exaggerated. She had enormous eyes with long thick eyelashes and large pouty lips. Her waist was tiny; she had rounded hips and a forty-four-inch bust that made plain tailored blouses look provocative. She worked in the dancehall because on every other job she'd had, men had made her life miserable by not being able to leave her alone. In there, it made sense. She was one of the top girls without trying. She had a college degree and could type eighty words a minute, spoke several languages and read everything.

All that didn't matter.

That dark-haired beauty could never earn as much out there, as she did in here, by just being here. If Helen had been a deaf mute or lacked the ability to tie her own shoelaces, it wouldn't have mattered at all. She must be desperate, I thought, to even consider leaving.

"Take it easy Helen, nobody said you had to date these jerks. Anyway, every once in a while, something good wanders in."

"I'm sorry. I forgot you find boyfriends in here."

"Are you saying that I have lousy taste in men?"

"Well, I don't want to be insulting but look around. Let's just say you're not too discriminating."

I had to laugh with her. She was right, of course, they were there in full force that night. The slider had a new girl, and he was running across the floor with her. When he got halfway across the hall, he slid the rest of the way, hanging on to his partner, so that the girl had to slide with him, or risk being dragged across that splintered floor on her knees.

Then there was the tail gunner. Only a new girl would dance with him because of his hand placements. He was persistent, even though he had been admonished, many times, by the management. Sam once made him stay away for six weeks, until he could behave himself. Big Louie kept an eye on him, and the girls would avoid him.

There was always one innocent new girl.

Also, I saw Mervin standing by the snack bar counter. He was a lot of fun, because he could hardly hear the music, due to the bells and birds that were making so much noise in his head. To control the noise, he had tinfoil wrapped around his ankles, and he smeared some kind of smelly ointment in his mouth and ears. It almost made sense when he explained it. It was just awful to try to get close enough to dance with the poor guy.

One of the things I hated about Tony, was the way he talked to everybody. We had all kinds of women working there including one with a bunch of kids who had a daytime job, too, and he called them all "lazy cunts." I'll bet you guessed that he was not in love with me either, but the owner, Sam knew me for being a straight person. I never fooled around with alcohol or drugs, and I kept my private life private, so he had nothing on me. Also, I was one of the top five ticket makers in the place, so he couldn't get rid, of me on the grounds of my being non-productive. It was a standoff.

"What are you sitting on your ass for?" Tony always said hello so politely. "I thought you had early customers, Miss Hollywood. So, where the fuck are they?"

"Dead or in jail." What a sweet, gentle man.

Being the enlightened, civilized person that I was, I repressed my urge to leap up and rip his face off. I just sipped my tea, smiling sweetly, while

I flicked the ash from my cigarette on his blue suede shoes. "So nice to see you again. You're looking well. I see you're still kicking dogs and pulling wings off flies."

He flipped me off, turned, and walked away.

Greek Helen called after him, "Why don't you sing us a song. We can't leave until two."

We shouldn't laugh at him, he just gets meaner, and then he takes it out on people who can't defend themselves, like some of those poor little undocumented women who don't speak English. He's been hiring and firing a lot of them lately. It seemed to reinforce, the idea that he might have other business going on. I wondered about drugs, or, maybe some kind of prostitution.

Theoretically, everyone who worked in the dancehall had to have a police license to work there. We were fingerprinted, and everything. That was supposed to keep the criminal element, also the illegals or undocumented workers, out of the dancehall. I was sure that Tony had a way around the rules. Fake IDs? Not that hard in a city like Los Angeles. L.A. is a place where you can get anything for a price, and if there was enough demand, you could, probably, get it wholesale. I knew that something was going on that Sam wasn't dealing with. Either he didn't know, or he was just looking the other way. Things might have been different if he weren't spending so much time in the hospital, I do not believe, that he thought anything illegal, could be good for business. Maybe, he wasn't noticing because his illness, had taken over his life. He was away from Musicland more that he was there.

I didn't have long to dwell on this because the next thing I knew, Danny, accompanied by a group of men, got off the elevator, and I became extremely interested in dancing with him. He was not very tall, about five seven, but he had the most interesting face. Obviously Chinese, I guessed Mandarin, northern Chinese. He possessed a very fair complexion, all pink and white. He had large, beautiful eyes and high cheekbones and such an air of refinement. His tailoring was impeccable and very British. I noticed his hands, slender and elegant, everything about him looked like money and breeding. Even the way he held his cup and the way other men walked over to speak to him at his table told me something about him.

I didn't want to be obvious, but he intrigued me. Actually, a plan for revenge began to take shape in my mind.

Danny walked purposely over to the line where I was sitting. I felt a little edgy about him. There was a reason that Mei Ling was so nervous about him. I had never asked her about what she was afraid of. She never confided in me about what it was about the man that seemed to unnerve her. He was always accompanied by a group of men, who seemed to be his retinue. Yes, there was something regal about him. It wasn't his bearing, when I thought of him after this time, I thought that it was a kind of arrogance. It was like a king or prince bestowing his attention on a peasant.

Danny offered me his hand. There was a faint scent that I recognized that followed him. I also think that there was a slight aura, very masculine, surrounding him. It reminded me of something, I had heard about pheromones. He might have been blessed with that glamorous scent or aura. I felt a little excitement.

There was also an element of feeling a little grateful. I was happy to be invited to the party one more time. It is nice to be noticed.

We danced; and he spoke little. His accent was British and Chinese, confusing me that he might be from Hong Kong. No, my first impression was correct, he was from Taiwan. His father had been in politics when the Communists took over. He was an aristocrat, and we were definitely from separate universes.

He leaned close enough to me on the dance floor to whisper something, and his eyelashes touched my cheek. "I want to make love to you.," he said.

When I put my left hand on his shoulder, he moved my right hand to his other shoulder. Then, he put both of his hands, on the back of my waist. That put us even closer together, while we were swaying to the music. Good dancers are appreciated even up there, but I couldn't seem to trust the situation. It felt more like acting, than anything I'd been involved with lately.

I was glad that I was wearing a simple long white gown, and very simple, jewelry. Nothing flashy, but tasteful. I wanted to forget Toshi for a little while.

Even though I knew he would when he asked me to spend the night with him, I hesitated. I don't have anything against sex. I was no longer attached; he was attractive and compelling in his own way. Still, there was something about him that made me uneasy, I wondered, why Mei Ling seemed a little afraid of him.

"You're not insulted, are you?" I couldn't help thinking about that night with Toshi. I almost burst into tears, thinking about it. He was an attractive man. Not that I had anything to prove after being ditched, by Toshi.

"Not insulted, just cautious. You've known me for a while. You've even danced with me. It's been a while. You never really flirted with me before. Why this sudden notice?"

"I want to make love to you. You are more available now, with Toshi out of the picture. I know a nice motel. We could have breakfast, spend some time together. I would bring you back to your car."

His confidence was not appealing.

"Maybe, we could talk about that, but not tonight. Let me think about it."

"I see. I think that I have offended you. I apologize. I didn't mean to upset you, I meant to compliment you. I think you are genuinely nice to be with. I would like you to be my exclusive friend. I know that you have just had a bad breakup. If you would like that arrangement with me, I think you will find me generous. I also promise not to humiliate you in front of all of your friends."

Danny was right about that, about the humiliation. Maybe, he thought that by reminding me, it would make me more vulnerable to his plan.

"It's up to you, Frankie. I think it could be very pleasant. You don't have to give up your acting career, since I won't be here forever. It's just that while we are together, I don't want you to go out with anyone else."

Men, I swear, especially Asian men. If he weren't so attractive in other ways, I think I would have picked up that slender, beautiful body, and thrown it out a window. Oh hell, I thought, you might as well let him think that you might go along with the plan. If he gets to be a real pain in the ass, there's more where he came from. I thought about China's teeming millions and burst out laughing.

"I promise to think about it. Give me a little time." I smiled but gazing up at him. I didn't want to commit myself before I know him better.

"I'll be back before the end of the week. Let me know." When he checked me out, he made my sum for the evening look like my envelope on Friday, in a good week.

There was also the "Dance Hall Rule Number One." There were a few things that I knew and anyone up there who planned to be there for a while needed to remember. The first rule was "Never give a Customer a Definite No." The second rule was "Never Give a Customer a Definite Yes." Either one of those could cost you friends, tickets, and respect.

The correct answer to those first two rules was "Always make it a definite maybe."

So, there it was, my sex life didn't have to suffer with the loss of Toshi's attention. If I had any concerns about it. Which, by the way, I didn't. We both knew that what he was offering was a relationship as meaningful, as catching a bus.

In fact, this little episode with Danny, two days after losing Toshi, reinforced my conviction that men are like buses, another one will be along any minute.

Going home that night I thought about Lupe, Linda and all the other women whose bodies had been found. Maybe there were more from Musicland. Tony had hired a lot of undocumented women, and there were so many that disappeared. It seemed like nobody was keeping track, anyway.

The rain had stopped, and the streets were almost empty. It was strange about the downtown that after midnight, actually before that, the streets were empty. It was an eerie feeling; like being the last person alive in an empty city. During the day traffic made it nearly impossible to drive faster than ten miles an hour, sometimes less. I lived so close to downtown, that it only took ten minutes to drive home at night and a half hour to get there, during daylight, on time.

The problem in a city as big as L.A. is that there are a lot of people who live outside of the regular ways of identifying people. Even if they found their bodies, who could or would identify them without giving their own, maybe illegal, status away? I wondered who else might suspect what was happening? I couldn't talk to Sam about it because of his illness. Big Louie was the most official person I could share my concerns with. Besides Sam, me and a few of their friends, nobody else seemed concerned.

Brian, the dirty cop, especially scared me. He would hurt anyone if they got in his way. Nobody was able to say how or what they knew about him, but I don't think that I was the only one who felt that he was corrupt. I knew that in my heart, and I also felt that he had something to do with what was happening.

How to prove it though?

I could feel his intense, ruthless attitude. He didn't like me. His eyes were cold and unforgiving . . . I doubted that he was a safe person to be around. Even Bev, seemed very tense when he dropped by, even if all they did, was have coffee, at a table. I'd never seen him dance with her. Maybe he thought she was crazy enough or dumb enough, to tell him any rumors going around about what was happening?

I was afraid for her and me.

I got home, closed the door, and felt a chill that caused me to shudder. That quickly reinforced my decision about the séance. I was determined to try to do something about the ongoing situation in my house. I really didn't know what to do about the disappearing women. The séance was about the real problem of that cloying scent, and the unwanted intrusion into my private life.

It was obvious that something had to be done and I was counting on my friends, Adriana and Teji to do something about it.

I wondered if the two things that worried me could somehow be related?

CHAPTER NINE

SEX AND MONEY

That Thursday morning, I was glad that the séance was just a few days away. Remembering that shadowy image of Linda, was more than creepy. I wasn't terrified, at least not like that Friday, when I heard the sobbing. I felt sad that it was my friend, Linda who was trying to let me know something. I was almost sure about that. Then, I wondered about why Tony, had wanted to talk to me. It couldn't be anything good.

Toshi, even though he was in the hospital, was not the first thing I thought about. He was alive and they said, not seriously injured. I had questions about what happened, but those answers would come later.

My day was spent doing some important things that I had neglected lately. I called my agent. He wasn't available but I left a message.

Not a good sign.

When he did call back, he offered me a small list of "cattle calls" Not a very promising response. I asked him about the ad that he had mentioned two weeks ago.

He sounded embarrassed.

"They wanted someone who was older, who looked younger," he explained.

"What does that mean?" I was creeped out, for a very different reason.

"It means that you look like a sophisticated woman in her middle-to late twenties. They said that they wanted someone who looked like a teenager, but they wanted her older, at least twenty-one."

"What kind of add for what?" I was infuriated. "What was it, Porn?"

"Not exactly. Well, I have another call coming in. I'm checking something else out for you. If I get you an interview, are you open next week?"

"Of course." I hung up the phone and was angry, but I thought about it for a minute.

Thursday night seemed uneventful, at first. Even, the women on the line didn't seem inclined to talk about any of the things that were topics the night before. I had a headache and I felt like I was barely able to walk around with the buzzing in my head. I didn't feel like dancing, and it showed, later, in my ticket count when I was getting ready to go home.

Even after the romance from the night before, I wasn't expecting Danny, especially. He was not the kind of nightly customer that some were. It wouldn't be a surprise if we didn't see him for as much as a week. The rumor was that he was a businessman, and that he was involved with some of the high finance and maybe somewhat illegal things, going on, in Chinatown.

I was on the floor with one of my favorite customers who happened to be, a very good dancer. I glanced up and saw Danny dancing with Choug. They were doing the Tango and they were good together as I saw people had stopped dancing to watch their maneuvers.

It was a public humiliation. After he had made such a public display of courting me, he had turned around and made a display of his intimate form of dancing with my friend. It was a small loss of face.

Well, I thought, it serves me right for thinking of him as anything but business., I thought. Shit! Men! Damn his eyes!

Who does he think he is? Toshi, and now Danny, had both shown me how little I mattered in their scheme of things.

I was glad the night ended. I couldn't wait to get out of there. I got my things, headed to car, and sped off. I drove home thinking about what was going on. They found Lupe, after Stan was arrested. Then, there were the threats from Brian and Tony. If Stan was the murderer, why was this happening? I was sure that there was more to the missing, and more bodies than I knew or could imagine. What was going on? What happened to Toshi? I couldn't stand to think that I caused or had anything to do with that accident.

There wasn't any evidence that anyone at Musicland had anything to do with the murdered woman, except that meeting with Tony, Brian, and Henry, but I was sure that they had some knowledge, even if they weren't involved. How could I find out what was happening?

My next step would be to check with Choug. Her brothers would know if there was something going on. They were friends of friends who knew what was happening in their city.

A new world's record was established in the 20-yard dash between my car and my front door. I got inside the house and instantly, I felt the cold impending rain in my bones.

There was nothing was really on TV, after the sports report on my favorite team. I picked myself up, got undressed, and went to bed. I laid there, unable to sleep, as the phone rang, five or six rings several times during the night. I thought it might be Tony, so I didn't answer, but it didn't help the awful lonely feeling.

In bed, I didn't sleep, but I hovered on the edge of sleep until the overpowering scent engulfed my room. I pulled the covers up over my chin, until I heard the sobbing. I sat up in bed in time to see a shadowy figure. It behaved as though it was weeping, with her head in her hands, by the window. The room was suffused with moonlight, but her figure was almost solid. I knew she wasn't there, but still, there she was.

Maybe, the next step would be to communicate. I said, "Linda. I know it's you. How can I help you? Can you tell me what you need? What can I do? Tell me!"

She didn't respond except that her image faded into the moonlight. The room was empty, and the cold feeling began to disperse.

While I lay awake wondering, while going over everything in my mind, until daylight, it occurred to me that since Lupe had been killed after Stan was arrested, there was some proof that Stan wasn't the only one involved. Then I was right, that there could be more murders, more bodies discovered, and more going on. Did he have a partner or was it bigger than that? Could it just be a copycat?

Maybe I was wrong. Maybe they found her after they arrested Stan. What if he killed her before he was arrested? Were there others? Maybe I was exaggerating the possible body count in my mind. There were a lot more women missing, who could potentially have been victims.

Stan had never seemed to have any friends up there. Some of the guys would show up occasionally with pals, but I had never even seen Stan talking to another guy, except Filipino Henry. I guess all of the guys talked to a pimp, once in a while. I thought that I would toss and turn all night, but I was so tired, I ached. Then, I drifted off till noon. By then, my house was quiet, with no sobbing, no overpowering scents and only a comfortable bed. I slept until mid-morning. I awoke feeling like I had been a little restored.

CHAPTER TEN

ENGAGED

On Friday, the sport pages were still rehashing the Dodgers last game. Sometimes it seemed like the Dodgers were hexed by witchcraft or something; the dumbest things happened to that team. Like the time an outfielder was beaned by a paper cup thrown by an excited fan. Things were not going well since Koufax was forced to retire even with Drysdale pitching. I couldn't fix my mind on what I was reading, so I tossed the paper in the trash. Even my favorite team couldn't get me too interested on a morning like that.

That Lupe's body had been found, was not just depressing, it was terrifying. I had to get over it. There were lots of other things to think about. George was a problem, but I thought he would be easy to eliminate from the confusion.

Oh boy, was I wrong about that!

While I went around the house opening the windows, muttering to myself, I thought about how to get rid of Linda. Spirit or not, she was more than a nuisance, and taking an unwarranted interest in my sex life. It had to stop! I wasn't kinky enough to appreciate the presence of another being, even a disembodied one, in my bed. Orgies have never been my thing. Just the thought of all those elbows, and knees, and sweaty armpits, just puts me off.

Even a three-some would be distasteful.

I like one-on-one intimacy with a large lacing of romance.

Also, there was a small nagging doubt about her, Linda's, behavior. I had no way of knowing whether she'd had anything to do with Toshi's accident. If she did, then she could be dangerous.

So, how was I going to get rid of her?

I didn't really have any idea about why she was bothering me in the first place. Would the séance give us a clue? I sniffed the air. She didn't seem to be anywhere around at that moment. Communication with her had been pretty one-sided, so far, I wanted some answers.

Finally, I was glad that the séance was scheduled in the next few days, I was ready. If it didn't work, I was prepared for that. If it did work, well, I trusted Adriana because she knew her stuff.

It was payday, and that meant that I would have to visit Tony, in his office to straighten out my check. As usual, I was shorted about two hundred tickets. I kept totals of my tickets in a notebook, and checked my check, and timecards because he was always trying to slide away with a little chunk of my pay. Not because he got to keep it, it was just for meanness. He had done it so many times, that Sam expected to see me in his office the day after payday, to have the bookkeeper check the records.

It could wait till Sam was here tomorrow. If he weren't in the hospital, he would be in to check on the operation. Tony had been trying to get me alone in his office, for a couple of nights.

When I got to work, the first thing, I noticed was that Sam was back. There he was with Mei Ling, sitting at a table drinking coffee, and smoking his ever-present stogie. His appearance scared me as he was thinner, and his condition more fragile, every time I saw him.

I made a big show of smelling his cigar. I sighed, "Very mellow, Sam. If I could find out where you get them, I'd start up."

Sam laughed; I could always make him laugh. The boss was an old friend of mine. He'd been in love with me two years ago, in vain, I might add. We were good friends and even though I turned him down to being more than my boss, we still clicked.

He put down the cigar, stood up, and gave me a hug, and said I looked terrific. He was a sweet old dear. He looked very pale, and vulnerable to me. Mei Ling was sitting at the table with him, holding hands, probably causing no end of gossip. We sat down, I ordered a tea from the waitress and the three of us had tea, and chatted for a while to an old Sinatra song, "When I Was Seventeen . . ."

When Mei Ling excused herself and went back to the line before I started to leave with my paycheck, and Sam stopped me. He had some questions about Tony, and how things were going. It was the first chance I'd had to talk to him in a while. I wondered if he knew about Linda.

"Did you ask Mei Ling?" I was in big enough trouble with Tony, without having it get back to him that I ratted him out to the boss.

"You know her. She can't say anything bad about anybody. I know that she's afraid of him. I had to tell him that there are limits to what I'll put up with. Has he been pushing you around?"

"Not more than usual. You heard about French Linda and Stan?"

He looked sad. "Yes, I feel bad about that. I know it probably would have happened whether I was here or not, but I wish we could have protected her better."

"You don't have any control over things that happen out there, any more than any of us do. As far as Tony is concerned, he's what you would expect. There's been a lot of turnovers, with the Latinas."

I didn't want to worry him, but he would hear it from someone. Not from Mei Ling. I thought she didn't want to worry him, but he would hear about Lupe soon enough.

When I said I had to get back to the line, he smiled, and nodded. He waved me away. I didn't get very far past the snack bar when I saw George approaching. He motioned for me to join him at the time clock, where I could check in. So masterful, and what a natty dresser! I was always impressed by his appearance. I wondered what old movie had inspired the cigarette holder, he was sporting that night, and, of course, the ascot at his throat.

I tried not to laugh. It was so funny and also, he didn't smoke.

"You . . . okay?"

As I was checking in, he hooked his hand under my elbow as he steered me to a table. Obviously, he had something on his mind. I hoped he hadn't hired an orchestra and booked a church for the forthcoming event. I was close.

"I gotta surprise." He whipped out a little box.

Oh no, I thought. What to do! I shouldn't accept, but I wouldn't be true to the Gold Diggers Code if I refused a diamond, no matter how small.

"Oh George, I can't really . . . It's too much. I'm not ready. You're pushing things too fast." By his standards we were now a couple. After all, I did let him kiss me.

"Jus open. Put it on. Please. I wan' you see."

I opened the box and was stunned. For once George had exquisite taste. The stone was a little over two karats. I had a pretty good eye, and it was a beautiful, clear color. It had to be an H or I in clarity. I would check it with my loop later to find only a small flaw, but as far as the naked eye could discern it was an almost perfect stone, set as a solitaire.

I was overwhelmed. Why George? Why me? Why not? I am always a pragmatist. The bird in the hand, is always better than whatever is out there in the bush. Nobody else, that I could think of, was going to be buying me a diamond solitaire this night, or any near nights I could imagine. So, I accepted it.

We were leaving the table to go to the dance floor when Terrible Tony walked past the table. He couldn't resist a remark to George about dancing with the new girls.

George said he wanted Tony to know about us.

Shit. Of all the people in the world to tell anything to, Tony was the worst. Before I could stop him, the cat was out the bag.

"She's gonna marry me. Show him."

He pulled my hand up to show to Tony.

"What a rock! Congratulations," he turned insultingly to me. "It just proves there's one born every minute."

"What he'd say?" George didn't always get the conversational nuances.

"Nothing George, he's just a jerk who doesn't want anybody to be happy." I made up my mind to speak to Sam about Tony. The man was so up front about trying to ruin business for me. That kind of behavior had to be curbed.

"I'm happy," George said, and he was. He had the biggest dumb smile on his ugly face. It made me feel terrible, but I couldn't turn down that diamond.

I am not stupid. I was foolish, but I would do it again.

George ordered tea, and a couple of stale doughnuts, to celebrate the occasion. His face was split by the biggest grin. There was no chance that I was going to forget that we were now engaged.

His smile was as creepy as a Halloween mask. I shuddered at the idea of a closer relationship with my dear old lonesome friend. I had the uneasy suspicion that being haunted by the ever-present George, wasn't going to be much better, than keeping company with the dead.

Of course, I had to go to breakfast with George. He stayed around the hall for a couple of hours and promised to come back. He had business to take care of. As I walked him to the elevator, he handed me a hundred extra tickets with a flourish. Things were definitely picking up.

After he left, the next thing I knew, Ed Wong was walking off the next elevator.

I knew I had to ditch the ring before I talked to Ed. Then I had to get rid of Ed Wong before George came back to take me to breakfast. Also, I had forgotten that there were people in there who knew Ed, and some of the people who knew George. What if some of the same people knew both of those guys? The story of that enormous diamond was going to be spreading all over the damn place.

Maybe I would have to explain it to Ed. Could I?

The cashier had some experience in these things, so she placed the diamond in my little envelope that would hold my tickets until the end of the evening, with a folded piece of paper around the ring, inside the register.

I told her that I would pick it up at two. We're friendly, but I don't trust her. However, I know how she augments her salary from the register, and I can prove it. I am sure that she has figured out that I know, so she will behave for at least a couple of hours. Basically, she was a nice person except about money.

Ed spotted me and asked me to dance. I remember that the jukebox played, "Unchained Melody" and it sounded like a dirge to me. We moved to the music for a while.

"I'm sorry, Frankie, but I find this particular tune depressing," Ed said. "Let's sit the rest of this one out."

I couldn't agree with him more, as we sat down at a table. Both elbows on the table, and a serious expression on his face; had me sitting up straight in my chair.

"Have you given any thought about what I said the last time I saw you? I spoke with someone else about it." Concern was written all over him. It was flattering but it also made me feel that Ed was a true friend.

"About what?" So much had happened that I really couldn't remember what we had talked about the last time.

"Real estate, Frankie; I'll sponsor you in Real Estate School, and even pay for your school, if you're interested."

He patted my hand. He was serious and he really meant it. If I said no, it might be a real opportunity passing me by.

Truthfully, I had not given it much thought, until yesterday, but I didn't want to say no. It might be a way out of the Musicland, and still not be as confining as an office job. "I am thinking about it. I just haven't made up my mind."

I asked him for a pen, and I wrote my phone number on a napkin, and gave it to him. He had to leave early, but I was glad that he'd come in.

"Maybe you could give me a call and let me know the name of the school and a number I should call to set it up." I thought about it for a minute. "It couldn't hurt to check it out. Thanks Ed."

When we parted, he held my hand and said that he would give me a call in a couple of days. I told him Monday or Wednesday would be good. I knew that I was holding a séance in my house on Tuesday. I could hardly wait. It was beginning to sound exciting, but I had things to work out with George.

Big Louie, our Latino assistant manager, was dancing with one of the newer illegals. Because I didn't speak Spanish, I had never spoken to her, but she looked like a sweet child tossed into a pen full of ravening crocodiles, if crocodiles could raven. He sometimes spent his own money, to make some of the girls less terrified, when things were slow. Like Sam, the owner, he was unusual in the annals of dancehall management. Tony was worse than average, Louie, and Sam were way better, than average. I watched him do a mean fox trot, then a quick step, while keeping up a polite conversation with the little one. He was light on his feet for a guy that must have weighed over three hundred pounds. He nodded at me, I guessed that he wanted to talk to me, after he finished giving his chosen an hour's worth of tickets.

His nod told me he wanted to speak to me and since thirst had overtaken me anyway, I walked over, and I leaned against the Snack Bar and waited for him. I liked Big Louie. The trouble was that he was often honest with me. I used to joke about it and tell him that I would prefer having him talk behind my back than to tell me stuff I didn't want to hear, to my face.

He checked her out and made a beeline for me, but he didn't check me in. We both knew that I wasn't hurting for tickets, and that I wouldn't mind a couple of minutes of conversation, at the corner of the snack bar.

"Can I buy you a Coke?"

I nodded, he signaled to the waitress, and she went to get my drink.

"I heard about you and George, Frankie." Louie was what I thought it would have been like to have a brother.

"Look," I said. "It wasn't my idea. He's been on this for I don't know how long. He wore me down." Well, it was true, in a way if you left out the two-karat diamond.

"You mean he wore you down and you are really going to marry him?" Louie looked at me waiting patiently for me to admit that I was a gold-digging dancehall girl.

"Come on, Louie. You know me better than that. I won't say that I'm sorry. He's asking for this."

"No doubt, you're right, Frankie, but I don't think that you've thought this through. George is a good customer. He has lots of friends who will be unhappy, when you make him look like a fool. If he gets mad, he could go off like a bomb."

Louie was like a sweet, big brother to me as put his arm around my shoulder. He was a nice guy. What he said was about the same kind of thing I'd been thinking.

"Don't think I haven't thought about it. I swear that I will try to save his face, his feelings and everything except his wallet."

Louie took his arm from my shoulder and gave it a little punch.

"You're hopeless. Did you see me dancing with the new girl? Her name is Alicia. She is so scared. Try to be nice to her, Frankie."

"I don't speak Spanish. Maybe Choug could take her under her wing a little bit. I'll mention it."

"Thanks. lady. Did you hear about Lupe?" I think I'm going to have a talk with the Latinas. They need to know that there is something going on.

His eyes looked up in the direction of the elevator and his face changed, and I knew that someone had come in that was familiar to us. "Oh, oh it looks like someone is looking for you."

Without turning around, I knew that George had come back.

CHAPTER ELEVEN

WORKING THINGS OUT

Breakfast with George after work was quite an event. He knew the waiters, workers, and the patrons. and apparently everyone else in Chinatown. They all stopped to talk to him at the table, mostly in Chinese. Then, nodding and smiling at me, they left in time for the next batch to arrive. I had a feeling I knew what the good news was. I was concerned because I had no real intention of becoming Mrs. Lonesome George.

Between the appetizers, and the arrival of the steamed rice accompanied by all kinds of goodies, including fried oysters, I spent some time working it out. The best plan would be one in which he decided that I wouldn't make a proper wife and drop me. Then he would save face, and I could keep the ring without a problem

Dream on, Frankie, I told myself. Dream on.

This plan could be tricky, because I didn't want him to end our relationship with a lot of hostility. Then, there was plan B, where if all else failed, I could lose the ring, and then break the engagement. This could be even trickier and might mean a vacation away from the dancehall until things cooled off. If he was serious about a wedding, I might pick up trousseau money ahead of the breakup, which could help pay for a vacation.

My mind worked on all this while George beamed at me across the table. I stifled an urge to scream, I would be cool, while I thought of something.

"George, maybe you shouldn't tell everyone we are engaged. It's too soon. I still have to work up there. If you tell everyone, it might be bad for business. Nobody wants to dance with your future wife."

"Thas' right. So, we wanna get married tomorrow, and you stay home."

"We can't get married for at least a couple of weeks, and I have to keep working until we do."

"If you need money, I give you money. If you wanna work, get a different job."

This wasn't going to be easy. What a stubborn clod! I felt the weight of the diamond on my finger. It was worth the effort.

"I don't feel well. If it's okay with you, George, I'm going to go home. Maybe I won't work tomorrow."

"It's okay. You don' work tomorrow, I give you money." He looked so concerned that I felt more than a little ashamed of myself.

When we were saying goodbye in the parking lot, George handed me two twenties, and asked me if I needed anything. He had his car, I had mine, so, I was driving myself home.

George let me know that he didn't expect anything from me, till after the wedding, but I decided to give him my phone number. After all, we were now somewhat officially engaged.

I kissed him goodnight, he lingered, and I tried not to lose my patience. Is there anything worse, than being mooned over by someone you can hardly stand the sight of?

I was exhausted. The strain of all that lying was getting to me. It was hard not to hate someone who insisted on being kind to me, adoring me, when I couldn't reciprocate. I'm not proud of myself, especially in this matter. I was a survivor. I had decided long before this happened, that no man would ever take advantage of me.

My stepmother had called me stupid. She said that I was so gullible that any man could and would take advantage of me. She had also said, "Once an alley cat, always an alley cat." I had spent all of my adult life proving that at least some of what she'd said wasn't true.

I went to sleep thinking that I could still smell a lingering odor of Linda's perfume. "Sorry sweetie, I'm sleeping alone." I addressed the dark, but I was too tired to try to communicate with her about permanently disappearing out of my life. The séance might take care of that, as I enjoyed her imagined disappointment. What did she want from me anyway?

Sleep didn't come easily. I was too tired to think about what to do. A ghost was just one more worry compared to the way everything else was working out. There was still a question in my mind about her involvement in the coincidence of Toshi's accident. Then, I wondered how he was doing? Should I call the hospital? No, he knew that I must know about the accident, and that he hadn't been alone.

To hell with him!

Then, the question of why those three creeps, Tony, Henry, and Brian, wanted to know something? They thought I might know more than I did. What would I know that would interest them? Or worse, what could I possibly know that would scare them enough to hurt me? To keep me from telling? What? It didn't make sense. They showed an interest in what Stan might have told me.

About what?

Thinking about all of this, and poor Lonesome George, made me feel lonely and overwhelmed.

That night I dreamed of being George's wife, and it was a nightmare. He came home from work in the dream. I was in a house dress tending a pot on the stove. I could hear a baby crying. I fished some chicken feet out of the pot, and some spinach. He was delighted. There were more children, at least a dozen, running through the dream, knocking things over and yelling. Then I couldn't find the baby. George insisted on having his arm around me, while I tried to cope with everything else. It seemed like he wasn't being affectionate, but that he was strangling me. There I was locked in a house forever, with that ugly brute drooling and slobbering all over me. There was no way out!

CHAPTER TWELVE

THINGS ARE NOT WORKING OUT

I woke up screaming, and I was resolved to get out of this engagement as quickly as possible. I was determined, even if it meant that I might have to give the ring back. I hated that greed that had gotten me into this mess to begin with. Nothing was worth this aggravation.

That night I walked into Musicland, with a confident smile. I said a friendly, charming good evening to the Hungarian waitress who was back at her job, with a bandage on her arm. I wanted to show no hard feelings on my part. She looked nervous, like she was afraid of me.

It's so ridiculous, when I'm such an amiable person. Choug and I worked out a little routine with Tony. She stood in front of him, rubbing her pelvic bones against him while she complained about her check.

While he came on to her, I took some red nail polish and wrote "asshole" on his back. It looked lovely, he was wearing a white suit, with sequins.

Nobody told him about it until halfway through the evening when he took his jacket off. All of the customers were careful not to laugh, but everyone looked pleased. Tony was blind with fury, but he didn't know, for sure, who to take it out on.

Of course, the undocumented women got it first. He called three of them up to the cashier's desk and fired them in plain sight of everyone on the line, and in the bullpen. One poor little one started crying and begging him. Alicia, her name was Alicia, the girl that Big Louie liked. Tony wrote something on a card and handed it to her.

I suddenly wanted to see that card more than anything. Why did this have to happen on Big Louie's night off? It was my fault, partly anyway. I don't speak very much Spanish, but I was going to try. I knew that this could be important and might answer some questions about what happened to Lupe.

The poor babies went to the locker room next to the john, so I went to the john. I didn't want Tony to see me talking to them.

Alicia was there all right, crying her eyes out. I really felt sorry for her. This was a hard job when you knew what you were doing and could speak the language. Up close she looked about fifteen. She was very thin, and pretty with the dark Latin eyes, and small delicate features. Her hair was long and somewhat unkempt. She wore a black cocktail dress that was too big for her and that she probably got from a thrift shop. Her shoes were cheap high heeled sandals, with one strap that had broken and been tied together. I would have hated to have that rubbing my heel while I was dancing all night.

Since Tony was known to disregard all the rules of decency, bouncing in and out of the dressing room, and the john without bothering to knock, I had to hurry so as not to get caught. His reasoning was that if we weren't doing anything wrong, like shooting up dope, it shouldn't matter whether he was there or not. Why should a bunch of down-at-the-heel-broads care whether he watched us dress or not? What a creep!

I motioned to her, "Por favor," politely, I didn't want to offend her. "Su tienes el papel que escribe Tony para oustad?" It was my best pigeon, Spanish.

She looked puzzled, then she nodded, but it didn't look like she wanted me to share whatever information he'd given her. I motioned, finger to lips for secrecy, and then pointed to the door. I said, "Shhh Tony."

I guess she decided that I meant that I didn't want Tony to know, so she let me see it. A phone number, I thought, harmless enough. I didn't write it down, I didn't want to worry her; so, I memorized it, telling her "Gracias." Then, I hurried to my locker and wrote it down while I was putting on my lipstick. It was easy to write it on my plastic makeup bag with my eyebrow pencil. I'm sure that nobody saw me. The three orphans were hanging on to each other and talking in rapid Spanish. I could only understand a few words. They had problems. The little one's husband, Alicia's had been picked up by the immigration agents, and sent back. She was pregnant. If she could stay long enough to have the baby, and if the husband could get back, with their own little citizen in the family, they could probably stay.

I don't know if her figuring was true, but I sure admired their spirit. I hoped that she made it, but if Tony was helping, I feared for her safety. I feared the worst.

I didn't have Big Louie's number, or I would have called him to see what could be done. Sam was gone. I didn't have a chance to ask Mei Ling, I just assumed that he was too ill to come into Musicland.

Speak of the devil and he appears. Tony burst in. "Quietes cabronas!" Leave it to him to always have just the right thing to say.

I started to leave before he could get into it with one of the other girls. A more assertive type was warming up, to tell him where to put it in thirty-five thousand words or more. It could get violent, so I started to go into a stall, but he grabbed my arm.

"What are you hanging around here for Hollywood? Trying to score a little grass? These losers can't help you."

"Lay off, Tony. I've got people waiting for me out there. I just needed a little pit stop. Don't put your hands on me."

"I'd like to put a little more than my hands on you. I would like to lay you out and call in some friends."

"Don't push me or I'm going to Sam. He should know about some of the crap you pull. I'm warning you to get off my back or you'll regret it"

"Big talk! Don't mess with me, lady. Just get your ass out on that line. I don't want to see you hanging around these beaners either."

I came storming out of there fuming. "He can't tell me who I can talk to and who I can't." I was muttering under my breath. I was so upset that I almost ran down James, an engineer, who was polite and enjoyable conversation. I was so mad that I couldn't speak. I just nodded and checked in.

We danced silently for a few moments and then he ushered me to a table, where we could sit and talk. The waitress was a little sullen, but I was perfectly friendly to her.

James was from Shanghai, and he spoke with a British accent. He passed the time regaling me with stories of his adventures as a construction engineer. Although he flirted with me, he wasn't exclusively mine. When he asked me about the morals and habits of some of the other women, I tried not to look offended. He was looking for sex. I think he had given up on me, but apparently, he liked to chat with me. I was amused by his honesty.

James looked at his watch, and then, hurriedly checked me out. He tipped me and bought fifty extra tickets.

How sweet, I thought. I could always use the extra tickets.

I noticed that George had just come in and was leaning against the snack bar counter smiling smugly, waiting for me.

"One of these days, you'll weaken and go out with me." James steered me to the check out. "I'll be waiting," he joked.

George grabbed my elbow, before the elevator door closed behind James' back. He steered me to the time clock.

"What did he say? What was he saying?"

"Nothing, George. It was nothing important, honestly. What's the matter with you?"

"You're making dates with him after work. You are not honest with me. You think I don' know. You think I don' hear. I hear what he is saying."

Great, I thought, and this is going to get worse.

CHAPTER THIRTEEN

MONDAY

Sunday passed without much incident. I danced with the regulars, had tea with No-Nose Harry and passed the time with Annie, on the line. Hardly anyone was there that night. I think that there were about forty girls because they were concerned with their checks being docked. Even the bullpen, usually full, had about four or five guys there that night.

I had danced with George, but I told him that I needed to rest, and that I would surely see him tomorrow night. He had some business later with his uncle so he might not stay till closing. I went upstairs, counted my tickets. I did sit in the locker area and tried to rest. I had some aspirin in my purse, so I took a couple, and waited to see if the headache would abate.

When I came back down, some time had passed. Tony didn't buy the headache, but it was all I had to offer. I thought that George had given up and gone home.

The rest of the girls on the line were counting their tickets. I mentioned my plans for Tuesday to a couple of them, including Choug and Greek Helen. They would be there, they both confirmed. I went to my car and began the lonely ride home.

I noticed the car following me. It looked familiar. It was George and it gave me the creeps! Why was he following me? He didn't trust me, and he thought he was going to catch me. The nerve of that jerk! He could take that diamond and shove it "where the sun doesn't shine", as far as I was concerned. I just had to make it from the car to my house before he could confront me.

I had the advantage that he didn't know that I'd made him and his Jaguar. I had the keys in my hand when I parked my car as close to the front door as the curb allowed. I almost didn't have a front yard, so it was about a 15-20 ft.' sprint ahead of me. I took off my heels put them in my bag and put the shoulder strap over my shoulder. Then, with my house key in my hand, aimed and ready to insert in the lock, I made a dash for it!

I made it! I waited for a knock on the door. Nothing but silence. I waited for a few minutes in my semi-darkened living room. There was a night light that was always on when I was gone, but no sound.

There was nothing. I went to the frig for a glass of wine and changed into a robe and nightie.

I put my feet up and turned on the TV without the sound. That's the best way to watch the Three Stooges anyway. I relaxed.

Then, I checked and yup, his car was still out there.

I laughed.

He was waiting for someone to show up. Great! Have a ball, George, all by yourself out there. I'm not going to worry about it. If you even knock on that door, I'll call the police and tell them you're a customer, that followed me home. I will embarrass you.

The morning would be soon enough to get ready for my little get together. I was going to get some sleep. I really hadn't been sleeping very well. Everything was beginning to get on my nerves. Add George to a murder, what might be the ghost of Linda, and Toshi's defection, then accident, to the missing women, and I was feeling the stress.

Maybe my friend Ed Wong was right. He kept insisting that I consider another way to make a living. He could have a point. I wanted to hang in until there were some answers, but what he had to offer was worth considering. Ed never made it sound like there were any strings attached.

He really seemed like a friend. Yup, he could have a point.

I didn't check again but I went to sleep knowing that Lonesome George was out there waiting for something to happen. I think I was smiling as I drifted off with the familiar flower scent in my nostrils.

"Goodnight, Linda," I said out loud and smiled. I wasn't afraid of either haunting.

CHAPTER FOURTEEN

THE SÉANCE

They'll be here any minute, I thought. Maybe I should have made a dip. It's hard to know what's proper for a séance.

I placed a couple of brass candle holders, complete with large red candles on the table, without lighting them. I also had some other white candles in case that would be more in keeping.

I checked around the living room, it was tidy. The dining room had eight chairs, enough, if they wanted to use the table. I opened windows and checked the guest towels.

Annie showed up first. I really appreciated her being there on her night off. She sank into the big, upholstered armchair looking like a thin, edgy schoolteacher in her plaid granny dress and white collar.

"Relax. I'll get you anything you want to drink, except alcohol. Adriana says the spirits don't like spirits."

I babbled on and watched Annie try to get comfortable. As long as we'd worked together, this was the first time she'd ever been to my house.

"Of course," I gave her a choice pointing at the coffee and soft drinks on ice on the sideboard, "she didn't know Linda, who still seems to enjoy, second hand, of course, champagne." I was glad that I had put a couple of dishes with chips and peanuts near the drinks. Annie wasn't paying attention.

"Annie, are you going to share what's on your mind? Do you want me to guess?" I wasn't totally impatient; I was just tired of the mystery. It could be any number of things.

"Frankie, I'm pregnant." She blurted it out, just like that.

"For god's sake, Annie! Why haven't you said something?" She looked tired and thinner than I had ever seen her. "How long have you known?"

"A few weeks. I just found out for sure. Don't say anything to anybody. Please." She opened a can of orange soda and poured it in a glass. She probably thought that it would be healthier than a coke.

Oh hell, my mind was working on any clue.

"What are you going to do? Who's the father?"

She looked like she wanted to tell me, or somebody, but the doorbell interrupted.

"Of course."

I answered the door to Adriana, who was resplendent in flowing garments and dripping beads. The slender guy with a beard, wearing a white muslin shirt, jeans, sandals, and beads, was sort of cute, too.

"Adriana, this is my friend, Annie," I motioned to my friend.

"This is Teji. His contacts are more dependable than mine. Besides," she tossed her hair back with a gesture of her head, "I thought we needed some yang to balance all of this yin."

This time the phone, and the door went off together. I got the phone, and one of the others opened the door. The phone was George. "What's up?" I laid it on thick. "What do you want?" I was so disgusted with him after being stalked the night before. Anyway, I was really sick and tired of his clinging and the whole engagement thing. Although it was a lot easier to be friendly on the phone, than it was when he was hanging over me.

"How come you're not here?" I could hear the music, so I assumed he meant the dancehall.

"It's none of your business, but I took the night off, George. It's my day off. I take Monday or Tuesday off a lot of the time."

Thas' okay. We can go out." George was great. He would take me to the opera if I wanted to go and I didn't mind showing up with a guy in brown and white saddle shoes and an old movie version of an ascot over a suit that was too short and twenty years plus thousands of miles out of style.

"No, I can't go out. I have something else to do."

"Who's there?"

You can't fool George. By now the place was filling up with female squeals and laughter. "That's why we can't go out. Some of my friends from work are here. Just a little group of women." I could hear the deep booming male laugh that belonged to Teji.

"I hear a man."

Shoot! "Greek Helen just stopped by. Her brother brought her."

There was a silence.

"I wan' your address. I like a party." Well, there it was again.

"For goodness' sake, George, don't be silly. Her brother isn't staying. I don't believe you would like to be here alone with a bunch of women. Call me later, and maybe we can talk. Call me and say goodnight after midnight. Maybe we could go for a drive and look at the ocean," I said. Right on, I thought, while you paw me and slobber about getting married. You know where I live George; but I didn't say it aloud.

"It's okay."

Click.

He hung up leaving me a little troubled.

In the other room a crowd was forming. I should have had included a dip. "It looks like we're all here" I said and counted heads. "Everybody except Choug."

The doorbell went off again.

Annie opened it to Choug, wearing Levi's, a T-shirt and gang tattoos. She was carrying a rosary in her hand.

"Hey, I didn't know if I should dress up."

"Why do you have that with you?" I honestly couldn't figure it out.

"Protection, man. I'm a Catholic," as if that explained everything.

I looked at Adriana and she was looking at Teji. They were both shaking their heads in agreement. Protection from what? I didn't have time to get too creeped out.

"Are we going to sit at the table?" I motioned to the dining room area and the candles.

"Why not begin?" Adriana and Teji began to set up shop. The tarot cards came out of her large purse, and some white candles. She removed my red ones and put a different candle in the holders.

I said nothing.

Beverly was looking for a place to sit.

I had to ask, "Where's your Venusian?"

She said Marratz might join us later.

I said, "Swell. I'll just sit next to Adriana."

Adriana looked up and said, "No. You sit opposite me."

I moved around to that end of the table. Adriana sat at the head, Teji next to her on the right, then Choug, still clutching her beads. Then, on the other side of me, Big Beverly wearing an interesting latex outfit that fitted her six-foot frame like it had been molded on her. On the other side of Bev sat Annie. She clutched Helen's hand on her left. Helen, in a tailored pants suit, looked amused as she settled herself on Adriana's left.

Arrayed in my forest green pant suit, I surveyed the asymmetrically arranged table. There were seven of us waiting expectantly. We were ready to begin. I had been eager to get this together. Now, I wished for this to be over.

Adriana took charge. "Everyone! Put hands on the table! During the next few minutes try to keep holding hands, so that the circle of life will not be broken." As she talked, she lit the candles. "I have a small brass bell. I will use it for attention, if necessary. If you let go of the hand next to you, you are breaking the connection. Whatever you see or hear try to remain connected. It is a circle of light and protection. We need your serious intentions." She held Helen and Teji's hands. "This is not a game. Choug was correct in arming herself against the influence of darkness. Remember, we are here to listen and help souls who have tried to gain our attention."

Adriana freed a hand to motion to me. I dimmed the lights. There was now a silence and the flickering candlelight.

Teji broke in, "Before we start, I ask a blessing on what we are doing. Let us remain in the light and be protected from evil or the influence of evil. Let no evil enter here." There was a silence. He said, "Repeat after me. Let no evil enter here."

"Let no evil enter here." A chorus of voices responded.

He had our attention. I could see that even Helen, who could be counted on to be skeptical and amused about everything, looked serious.

Adriana let go of Helen's hand and shook the bell. It was incredibly quiet. The hair on the back of my neck ruffled from the faintest chill. I could see the faces of my friends in the flickering glow of the candlelight. Silence. I don't know when the others noticed, but the smell, subtle at first, began to engulf me. My hands clung to Beverly and Choug, as the room turned suddenly cold.

Annie whispered, "I'd know that perfume anywhere."

I think I moaned.

"Jesus and Maria!" The beads Choug had wrapped around her wrist rattled.

While all of this was going on, Teji inexplicably went to sleep. His head rolled backward in his chair.

"I don't have much time. Please help me." The woman's voice came from his lips. It was awfully familiar.

Adriana said, "We hear you, Linda. How can we help you? How can Frankie help you?"

"There are more murders. There is more than one murderer. They can't get away with it. We want justice."

"Who is we? They've got Stan." I wanted her to know.

"Frankie, you are in danger. He was not alone. He was only part of it. All of you are in danger. More women will die. There will be at least three attempts on your life. The dancers don't know the murderers are out there. Look for" the voice started to fade. "Look, . . . the film."

The voice was fading, and Teji was waking up.

"Wait! Wait a minute! Three attempts on all of us or three attempts on me? What film? Don't go!"

It was too late, of course. Teji was awake and the séance was over.

People got up and started milling around. I sat there feeling, and probably looking, stunned.

"Nice effects. I wonder how he made it sound so much like a woman." Helen had a glass in her hand. I should have made a dip. "The perfume was a neat touch," she said.

"Yeah," I said. "Would anyone like something a little stronger?" No affirmatives but I helped myself to a double scotch over ice. What an experience!

After some head shaking and comparing of notes, the group began to break up. I think that Helen said she was going in to work late. I said goodbye, and thank you, to Adriana.

I tried to give her some money, but she waved it off.

"You're in the middle of something, Frankie. She can't go to the light, unless she can let go of what she wants you to find. She thinks there is another murderer besides Stan. She's trying to warn you. I'd take it seriously if I were you." She and Teji departed in a swirl of fabric, a tinkle of bells, and beads, trailing a faint scent of sandalwood.

Choug hugged me, before she left and said that if I was scared of anything she and her brothers, home boys, would be there to help.

I thanked her. "I'll call you. We need to talk."

While I was saying goodbye to her, Beverly pressed my hand, and left with someone shadowy, lingering on the porch. I didn't get the chance to ask her about Brian. I planned to get a chance to have a heart to heart with her as soon as I could figure out how to get her alone.

That left Annie and me. Forgetting what she'd said, I offered her a drink.

She waved it away and asked for milk. I remembered.

"You're pregnant. I'm sorry, everything was happening . . . When?" I remembered how undone she'd been lately.

"December. You didn't press me about who the father is. That was nice." She drank her milk and had a white mustache like a little girl.

"It's not that I'm not interested." I stirred the ice in my glass. "I think that if you wanted me to know, then you'd tell me."

"I can't tell you, yet. I can't tell anybody. I hate him, and I want to get away from him. I don't want him to know about this. Nothing about this. When I go, I won't look back. I'll leave friends behind."

"Is he the only one you're afraid of? Who could scare you like that?"

"I can't tell you now. I will before I go, I promise."

She looked away.

Annie looked so scared that I didn't want to upset her by asking anything more.

"I hope that we can stay in touch. Do you realize this is the first time either one of us has been in the other's house?" I had never had anyone come to my house if you didn't count Linda. I'm still not too sure how to count that.

"I didn't expect to make real friends in the dance hall."

She laughed nervously. I agreed with Annie, but I also felt like it didn't have to be that way.

"You have more friends than you realize, including Choug and her brothers. I still feel bad about losing touch with Linda."

"In a way, you haven't."

"Do you believe it was her?" I did, but I wanted a friend to believe it too. Validation was what I craved.

"I think so. I'm not sure. I just wonder about the part where your life is in danger. I think I believe it enough to take it seriously." She paused and sipped her milk. "I think you should be careful, Frankie. You know that there is more to this than we thought."

"Thanks. I'll watch my step. You watch yours. If you ever need a space to hide out, this," I patted the sofa that I was sitting on, "makes into a very comfy bed. You're always welcome. No questions asked." I think that I only half meant it when I said it, but when Annie's eyes got shiny and moist, I realized that I did mean it. She was a nice person and an ally. I wondered who could be mean to Annie Fannie? He would have to be a really nasty creep.

What I found out later proved me more than right.

Just after Annie left, the phone rang. I looked at the clock and it showed twelve thirty. A nice time to be calling. It was George. He wanted to go out to breakfast.

I told him that it was too late, and I was tired. It was all too true.

"You don' love me."

"Don't start, George. Remember what happened the last time. I don't want to fight with you. Be nice and I'll see you and dance with you tomorrow."

"I love you."

"I know. Goodnight, George."

I wanted to scream. What a night! Death threats and George. Give me a break!

The number that Alicia had given to me popped into my head. I would call that and see what I could find out. I could get her address from Sam. I didn't want anything to happen to her. I took the message seriously. I just wasn't sure of what to do about it.

I went to sleep still wishing that I had served some chips and dip.

CHAPTER FIFTEEN

BAD NEWS

The next night, I was back in the hall, waiting for whatever was going to happen, to happen. Things were sticky, and I didn't have a plan or an idea about what to do about it. I wanted to talk to Choug. I had that number to call, the one my little Spanish speaking friend had given me, but I needed to have someone call for me. I could not pass as an illegal. I was concerned about the message from the séance. I needed to figure out what was going on.

When things are up in the air, and I don't know what else to do, I make sure that I look my best. I had my hair done and it was all teased into and swept up on one side and the glitter sprinkled on made it look almost like real copper. I sat on the line in a good copy of a Helen Rose original, a strapless, beaded, full length white gown, trying to exude a glamour and confidence that I wasn't feeling. I stared at the turning ball of mirrored light and seriously tried to think of a plan. The reflections of light against the tired old paint, seemed like my own personal efforts to bring a tiny bit of magic to the dance hall. The efforts of either one was just not enough. Neither the ball of glass, nor my Helen Rose copy, and sparkles in my hair, could hide the shabby surroundings or the equally shabby customers. Even some of the few other girls who were there early looked bedraggled, and sad. I was waiting for George. I couldn't pretend, and I couldn't ignore the squalor. It was depressing.

Just to make everything perfect, George showed up wearing, besides his usual sartorial splendor, what could only be described as a pout. The jukebox droned the song I always associated with him. Poor George and that god damned lonesome whippoorwill. Just looking at him irritated me, from the top of my upswept hair to the tip of my four-inch sandals.

George motioned me to a table. By the time I checked in, he was seated, and barely acknowledged my presence. I watched him flick his cigarette against the ashtray, his two fingers poised, and his pinkie raised. He continued to tap his cigarette and scrape non-existent ash on the filthy black plastic ashtray on top of the table along with the candle in a wine bottle decorated with plastic mesh. Tears coursed down his cheeks, and he sulked sipping his tea.

"I love you. You don't love me" I stifled an urge to scream.

I can't stand to see a man cry. I think that I could be sympathetic under the right circumstances. For instance, the loss of a loved one, or after totaling his new car, a man might conceivably cry in front of me, and receive his proper amount of sympathy. However, watching George across the table from me, whimpering and sniveling in his tea, as if someone had just shot his dog, was horrible, disgusting and revolting. I could easily have strangled him with his own ascot.

"Oh, for god's sake, George, stop it! Please stop it," I begged him. "People are watching us." I stifled the urge to bean him with the candle holder, which seemed like a good idea at the time.

It was true. It looked like everyone in the place had found a reason to walk close to our table. I guess you don't see a tall Chinese guy, in saddle shoes sobbing his heart out, and waving a cigarette around like Bette

Davis, every day. He had only recently started smoking but he used it as a prop for his drama.

"You're embarrassing me, George. I don't want you to be unhappy. I don't want to sit here and listen to this. I want to dance."

"I don' wanna dance. I'm not happy."

He was, for as long as I knew him, a master of the understatement.

I watched him puff and wave that damned cigarette dramatically while huge tears glided down his short nose.

"You don' love me. I know you don't wanna marry me."

"What can I say to you? I'm not going to leave and get married to you right this minute. I never said that I would not ever marry you."

"You, say that, but I know. Everybody knows. You date other guys. You never sleep with me."

The last was a sticky subject, that I wanted to avoid as long as possible. I had no intention of sleeping with him. I was really afraid that I couldn't get away from dancing with him. "Really George," I said, "I don't know why I like you, when you listen to all that gossip. If you love me, you should listen to me, once in a while. Just because somebody tells you that about me, why do you believe them? Everybody gossips around here. Nobody wants anybody else to be happy. I want you to be happy."

It was almost true. I didn't want to make him unhappy. If he hadn't pressed the issue, including a cash incentive, plus the diamond, I would have left the man alone. It certainly wasn't an idea I woke up with one morning. I never started a day thinking, I'll make good old Lonesome George miserable, but here it was. After last night and that whole mess, he was forcing me to decide if the diamond was worth it.

It was a really nice diamond.

"You lie to me. I wanna get married and you don' wanna get married. You don' love me."

He put his head down on his arm and huge sobs began coming out of him accompanied by horrible gulping noises.

"Stop it! Please George, couldn't we talk about this some other place?" That was my first mistake. I should have known better.

"I never see you. The only place is here. I don' like to see you here. I don't like a see you dancing with other men. I wanna marry you. You don't wanna marry me."

At that moment it wasn't worth it. I felt a cold distaste building in me for George and his ridiculous performance. It wouldn't do any good to give him back the diamond. I could see that clearly. The trouble was exactly as he expressed it. He loved me, and I didn't love him. Nothing could change that. Whatever ended this relationship would be awful for both of us. We were both trapped inside this disaster.

"Stop it and dance with me, George or I'll check you out, and I won't dance with you again. Ever." Something in my voice got his attention. I said it quietly, but I meant it.

He pulled himself together. We walked to the dance floor like a dignified old couple; he had his hand on my elbow. I think that I managed to look almost expressionless, maybe as if I were mildly amused, at something he'd said. I tried to act as if nothing had happened, and he behaved himself.

George was so quiet, in fact, that I was forced to look up at him. I was amazed to see him dancing with his eyes closed, smiling ecstatically, as if he were indulging in a major pleasure. I was only included, because I happened to be there. It was odd how left out I felt.

I suddenly understood something else. George didn't love me, he loved love and the anguish and the drama of love. It wasn't necessary for me to love George back. He hardly knew me. In fact, if I had loved him back, it might have spoiled half the fun.

I wanted him to leave. I wanted to go home and take a bath. I was sick of his fantasies. I remembered the warning. I had a premonition that this would end badly, and that I would not be able to stop the march of events that were sweeping me along.

George looked at the clock and acted like Cinderella at the ball. He shoved money in my hand to pay for his tickets, and literally ran to catch the elevator. I would have enjoyed seeing him leave a brown and white saddle shoe behind, or seeing his scarf get caught in the elevator door, but he made his hurried exit in one piece. I was relieved to see the door close behind him.

I was on my way back to the line when Tony stopped me.

"Maybe I ought to get a cut to keep my mouth shut. I hate to see these suckers taken by a dumb cunt like you. What do you say, Hollywood? Do I get my share, or do I blow the whistle? George seemed kind of interested in who you've been hanging around with. I got a lot I could tell, and I would do it just for the hell of it."

He smoothed his sideburns and watched the line over my shoulder while he was speaking. I noticed that he had developed a growing roll of flesh around his middle.

"If there's a god in heaven or justice on earth Tony, I promise you'll get yours. What do you think you're cut should be?"

"I'm not a hog. I'll take half. Half of everything you screw him for."

"Well, what an attractive offer. One thing about having you to work for, you sure make the rest of these guys look good. I haven't screwed him out of anything as you so charmingly put it. You're talking about a man I'm fond of, so don't press your luck. I think your attitude is bad for business and Sam might think so too." I took a breath. "I wonder if he knows about the illegals?"

It was a shot in the dark, but it got a bigger reaction than I'd expected. I was shocked by the look on his face. He knew more than I did, and it couldn't have been good.

"You talk to Sam or anybody else and you're gonna' have trouble talking to anybody else. Ever." He turned and walked away before I could rip his face off.

I was angry, but I was also scared. He thought I knew more than I did. Was he involved with the deaths? He was scary. I don't like being threatened. Ordinarily, I would consider his threat a bluff, but if he were involved, he had a lot to lose. He would be rough if he got the chance and thought he could get away with it. I shuddered. It was physical but it was also as I thought of what happened with George, now Tony, and with Linda's warning from the seance.

There was George and now Tony. Shit! What a week this was shaping up to be. I should have read my horoscope before I came to work. I wished with all my heart that Toshi was still hanging around. I had always felt protected when he was there.

I sat next to Choug, for a while. I wanted her to make a call for me and pretend to be an illegal that Tony had fired. She started to ask me about it when we were interrupted by Filipino Henry. He wanted me to dance with him, always a treat. At eighty something, he could still cut a mean rug and was one of the best jitterbugs I've ever seen. He told me that at one time he was not only a zoot suiter, but he had participated in the Zoot Suit Wars, that historic dancehall event that took place during WWII. Actually, I'd heard the story before. He was also the oldest pimp still hanging around the dancehall, maybe the oldest anywhere. I'll say one thing for him, he was a gentleman around me, and since I never saw him outside of the hall, I couldn't really feel anything about his profession. It seemed like none of my business. I hate pimps in general, and on principal. With Henry, I don't think that he was especially predatory or unkind to his girls. Several people I'd known had worked for him. The story was that they were all one big happy family.

There was an urgency to his stride as he checked me in then we walked to the dance floor.

"Listen up my pretty, I've got stuff to tell you. I saw you talking to Tony. Stay away from that guy; he's bad news for a lot of people."

My favorite gossip, he always had the latest scoop on everyone. With little or no encouragement Henry was the best source of information in the dancehall. He knew something, if not all, about everybody.

"Have you heard anything about Tony and the illegals?" I watched his face for clues. I was beginning to think that everyone knew more than I did.

"Like I told you already, the guy is bad news; he's not nice to women. Not like me, I know how to treat a lady."

"That's not what I asked you. Why can't you give me a straight answer?"

"You want me to bad mouth the competition? I don't know, but I think he's got an angle. He is mixed up with some bad dudes. If you go around asking, he'll know. You could get hurt, honey."

"A gang?"

"Something like that. More like businessmen. Not from here, maybe South American or China. I think they are from somewhere out of the states. I'm telling you to keep out of his way. He doesn't like you, and he doesn't like to hear that you're asking questions. He told me you were engaged to George, so I won't dance with you."

"I owe him for that!"

"Listen to me," he leaned forward, he was serious. "I heard him talking to George. I think he's trying to push some buttons and get you some trouble. Usually, I wouldn't say anything, but we're friends, right?"

Were we friends? I wondered. He was around when I needed him. If I had any reservations about our "friendship" this didn't seem like the right time to voice them.

"You bet! Thanks Henry. Could you do me a favor and kind of listen around? If he's mixed up in something, I'd like to know. You know, so I won't say the wrong thing." I told Henry about the illegals being fired. I didn't tell him I had the phone number. I remembered that he was in the office with Tony's buddies, the day after they arrested Stan. I wasn't completely sure what side he was on. I was beginning to believe that he was involved, in some way.

He said that he knew nothing for sure, but he wanted me to stay out of it. He couldn't look me in the eye. There was something bothering him. When I mentioned Tony giving the phone number to one of the girls he fired, I saw something in his face. "It could be serious Frankie. I found something out about Linda."

"Tell me the truth. Was she working for you?"

"For a while, then she wasn't happy, so she left, and went to work in the restaurant. That's what I wanted to tell you. She was afraid of a customer. I didn't know if it was Stan, or I would have told you, but I didn't know if it was him. To tell the truth I thought it was somebody else. I found out who told Stan where she was."

"Who would do that?"

"Tony. Tony did it. I couldn't believe it. He wasn't mad at her for anything except that she didn't want to have anything to do with him. I think he was jealous that she went with me. Maybe."

"Did Tony know she was afraid of Stan? Did he know that Stan was dangerous?"

"Well, he told me. He laughed about it. It was funny to him. That's why I tell you to stay away from him. We're friends. I don't want to read about you in the papers. Okay?"

"I appreciate you're telling me, Henry. Thanks." I looked at his yellow suit and red shirt. Henry looked so ugly and outrageous, but I thought that there was something sweet about him, outside of business. Boy! When I'm wrong, I'm wrong.

After we checked out, I had some time on the line to think about what he'd said. I didn't want to find myself the subject of a news item either. On the other hand, I could hardly sit there like a nice rabbit waiting for the stew pot either. I refused to be a victim of Tony or anybody or anything. That's it. I refused.

While I was thinking earnestly about Linda, Elena, Tony and whatever that mess was, Annie sat down next to me.

"I saw you talking to Tony," she looked away from me to the dance floor, while she talked to me. "He asked me, after you walked away, if I knew anything about those illegals."

"I'm not surprised. What did you tell him?"

"I didn't know what the fuck was he talking about? I told him the only thing you were talking about lately was baseball and those damned Dodgers."

"That's true enough. So . . . ?"

"So . . ." Annie watched the dance floor and talked without moving her lips. It was like talking to a ventriloquist. "So, tell me about the illegals. He's in the office with Sam, and I'm going to be pulled away in minute. Be quick! Tell me."

"I think they have a little scam going, wherein they use the bodies, of some of the more desperate women. Some have disappeared or turned up dead. At least two and maybe three that I know of. I don't really know anything, but I guess I made Tony think that I do." I watched her face while I told her this. "It might be some kind of porno."

"You're crazy! If it's true that he had something to do with it, that guy can be bad news. You better watch your step. I know."

I looked at sweet, hard-working Annie, and wondered what the creep had done to her. I didn't want to ask.

"I'll watch out," I said. "I promise. Maybe I'll talk to Sam. He's a friend."

That was our only chance for conversation for the rest of the evening. It weighed on my mind. I kept thinking about the way Tony had threatened me. I didn't trust him on a good day, and now two different people in a row had tried to warn me. I felt a little scared.

I was about to head to my locker when I noticed Sam was in his office. I found him there but there was something not right with him. He hadn't been feeling good for a while, and lately he'd been gone for days at a time. He'd been in, and out of the hospital for tests. On the rare occasions that he was in his office at the Musicland, he looked like it took most of his strength and energy just to get there. The truth was, that he didn't seem to be getting better.

Before I could bring up my uneasiness about what Terrible Tony was up to, he motioned me to a seat.

"Hi, honey. What's new?"

"What's new with you?" I knew my man. He wanted to chat about something. He looked old for the first time that I could remember. It was hard, usually, to remember that he was seventy.

"You look done in, Sam. Don't you feel well?"

"Hollywood. Tony calls you that, but I think you're one hundred percent real. Nothing phony about you."

"Shucks. You'll get me tossed out of the Gold Diggers of America if you keep that up."

"They ask for it." He stood up from the desk and pulled a manila envelope off the top of the file cabinet. "Look at these." He smiled, but it made me shudder.

"What are they?" Then, as I opened it, I could see that they were chest x-rays. "What do they mean?"

"Well, that white spot, see it? No, down a little. Yeah, that one. That's a death sentence. It's simply a question of how long."

"Oh Sam!" I felt sick. It was like losing a family member. He had always been like a dear old uncle to me.

"Don't tell anybody. I'm going to stay right here, until I have to be hospitalized. I'm just not up to dealing with everybody if they knew. I don't trust Tony to know. Well, I don't trust Tony. Period."

I could understand that. It was hard to know why he didn't replace him, but knowing Sam, he must have had a good reason. I didn't want to burden him, with my suspicions about Tony. I decided to handle it myself.

Before I could ask Sam for Alicia's address, Tony came in to get Sam to sign a check for a supplier. Sam motioned me out.

I was sitting back on the line a little while later trying to decide what to do, when Choug sat down next to me and gave me the play-by-play conversation between her and her sister.

"So, I told her . . ."

"Can you sound like an illegal?"

"I beg your pardon. I speak one hundred percent pure American L.A. Spanish."

"Look babe, this is important, or I wouldn't ask you. Tony has some scheme going with the illegals, that he's hiring, and firing all the time. Some of them are pretty young, and I don't like to see Tony get away with something slimy."

"Like what?"

"I'm not sure. I just want you to sound like an illegal and call this number. Say that Tony sent you, give a common name if they ask you, like Maria. Just go along with whatever they say and tell me. Okay?"

"If I get into any trouble with this it's on your head." She gave me a look that made me believe she wasn't kidding.

We went to the phones where some of the ladies were calling to try to get customers out from the little rocks, they crawl under, during the day to come out, and play. I handed her some change, and she dialed the number written in eyebrow pencil, just inside my makeup bag. The conversation went in Spanish. She talked, and I listened, watching for Tony.

She hung up with a frown on her face. "They wanted me to meet somebody over by Echo Park, tomorrow. They sounded like those kind of home boys you don't want to know. I'm not going near that place. I don't want to meet nobody."

"Calm down. Nobody asked you to go. I'm going."

"You don't look like an illegal. Don't be stupid. If they find out you're interested, you will just end up in the big frig downtown, with a tag on your toe."

"I've got to find out." I wondered about me. Brave? Smart? Stupid?

"Why? It's no sweat off your nose, if Tony is involved with putting women out on the street for himself, and his friends. Hey, it's business. You got to watch out for numero uno."

"You're right. Stay out of it. You know how to take care of yourself. I'm not sure that little illegal, Alicia does."

"Por Dios! Do you mean the one that was pregnant? The kid?"

"Yeah, I think Tony knows how desperate she is, and I don't think she has anybody here to help her. I wouldn't like to be alone here in the hands of that creep."

"I know he fired them. Why do you think he has any other plans?"

"I don't know for sure, but he gave her the number you called, and several people have given me a hint that he's up to something nasty."

"I wouldn't put it past him." She stood there quietly thinking. "I like her. She is a nice person. I don't know if she is worth getting hurt for."

"So, don't get involved, like you said." I could probably handle this better on my own anyway. If I got somebody else involved, I would feel responsible, especially if they get hurt."

"Don't be crazy, Frankie. What's the plan?"

That Choug was some piece of work.

When Danny came in, he was surrounded, as usual, with his little group of admirers, or guards or . . . who knows? He watched me dancing and I could feel his attention from the dance floor. When my partner and I checked out, he was standing by the time clock and asked me to dance. This was not the first time, but I had worked at being less interested since the last time. There was always something odd about the fact that I felt attracted to him and repelled by him at the same time. I wasn't the only one. I remembered how Mei Ling had avoided him by actually fleeing upstairs when she saw him.

"I heard that you and George are an item." This was a statement that didn't seem to need a response. "He does have good taste."

I really didn't know if I should thank him for the compliment or make some other remark. I am usually an easy conversationalist. This wasn't easy. He pulled me closer, and the slow music seemed to swirl around us, pulling us out to the middle of the floor. While my right hand was on his shoulder, he took my left hand and moved it behind me. I tried to resist, but for as slender as he was, he was stronger, and I would have had to make it obvious that I was resisting I didn't. Again, I felt how compelling his presence was, and at the same time how repellent. I was afraid. My heart was beating wildly out of control as he pulled me closer to him. Perspiration was running down my forehead. I couldn't talk. I wanted the music to end. The "Unchained Melody," was a dirge that continued during this odd ordeal. It must have looked romantic to other dancers. I didn't find it so.

When the music finally ended, I said, "Let go of me."

Danny dropped my hand and pulled back. "I'm sorry you seem so . . ." as if he was searching for words, "so uncooperative." He smiled showing perfect little white teeth. "I'll check you out, and you can wait on the line for your fiancé."

He put his hand under my arm and steered me to the cashier's desk.

The line looked like a safe harbor after that experience. I didn't mind being almost alone. My heart was still pounding. I had offended him. He didn't tip me and that made me laugh. I would have enjoyed it more if the hair on the back of my neck wasn't standing at attention. Asshole! What a jerk! I watched him leave surrounded by his entourage.

CHAPTER SIXTEEN

SAM ENTERS THE HOSPITAL

When Choug asked me what the plan was, I had to admit that I didn't have one. I wanted to see if I could find out anything, about the guys involved. I also wanted to find Alicia before anything happened to her. I wondered if she had called them. It was too risky to send Choug in to meet with them, even if she was game. So far, only Linda and Lupe had ever turned up again, of all the women that left the dancehall. Now that could be non-connected, and the two things could be non-related. After all, L.A. is a big town, and lots of people move on, and we don't hear from them again.

Still? At least two of them were dead.

"I wonder who the number connects to?"

Choug shrugged her shoulders.

"We could wait in my car, and, discreetly of course, try to see who shows up, and follow them. It would be nice to know who we should watch out for. Maybe we know already, maybe they hang out here, at the hall."

This sounded better to me than trying to actually meet with them and find out firsthand what they had in mind. Because of my red hair, and the fact that I don't speak very much Spanish, I don't think that I could fool them for long. They would probably notice that I might not be an illegal.

"Okay," Choug looked determined, "I'm going with you. We should bring one of my brothers." She wasn't kidding, and she wasn't being generous. Choug, had a lot of brothers, and they were all very protective of their sister. They were also home boys, but of a different stripe, she insisted. "They are good guys, not the rowdy gangster pachuco types."

"Not this time, but it's a good idea. We may need them later. Tomorrow afternoon we'll get there early and wait to see who shows up." It sounded simple enough, but I didn't want to make us a crowd as we were going there just to find out something about who the phone number connected to. I did not want to tip anyone off. Who was Tony sending those women too? We wouldn't do anything foolish or dangerous if we were by ourselves. Right?

That night I went home alone. Besides the phone call, I couldn't get past the little encounter with Danny. Those things were on my mind.

When I entered the house, the first thing I noticed was the scent, I had come to expect. I told Linda, my mystery guest, aloud, that I was doing my best to unravel the mystery of the illegals. I had no way of knowing if there was any connection to her mystery, except that I was fairly sure that Tony, was somehow involved with all of it. I just didn't know how. If she had any way of helping, I said I would appreciate it if she could find a way to let me know.

I tried to get some sleep because I was going to see Sam early, and I needed sleep. I was exhausted, but I had so much on my mind. It wasn't as if I didn't have enough problems with earning a living, coping with Toshi, and now I had to worry about Alicia, Tony, and his friends, and also George. Then there was Sam, and the worst news I could imagine. What about Mei Ling? I wondered if she knew. I was beginning to understand her aversion to Danny. I found him increasingly scary. Then there was Lonesome George, and his hangdog, sulking face following me uncomfortably around. My work was ceasing to be fun; I remember thinking. All of this stuff followed me into the land of nod. I had the same miserable dreams, which had wrecked my sleep, for the last couple of weeks.

I was awake and up early at the unheard-of hour, of nine-thirty a.m. I decided to call Sam. Besides being a good businessman, his son was an attorney. He would be able to find out what it would take to help Alicia, once I found her, if I found her. He could find things out, before I did some real wheel spinning. Also, Sam had her personnel file, and maybe I could find out where she was living. If I could get a phone number for her, I might be able to reach her and warn her off. Maybe Tony and friends had not gotten to her yet.

A vague plan regarding Alicia and her baby was beginning to form in my mind.

I called Sam and his housekeeper answered. She told me that he was in the hospital. I asked her his room number and she said that she was given instructions not to tell anybody. I knew that didn't apply to me, but I wasn't in a mood to argue with her.

I tried to remember the hospital he'd gone to for the tests. I had seen the name printed on the x-ray envelope. It started with St. I knew it, St. Vincent's. I called admitting, and they checked. Yes, they found that Sam Weintraub was being admitted today. I asked about visiting hours and they said that I could see him anytime between ten a.m. and eight p.m.

I glanced at the clock on my dresser, and it was only a quarter to ten. I looked in my closet to find something that looked as little like a dancehall as I could manage. I changed from my robe to a tasteful navy blue and white dress with a little matching jacket. I pulled my hair to the back of my neck with a clip and wore only a little lipstick and some eyebrow pencil. I looked like a teacher in a girl's school. From shower to ready in less than half an hour. I was setting a new record for myself.

On the way, I stopped and bought Sam some daisies. Now it was difficult because I hated having him in the hospital. He was a good man. In the dancehall world the good guys stood out. Each one was like a tiny oasis of good will. I have wondered why the men, who made so much money from the attractiveness and sexuality of women, didn't even have the good sense to be polite to them. They did not even the good sense to just treat those women decently. It was my observation that as soon as they had you in a position to make money for them, whether you were an attractive secretary, smashing cocktail waitress, sexy dancehall girl or dedicated hooker, then you were immediately diminished in their eyes, and they treated you as something a tad less than human. It's that about men that I don't like. I don't like their assumptions.

In this way Sam was different. He loved the girls that worked for him. He had often been a soft touch. A longtime customer, before he owned his own dancehall, he took care to provide an atmosphere of party and fun that, until his effort, no other dancehall owner had been moved to consider necessary. Women in this business were treated with a marked lack of respect by customer, owner, and manager, with few exceptions. Sam was definitely an exception.

At the hospital, I was standing by the admissions desk trying to find out Sam's room number with a handful of daisies, and my white pumps pinching my feet. I was trying to find out why they'd said he would be here, and now they said he wasn't. He was there. I looked up and spotted him across the admissions lounge. I was shocked that he was just a small old white-haired man, with his suitcase waiting for his room. I'd assumed that he'd already checked in. It just wasn't so. There he was, alone, looking as helpless, and vulnerable as new girls do, the first time they walk out to the line, and have to pass the bullpen.

I walked up behind him and touched his shoulder. He turned and registered surprise.

"My timing is terrible," I said. "I thought you'd be in your room, with all the nurses hovering around you. I was going to impress them with my devotion. If you want me to come back some other time, I will."

"No way, kiddo! Your timing is perfect. I'm glad you're here" he motioned with his head toward the waiting room. "I'm glad it's you and not somebody else. I didn't even tell Mei Ling I was checking in today." He picked up his suitcase, and I wrestled his briefcase away from him. "There's nothing to do but wait until they put me in my room. Then they'll draw blood for tests, and urine samples. If you don't mind all that, I'd be glad for your company. Maybe it'll take my mind off this crap."

I hugged the old dear and sat down with him. We didn't get to chat very long before the nun, in her long white habit, came and led us up to the elevator, Sam in his wheelchair, and me holding the daisies, his suitcase, and the briefcase under one arm. I was glad that I was there. If I ever go into a hospital to die, I want someone there. He didn't say that this was his last visit, but I had a feeling. I didn't ask about his son. I knew their relationship was a distant one. I was only glad that he wasn't alone, and it was true. I cared about him. We were friends.

After he'd been put to bed and they'd taken his blood once, they did it three times in my two-hour visit. He began talking about Mei Ling. It was no secret that he had a crush on our little fortune cookie. I had already heard that she'd made him dinner at her apartment, but he had said nothing to me about their relationship until now. I don't think he'd said anything to anyone about the stage of their attraction.

"She's a lady, Frankie, a real lady. I haven't known anyone like her for a long time. I love everything about her, the way she looks, her manners, her quiet good humor. She's lovely." He looked exhausted in general, but he certainly brightened when, he spoke of her.

"You're so good at hiding your emotions," I had to laugh. "Come on Sam, how do you really feel?"

"I guess it's common gossip around the hall." He was sitting up with his hands clasped over his stomach, looking pleased with himself.

"Well, it would be hard not to notice, but she hasn't said a word one way or the other to anyone. I'd have heard. She really is a lady. I like her a lot, even if she is beautiful and dresses like a dream."

"You're right. You and Mei Ling are the two classiest women in the place."

"Gee, thanks boss. So, what's happening? Why isn't she here?"

"She doesn't know. I don't want her pity. I care about her and I . . ." His voice trailed off and he cleared his throat. "She's too young and lovely to get mixed up with me . . . with this." His eyes wandered around the hospital room. "I had an idea to do something about her, you know, something for her, maybe in my will. Then I was afraid my son, would contest every nickel. I'm thinking to do something now. I tried to bring it up and she got upset."

"She cares about you," I said.

"Our relationship right now is . . ."

I interrupted, "You don't have to tell me."

"I'm devoted, and she is fond of me. At least, she treats me as if she was fond of me, but we haven't, you know, had an affair. We didn't make it to the sack. I'm not sure that I could've when I had the chance. You know, the medications and everything."

I swear he looked like he was blushing. His ears were definitely red.

I was close to breaking down, and sobbing.

"Wow! I'll bet she doesn't even know how rare it is for you to dig her. You've never had it this bad since I've known you." I tactfully avoided reminding him of his past attraction to me. It didn't amount to a hill of beans.

"That's not important. I would like to know that she wasn't at the mercy of Tony, or anybody else who takes over."

"Maybe all of this is because you're not feeling so good." Sometimes I can't keep my mouth shut.

"Don't patronize me, Frankie. That's what everyone thinks, I'm a sick, doddering old fool. She's twenty-five and I'm seventy. I'm dying and she's going to have a long life, and I want to leave her something to remember me by. Something to help her. Anyway, I have to think about what and how to do it without offending or embarrassing her. Don't let Tony pick on her."

I laughed at that. "Who's going to protect me from Tony? I'm not high on his list of favorites, and he's been firing a lot of people lately."

"As long as I'm alive he won't fire you. If he gets too far out of hand, you can call me. My son says he'll take over and send in his own manager; if I can't handle it." He paused as if he were thinking it over. "I don't want him to, because of Mei Ling, right this moment, but if things get too bad over there let me know. Okay?" I thought he was finished but he squeezed my hand and looked me in the eyes. "Promise me that if I need your help to work something out for Mei Ling, I can count on you. I trust you."

I would have cut my wrist and sworn in blood. I resisted the urge to hug him.

"Now, let's hear about your love life. I noticed something with Toshi and the Hungarian."

Sam loved all the stuff that happened up there, and he kept in touch with who was in love with who, like a soap opera addict. I made him laugh about me, and Lonesome George. He was a fan of Annie Fannie's too, and he liked the way Big Louie had tried to help Alicia with tickets. He always wanted to know Tony's latest bon mot. I talked and he listened until I noticed that the medication, they'd given him, was making him a little drowsy. I looked at my watch and saw that it was nearly time to meet Choug.

So, I kissed his forehead, and exited without telling him about the guys, we were going to meet. I didn't tell him about Alicia being fired because he had enough on his mind. I don't know that if I had, he could have changed anything. I thought he was right, that it wasn't time to have his son take over yet. Still, I thought that he could rely on Big Louie, if he'd just clued him in.

I looked at my watch. It was time to meet Choug. We were going to meet the voice over the phone. I was really nervous. As it turned out, I was right to be.

CHAPTER SEVENTEEN

BAD BOYS

I was supposed to meet Choug at two o'clock. I didn't have time to call her, but she was on time waiting for me, in the parking lot of the Denny's on Vermont. She was dressed in Levi's and a t-shirt, while I still had my girls-school teacher's disguise on.

She got in, looked me up and down, but earned her points as a friend by saying nothing.

We were supposed to meet the guys in Echo Park at two-thirty. We had plenty of time to get there early and find a way to look inconspicuous. That is not a mode that I practice much. A redhead in a red convertible is usually not inconspicuous. However, they were expecting some nervous little illegal, and they might overlook the two of us, if we could look like we were not waiting, for them or anyone.

Even though we were a half hour early, it was still difficult to find a place to park, that would give us a view of the place where she'd agreed to meet them, and still not be noticed. I was ready to throw in the towel, and just concentrate on getting out of there without being seen, when a parking place opened up around the corner of Lakeshore. We were facing the park, but we were not next to it, all but invisible behind a blue

Volkswagen hippy van. Choug slouched down as if napping. I pulled a map of L.A. out of the glove compartment and proceeded to look up imaginary addresses. I bought this map from a street hawker when I first came to the city. It was one of those maps of the homes of the stars. It was a phony, of course, but I kept hoping that maybe one day I would actually stumble across a star or two. I would love to find certain ones; Fred Astaire comes to mind.

Anyway, thus engaged, I noticed two men dressed like drug dealers in the movies, you know, white suits with black shirts and yellow neck ties. They had arrived and kind of casually strolled around, as if they were checking out the neighborhood. They definitely looked like they were looking for somebody.

Choug made a kind of gasping noise. She looked scared. "I know one of them, and I think I know who the other one is."

"Don't keep me in suspense." I was dealing with my own panic attack.

"The tall one, the call him Spider. The shorter one, I've never seen, but he must be Spider's partner, they call him Barbazul. That means Bluebeard. These are scary guys."

They hung around for a while, and then one of them looked at his watch. He said something to the second man, who nodded his head as if he was agreeing with him.

"I think they're gonna' split." Choug was sitting up and on the edge of her seat. "You gotta be careful, Frankie. If they are mixed up in this; it's something bad for sure."

"They sure don't dress like home boys." They were in their late twenties or early thirties. "Take a good look. Are you sure?"

The guys came strolling across the park. It looked as if they might have parked in the bank parking lot, which made a lot of sense, but it kept us from being able to see their license number, without following them.

Choug looked serious. "They are famous gangsters for sure. Heavyweights. Let's follow them."

"Are you crazy? Choug, we could get hurt."

"They are not pimps. You got it? Alicia could be in heavy trouble. We are not going to find her unless we find out more about where these guys are hanging out."

"There they go!" They came out of the driveway, and against my better judgment, I tried to follow at a discreet distance, without being noticed.

They headed for downtown. At a large office building on Sixth Street, they suddenly turned into a parking garage. I was a block away. I should have just gone on. We had their license number by then, but I turned after them, and followed them into the parking garage, taking my ticket and watching the barrier lift for my car. I pulled into the first available parking space.

I thought that we would be less noticeable on foot. Then I saw that they had simply skipped the first available space and had driven around that level and back.

They were waiting for us to get out of the car. It would have been great if I had noticed this before I pulled in and turned off the engine.

I tried to start the car as soon as I saw them, but they were on us before I could get it to turn over. Choug had started out of the car before she heard me scream. I did scream a warning at her.

Choug jumped back into the car, before the taller of the two, Spider, could grab her. It was her bad luck, that the window was rolled down on her side. While she kept one hand on the door lock, she tried to use the other to roll up the window. The overdressed tough guy was pulling at her, trying to grab her hair, her face, her clothes or anything he could reach.

I was just barely able to see what was happening to her, because I was engaged with the other thug on my side of the car. I never had a chance to get out, the door was closed. I was locked in, but he had a weapon in his hand which looked like a wrench. When he reached the car, the first thing he did was smash the windshield on my side.

Terrified, I was screaming. He was attacking the front of the car trying to get under the hood. I was so unnerved that I couldn't get the car to start for what seemed like a long time under the circumstances. It finally turned over and didn't catch. I tried again, pumping the gas and this time it seemed like it might have flooded. I could feel perspiration dripping off my body. I tried again. Choug was screaming like she was hurt.

"Hurry up, for Christ's sake," she screamed, and this time it caught, and I was in reverse gear. We went whizzing backward, and out of the parking space to hit the car parked in the aisle behind us. It was their Mercedes. Then I turned and streaked forward, not realizing that her foe was still clinging to her door. He had finally grabbed the lock by bending her finger, and the door swung open just as I was making a curve. The door flattened him against the wall, but we didn't slow down or look back as we made our way to the exit.

The guy in the booth asked about the windshield, I guess he felt he would have remembered it. I told him it was just an accident, happened a couple of days ago. We wanted to get out of there before those two guys got in their car and followed us.

Sure enough. Choug was looking in the rearview mirror and screamed, "Here they come!" We didn't even wait for our change; we just took off. They went through the barrier and followed us. We pushed ahead, and finally saw the Fifth Street onramp to the downtown over-change. The traffic was bumper to bumper; the time was four fifteen p.m. We finally made it to the Venice off-ramp on the San Pedro freeway. We carefully made our way back, watching to see if they could have followed us off the freeway, through back streets to Denny's parking lot where Choug's car was. We'd lost them.

Now we took stock. Choug was injured. It looked like her finger was dislocated and her face, neck and arms were a mass of bruises.

I had the sense that Choug was wishing she'd never involved herself with me in this adventure for any reason.

My car sustained some damage, but I had insurance, and had never had to use it. I had some consolation in that.

I was shaken and had a few bruises, but in better condition than my friend. I offered to buy her some coffee, it was the least I could do. I sat across the table and looked at her. Her face was bruised, and her finger was turning blue and swelling. She looked awful. She also looked angry and scared.

It was embarrassing that I was in better shape than her. My knees felt like they were joined to the rest of me by limp rubber bands and I was shaking, but I was all right. My car was a mess, but I still felt lucky.

Looking at Choug I realized that we were both lucky, and I said so. She was a little surprised that I felt that way.

"Those guys are bad news, Frankie. It won't take much for them to trace us back to Tony. You, at least. I don't consider that lucky."

"Look, if it was this bad and we got away, imagine how bad it would have been if we hadn't gotten away. We have their license number."

"What good will that do us?" Choug looked at me as if I had said something so stupid.

She was right, of course. Who would I take it to? The police would laugh their heads off if I told them the story. Who cares about one more illegal, and what about two dancehall girls getting more than they bargained for, when they met a couple of gangsters, for unspecified purposes? On the other hand, Spider, and friend would only have to describe my red hair to Tony, and I was revealed. They would connect us since Choug had called and used Tony's name as a reference.

"I hate to think about what will happen to us when we show up at work after they tell Tony. We are going to be sitting around waiting for the knife." I was quiet.

Choug didn't usually have this much to say. "I don't like to seem like a chicken, but I think that I'm going to take a couple of weeks off. You do what you want. but I don't like the risk. You and I are up to our necks with some heavyweight dudes who are famous stone killers. I am not stupid, and none of this is my business." She sipped her coffee. "I don't even want to get my brothers involved in this. Maybe you should consider going away for a while yourself." Choug drummed the fingers of her uninjured hand on the table.

I offered to take her to the hospital emergency room, where she could get ex-rays of her hand. She refused at first but changed her mind, when she forgot herself enough to try to pick up her cup with both hands.

I thought about what she'd said. They were not pimps. They were something more dangerous. What would happen to Alicia if they got to her first? I had to find her if I could.

We finished our coffee without saying much more. She was right, I was scared of Tony, and his friends. Any fool could see that human life was not something they had a lot of respect for. Again, I wished that I still had Toshi on my team.

It took a while for the emergency room. Neither one of us had much to say. The nurse came, got her, and almost an hour later, Choug was done. She was finally pronounced sprained, but not broken and bandaged with a splint on her hand.

Back at the car, she decided that she could get herself home. I offered to take her or call a brother, but she declined. I really felt alone when Choug got into her car, and I waved goodbye.

What about Alicia? I still hadn't found a way to get to those files in Tony's office. What if I did find her, and help her get away from whatever Tony and friends had planned for her? I was sure that it was something really evil, but what? Even if I rescued her, then what? Would they just ship her back anyway? I couldn't think about that yet. First, I had to find her. It was becoming an obsession.

That night I spent at home. The phone rang once, but when I answered it there was no one on the other end, just a click. It could have been George.

Right. Who was I kidding?

I felt like screaming. Nothing was all right.

I must have dozed off because I woke somewhere between midnight and dawn, still in my dressing gown with the TV making noises, and snow, but no picture. The room was cold, and I could hear the sobbing, just like the first time. I felt the goose bumps rise along my arms.

"I want to help. I don't know what to do!" It burst out of me without thinking, and the room filled with her scent. "I wish I could help everyone, but I'm in trouble myself and I don't have anybody either."

I let go and really cried, for the first time in a long time, and it was strange that afterward, I felt comforted. She wasn't sobbing and neither was I.

I think that we were ready for whatever came next. I know that ghosts are not usually thought of as sympathetic, but somehow, I knew that Linda was still a friend, and that we would be there for each other. I was still afraid, but I no longer felt quite as alone as I had earlier in the day either.

I went to bed and slept. I wanted to be ready for the next night at Musicland.

CHAPTER EIGHTEEN

WHO'S COUNTING?

At work that night I was dressed in my absolute best. A long black gown with a gold lame bodice, topped with a high mandarin collar. It was my most elegant look. A French twist pulled my hair to the side in a classic evening style. It was very simple, and sophisticated. I had on long gold earrings with a white jade pendant. I always feel that when I am entering an uncomfortable, maybe now even dangerous, situation; I should dress in my absolutely sensational best so that I'll have more confidence.

Sometimes it works.

That night I pulled into the parking lot, and cautiously looked around. One of the younger Filipino pimps was there, and he offered to escort me upstairs. Little Louie was elegantly dressed himself, in a tailored suit, forest green with white piping trim. It was a little flashy, but certainly original.

He offered to check me in for a cup of tea, so that I could start early, and make some extra tickets while he waited for Laurie, his girl, to get there, which she seldom did before eight-thirty. So, I clocked in, before I got my coat off, and signed the list of people working that night. While I was signing in, Tony came up behind me, and said he would like to see me in his office.

I showed him the timecard. "I'm sorry. I'm already clocked in. Talk to you later."

I grabbed Little Louie and split for a table. He was one of the people I could talk to about what was going on. He belonged to a brotherhood that had more gossip to share than any Hollywood reporter. We were having coffee, and laughing about something cute Laurie had said, when George came in. Little Louie understood when I asked to check out so that I could talk to George, we would talk more later.

"Hi George," I tried to sound cheerful.

"You wanna dance?"

The juke box was playing a rock tune, but George put his hand on my waist, and using his other hand to steer me with, tripped around doing his two-step to his own rhythm. We said nothing while he paid no attention to the music. We just danced around, and around under the ball of glass turning above us. It turned and sparkled throwing off the broken bits of light on all the dancers. I felt like the couple on top of a music box, performing this same damned two-step around, and around, and around.

How could I get George to break up with me? How could I do it, without another painful scene? He was pretty stubborn and inflexible. Now he had invested so much face in our engagement, that even if I were foolish enough to give him back his ring it wouldn't help. Besides, I had already tried once. I didn't think he would let me get away gracefully.

It was because of his unspoken agenda.

There was what he wanted from me. He wanted sex, but he couldn't say it, or maybe even admit it to me. That would make us like the others.

So, he insisted on romance, but the other was there. He only referred to "it" in the context of being "happy" after the wedding. It was an oblique reference to the honeymoon. I despised the dishonesty between us, even if half of it was mine. At the same time, I knew that any real honesty would make me despise him just the same. I couldn't think of anything more distasteful, more hideous, than a "honeymoon" with Lonesome George. It made my flesh crawl.

I had tried to give him back the ring. As long as he refused to take it, I was still technically engaged to him. Was it till death do us part? That, and other things crossed my mind as we glided across the floor, in his eternal two-step. Other couples gyrated in time to the music they were playing now. "I feel good" the singer insisted, "so good," and then "the way that I should . . ."

George paid no attention to the music. He was like a wind-up toy. The music began again and he two-stepped, no slower, no faster than he always did. It was the lonesome whippoorwill again. " . . . so lonesome I could die."

Just like George.

"I gotta go. I have business . . . sorry." He looked down at me and smiled a crooked broken-toothed smile.

"That's okay, George." What a relief! "Maybe I'll see you later." We checked out, and I walked him to the elevator. He insisted on kissing me on the lips.

I looked around for Tony's friends. They weren't in the bullpen, so I ignored Tony's request to see him in his office. I took a chance that someone would check me in quickly and returned to the line.

I didn't have to sit on the bench for more than a moment before Mervin of the bells and birds asked me to dance. He said that he couldn't really dance, because of the noise. Would I mind sitting down for a coke? He would be good for fifteen minutes.

Would I mind? "I'd be delighted. I'm happy to see you." I was nearly shouting, you had to speak loudly to be heard over his noises.

He couldn't hear much. He shouted back at me across the table. I tried to look like we were having an interesting conversation.

He showed me his new medicine. First, the ointment that looked like greenish black car grease and smelled abominable.

"Interesting," I shouted.

Then he showed me some little white pills that looked like a prescription. "The pills look like the doctor gave them to you." I tried to make myself heard.

"Of course. Where do you think I get my medicine?" His eyes were ablaze. "Do you think my mother makes it? Are you trying to make me mad?"

One tiny remark, and there I was in an amusing little shouting match with a maniac who had tinfoil on his ankles and heard noises that nobody else could hear.

"I'm sorry. It's okay, Mervin. Just check me out."

He glared at me and muttered under his breath all the way over to the cashier and refused to answer my "goodbye" when he left. It was an exasperating punctuation, to what was shaping up to be one of my more nerve-racking nights in the hall.

Still, he had given me a good laugh on a night like that.

Now, I decided, was the best time to visit Terrible Tony's office. He couldn't do too much to me with a whole dancehall full of people who knew me. Also, if I could get his attention away from me or if he left me an opening, I might be able to get into the personnel files, and find Alicia's address on her W4 form. It was probably going to be my only chance to get into those files, with Sam in the hospital.

Tony was at his desk reading something, which he put his hand over, and then slid into a side drawer, while he was talking to me. "Well, you finally had a moment to spare." He looked at the clock. It was a quarter to eleven.

"Well, I don't get paid for the time I spend sitting around chewing the fat with management. Unless you'd like to check me in . . . ? No? What's on your mind?"

"Don't crack wise with me, Hollywood. I'm on to you. Just because you're tight with Sam doesn't mean didley to me. I'm just trying to warn you to stay out of stuff that's not in your league. Dig? I hate to see a big money maker being replaced, which is always possible. Dig?" He pulled the high collar of his black Elvis shirt up and shrugged his shoulders. By the end of his little soliloquy, he was pointing a finger in my face.

I pushed his hand away and put my face in his.

"You don't scare me. Dig? I don't care what's on your mind, or what you think about me. Dig? You can't replace me because Sam told you to leave me alone. Dig?"

There was a knock on the office door which immediately swung open, and Big Louie was standing there looking very agitated. "Come on, Tony. You gotta talk to these guys. They say they're friends of yours and they don't want to pay admission."

"Wait here. I'm not finished with you." He nodded to me and smoothed back his hair.

As soon as the door closed, I was up rifling the file cabinet. I had to find Alicia's name, and Social Security form. It took a minute to figure out his unique filing system. The names were filed according to the month they were hired. So, all I had to do was remember when she was hired, and then it was a cinch to find her form. She'd told me her name was Alicia Cruz, but on her form, it said Devilla.

Oh well, there was only one Alicia working there during that time. I had it folded, and tucked into my bra before they came back in. I tried to get into the drawer that Tony had put whatever he was reading. I had just gotten it open enough to see that it was a news clipping. I should have been a little quicker.

The two guys I had been expecting entered in front of Tony. I'm proud to say that Spider was sporting a sling and Barbazul was definitely walking carefully.

"Well, Hollywood. I know you'll be glad to see these two admirers of yours. They remember you."

"I'll bet they do."

I started thinking fast. All I wanted to do was get away from there.

"See something interesting in the drawer?" Tony slammed it shut almost catching my hand in it.

"Nothing I had a chance to read." The guys looked like they were holding a grudge. I was interested in nothing, but how to get out of there in one piece.

"Here she is guys. I know you're happy to find her. Our own little Miss Hollywood."

"Hey, the good-looking redhead. Yeah." Barbazul leered in as sinister a manner as I cared to be leered at.

"You friend looks like he ran into a door or something. I hope you got the number." I wasn't going to let them see me even a little scared.

Actually, I was terrified. I wanted out of that office in the worst way. Well, almost the worst way.

"What do you say we take red out of here a little early for a little talk, and whatever. You're the boss, Tony. You think that we could bend the rules, and get our lady out of here before closing?"

"Hey, I have never been known to stand in the way of a guy, and a girl working things out. I'm sure we can fix it, so nobody even knows she's gone. What do you say, Frankie?"

"You're dumber than you look if you think you can get me out of here without a struggle. People will know something is going on as soon as I start screaming. Besides, I've got somebody special waiting for me outside."

Spider pulled a gun out of the sling on his arm. "I don't think you're dumb either Frankie. I'll use this if I have to. I don't think there are a lot of willing witnesses up here who would be willing to remember in an official way what happened to the redhead."

"Like Alicia?" I was fishing in the dark, but they didn't know it.

Their faces registered a certain tightening.

"I told you she was nosing into things." Tony turned to Spider. "Get her out of here. Do what you have to do."

I was trying to decide what my next move would be if they tried to get me out of the office with them. I would definitely try to break for it.

There was a knock on the door, and before Spider could put the gun away Big Louie poked his head in and said, "Wong's here. He's waiting for Frankie. I told him that I would get her."

The Calvary, I thought. "Wait Louie! I'll go with you." I climbed onto the chair, and onto the desk. I jumped off the desk, and none of them were quick enough to do anything about it, before I grabbed Big Louie's arm.

Outside the office, Louie seemed puzzled.

"You want to tell me what's going on. Who was the guy with the gun?"

So, I told him. There didn't seem to be much point in keeping any of this to myself. I was in some physical danger, and I needed help. Louie listened, and then he offered some sound advice. "Change your name, dye your hair black, and get out of town."

He had a point.

"Now that Tony and the guys know that everyone knows that they are after you, and Choug, they won't be able to do much. Not up here anyway. I wonder what they're into. Why has no one around the hall heard anything about it? It must be very expensive big-time trafficking of something I can't even imagine. Those guys have been seen around here, but they're not regulars. I think that Brian knows them. I wonder what they're up to, I wonder what it is."

"Thanks, Louie. Now all I have to do is get through this evening and get home. I wonder if they'll try to get me there?"

"You might consider staying somewhere else tonight. If I were Tony, I would expect you to."

He left and I was standing at the snack counter ready to buy myself something to drink and take a break when someone touched me on the shoulder.

To say that I was a little edgy was to put it mildly. I jumped and screamed.

Ed Wong was hardly prepared for that. I had forgotten that he was there, which just shows how badly they'd upset me. He was maybe the best customer around, and certainly my all-time favorite.

"Wow, are you trying to give me a heart attack?"

"I didn't know it was you. I'm sorry." I held his hand in both of mine.

"I told Louie to tell you that I was here. I was hoping that you'd be glad to see me."

"I am. You'll never know how much. Let's sit down and have some tea. I'll check in while you find us a table. Okay?"

I raced to the timecard rack and was just putting my card back up when I felt a pressure on my elbow. I didn't jump, I felt secure with Ed there.

It was Tony.

"I wanted to tell you to keep your mouth shut. I don't want you telling everyone that you had that little adventure today."

"Sorry, you'll read it in the Times in the morning. I have told everyone I can think of, so that if anything happens to me, or someone I know, they'll ask you and your friends first. I think there must be something going on that you don't want anyone official to know about, or why would you both try intimidating me? Right? Oh, and by the way, is Vice-cop Brian in on all this?"

"Stay out of this. You are already up to your ass in alligators. My friends play for keeps, watch your step. They eat people like you for breakfast."

"I would find your concern touching any other time, but as you can see, I'm in a hurry. I have someone more important waiting for me. Someone nice."

I pulled free and made my way past all the little tables for two and found Ed waiting for me. His navy-blue blazer and tie looked like he'd just left his office. I could just imagine him working late, and making a call, so that the last hour of the night could be his, and he wouldn't have to wait for me, while I was with another customer. He was a busy man, maybe too busy to make dates, and maybe too shy, so here he was welcome, anytime. I put on my best smile, like fresh lipstick, and slid into the chair opposite the pudgy gentleman.

"You seem nervous, Frankie. Want to talk about it?"

"It's just this place," I assured him. "Sometimes it gets on my nerves."

A major understatement on my part.

"If you ever decide to get out of here, and look for serious employment . . . oh well, we've talked about this before." He smiled, and I remembered his Real Estate offer.

"When are you going to give me the phone number so that I can look into it?"

He surprised me with a business card from the Real Estate School. I took it and we both laughed.

When Ed asked me if I'd like to have breakfast after work, I regretfully declined. I would have liked to, but I didn't want to involve him in this mess. Not at all. The whole thing felt grungy, and sordid. He was a nice man, too nice and too much of a gentleman to have to deal with the sleazy types who were out for my blood.

I asked him for a rain check, and suggested that maybe Saturday night, we could go for breakfast after work. If he wanted to, I would plan on it. He seemed pleased, but I knew something about him. He would probably not show up. I thought he would talk himself out of it, and he half knew that when I asked him.

Complicated, I thought, these sensitive egos, but also somewhat transparent.

We strolled arm in arm to the cashier with my timecard and she gave him a figure like eighty tickets; he made it an even three hundred. Then he gave me a twenty, and a kiss on the cheek.

I waved him goodbye, while I stood at the cashier's desk, and made out my envelope, noting the number of tickets, to write in my notebook later. I didn't have a moment to waste, I wanted out of there before Tony could pull anything. I was the first person ready and waiting for the down elevator.

Then, I saw Tony pop out of his office, and step towards me as the elevator door opened, and I was inside. The door closed on the last girl. I spent the ride down getting my keys ready for entering my car in a hurry. When I stepped off the elevator the scent of flowers suddenly engulfed me, and there was Filipino Henry at my side, linking his arm through mine. Ordinarily, I would have been upset at the familiarity, but I found his presence reassuring.

"Where's your car?" I asked him as he just steered me to mine.

"Did you see Big Louie?" he asked. "They're out here. Just do what I tell you."

Filipino Henry was my friend at that moment; I trusted him.

It bothered me that I had not found time to call the number in Alicia's file. There would be time tomorrow, if everything worked out, and I had one; a tomorrow that is.

After it was all over, I counted this the second attempt on my life if the psychic was right. But hey! Who's counting?

I made an effort to listen and do what he told me. I hoped he knew what he was doing.

CHAPTER NINETEEN

THE GETAWAY

Filipino Henry had his hand on my elbow as we left by the front door. Big Louie walked behind us. His larger-than-life presence was reassuring.

There seemed to be a lot of people milling around in the parking lot. I focused on getting to my car. I had my key in the door lock when Spider moved toward me.

I heard Louie say, "Back off!"

Henry held the door while I got in and closed it behind me. I started the engine and pulled out of the parking space. Someone pulled out behind me blocking one lane to the exit. I moved forward, and I saw Greek Helen give me a thumbs-up, she had her car blocking all the cars trying to get out of the exit on the left, and there was Annie blocking the exit to the right.

I could see the Mercedes behind Annie, but they couldn't get past her, and they couldn't get over her. I had a few minutes, to get the hell out of there before they did. It was neatly done.

Before I could finish admiring the technique, it looked like the Mercedes turned out of the side of the parking lot, where there was no fence, rolled down the sidewalk, and over the curb going the wrong way on a one-way street. Never underestimate criminals, I always say, they don't play by the rules.

When I saw them coming after me, I put my foot down on the gas, and shot through a yellow light. They followed me through a red light as I swung around the corner. They were right behind me. Downtown L.A. is not a good place for this kind of thing, even at 2 a.m. I was scared to death. There was every chance that they were going to catch me in a place where I couldn't get away, and they had a gun.

There was never a cop around when you could use one.

A flood of that pungent scent of flowers signaled the presence of my unseen friend. How reassuring to have her with me right there in the car. I wished that she could talk, and offer a suggestion regarding what to do next, as I came down Third. After I passed one freeway onramp, I turned left and went back up to Fourth. I wanted to find a place where they would get confused, and I could get away. Nothing suggested itself to me.

Then I made a turn right on Flower. I pulled over to the right and made a U-turn in a hotel driveway.

The black Mercedes was right behind, and they saw me make the turn, and tried to make it. A truck parked in the driveway at the service entrance without a driver, suddenly rolled backward into the street.

The Mercedes following me had tried to make the turn at the service entrance, and they hit the truck head on. Dead on.

There was a terrific noise and a fire. I pulled over and got out of my car. I wanted to get away from those guys, but I hadn't intended to kill them. People were trying to get the doors open. The front was so crumpled that I wondered how anyone could have survived.

"I set the brake!" The driver was running and pushing people out of his way. There were a lot of people for that time of the morning. "I set the brake. It couldn't have rolled." He was explaining to anyone who would listen. I believed him. The scent was hovering around me, and I knew in my heart that Linda had something to do with the brake release. I knew it.

The ambulance could be heard screaming closer. I crossed the street and got back into my car. My mind and body were numb; I think that I was in shock. I watched the car burn, as paramedics dragged the apparently unconscious Barbazul, and Spider away from the burning car. There was nothing I could do, and I didn't want to stay around to be a witness. I figured those two would be out of commission if they were still alive. They were not walking away from this one. I wondered what they knew, if anything, about Alicia? What did they know about any of the other illegals?

The scent in the car was so strong it made my eyes water. No one seemed to pay any attention to me. The crowd was focused on the fire. I started my car, and drove down the block, headed for home. I never looked back. All the way home I thought about Linda, the séance, the missing Alicia, and Tony.

Linda wanted something from me. I don't think that it was participation in my sex life that was keeping her hanging around. This was an attempt on my life. I am sure that if these guys had caught up with me, they wouldn't have just roughed me up with a warning. What connection did they have to Tony? Why did he give their number to at least one desperate illegal? What connection, if any, did all of this have to Linda?

I started reviewing what I knew from the beginning. Linda left the dance hall to get away from someone she was afraid of. Was it Stan? Was it Tony? Stan found her and killed her. If I could believe No-nose Harry, Tony helped him find her. Did Tony know that Stan would kill her? Tony must have told Filipino Henry, and No-Nose overheard him. He was probably bragging about it. Stan killed her after he tortured her. I didn't want to forget that. How did Tony know where to find her? How did Tony know where she was? Why, and how was Henry involved? What part of this had anything to do with Brian?

Who did customers ask when they wanted to know something? Sam? No. Sam was cool. He never told on anybody. Big Louie could be trusted, and he was street wise like Filipino Henry. Would Henry tell? He said no, but how much could he be trusted? He said he was a friend, but he was also a pimp. Pimps were not famous for their loyalty, or their veracity. He also seemed to be close to Tony. Right then, he had helped me get away from Spider and Company.

For the moment I trusted him; I had to.

Why would Tony tell Stan? Tony was not cool, but what did he have against Linda? Maybe, he told Stan just to give Linda something to sweat over. Or maybe, she was another girl who turned Tony down cold. He couldn't have known that Stan was a killer, could he?

Did any of this have to do with whatever Tony and friends were mixed up in? Maybe Linda found out something that she shouldn't have.

That left me with the mystery still unsolved. I didn't like the feeling. I've said it before, and I'll say it again; aside from dangerous car chases, physical violence against my person, unwanted attention from guys with guns, I just don't like roommates. An invisible one, with bad taste in perfume, and an unhealthy interest in my sex life, was not my idea of an ideal situation.

The connection between Linda and these guys wasn't an easy one to figure out, but I knew it was there. There was a piece missing. It was not a coincidence that she was there with me, whenever they were around, or was it? There was that thing with Toshi that had nothing to do with anything. I was pretty sure of that.

I needed to know more about Linda, and her relationship to Tony. Then something struck me that gave me a little tingle on the back of my neck. If Linda was trying to communicate with me, maybe it had something to do with my safety. I didn't have worries about Stan, he was out of commission, but if Tony and friends were connected to whatever made Linda disposable, which might explain Linda's warning.

Now some of the friends were out of commission, at least for the moment. I could check their license plate registration and see where they lived. Maybe, that could give me some insight if I check out their digs, while they were in the hospital, and before anyone knew they were gone. I was actually thinking of breaking into a house or apartment, or under their rock. This was crazy, even I have to admit, that I was getting caught up in the craziness around me. I hadn't even found Alicia yet.

I could only try to have Choug call the phone number, that I'd found in her unemployment record. I didn't speak enough Spanish to understand anything, when and if I found someone at home. I was lucky to have Choug for a translator. I would give her the number in the morning, if nothing else happened between now and then. Hopefully, she was still speaking to me.

I was getting paranoid. I obviously didn't know a damned thing. Even though I knew this for a fact, I felt edgy. Until I figured out what was going on, I didn't feel safe. My mistake was in making Tony and friends think that I knew more than I actually did. I also thought about the séance, and the warning. This was only the first or second attempt, tomorrow was another day. How long would my luck hold? How much can a ghost do to protect me?

All the questions, and nowhere to go for answers. I didn't feel safe, and I wasn't.

CHAPTER TWENTY

VISITING SAM

My house seemed like a safe place, but the guys had warned me that it wasn't. Big Louie's advice, about dying my hair black, changing my name, and getting out of town, wasn't too far off the mark. Still, after the accident, I felt safe enough in my own house. For all I knew good old Lonesome George might be sitting out there watching, to make sure I didn't have anything interesting going on. Who knows?

I slept because I was exhausted, but it wasn't a pleasant relief from one awful day and night.

I got up early, and decided to see Sam. I felt like there wouldn't be much more time for him. Who the heck knew, maybe for me?

Sam was lying very still. The blinds were almost closed, so that the tiniest amount of sunlight filtered across the foot of his bed.

I thought he was asleep for a moment. I was about to leave without disturbing him, when he fluttered blue veined eye lids, acknowledging my presence without speaking.

He's dying, I thought, gradually leaving. Every time I visit, there is less of his spirit here. "Hi, if you want to sleep, I can come back some other time."

"That's all I do, sleep. Sit." He motioned toward the chair with his hand. He didn't try to make his usual effort to sit up.

"How are you doing?" I realized when the words came out of my mouth, what a stupid, inane remark it was. He was doing terrible as any damned fool could see. There was a needle connecting his other arm to the dripping bag of medication that could be wheeled around. The oxygen cover was off, but I could see the equipment by him. I knew that it was only temporarily not in use. I handed the box of chocolates to the nurse, who said he could have one, and then placed the box on the stand that could be adjusted for trays and currently held his water carafe.

After the nurse checked his connections, she left us alone.

"I wish those were cigars," he said. It would be hard to imagine Sam giving up cigars for any other reason than dying.

"I do, too. I brought you some, but they wouldn't let me bring them in. The oxygen, I guess. You look pretty good," I lied.

"So do you." Still gallant even in this damned bed.

I wanted to run from death and decay. It wasn't fair. He was the best man I knew and there he was. We both pretended that he would be up and around until he said. "I'm going to have my son take over, Frankie. I have to; I'm worried about Tony, especially without anyone around to keep him in check. Tell me the truth about what you know. What's going on up there? All of it."

So, I did. I told him about Linda, about the illegals, Alicia, the phone number that Tony had given her, and the two guys that chased me after work the night before. I told him everything except the séance. I wasn't ready to explain why I thought I was haunted; it didn't seem appropriate under the circumstances. I told him that I believed that Tony was mixed up in something nasty. I had no proof, and nothing to go on, but I knew it in my heart.

Sam believed me. He asked questions. I could see that he was troubled. I could have left him in peace, but he loved the place, and selfishly I needed advice.

Like me, he was sure that Tony was up to something unsavory. He confided in me that he had reason to believe that Tony was stealing. He wanted his son to begin an audit on what was going on. After all, it would soon be his dancehall. Sam didn't want to alert Tony, because he was afraid that he would panic, and run before all the facts were in.

"I'm calling Carl, after you leave. I'll try to get him to start coming in tonight. Show him around. Talk to Big Louie and tell him that I said that Carl is going to need some help. Louie is wise about the score up there. He'll make a great manager. Carl's one of the good guys, but he doesn't know anything about dancehalls, and he is full of opinions."

"I will. I'll try to help with anything I can. Maybe I can get Choug to help me check out the address I found in Alicia's file. I feel like time is running out if I want to help her."

He asked me a good question. "How much do you want to help her? How far are you willing to go? You don't know her very well."

Sam was right. I had thought about what would happen after I found her. Alicia was a person with real problems and keeping her out of Tony's clutches would only solve one of those problems. The rest would be more complex. I didn't really want children around, but she was going to have one. That also meant medical expenses. The problem didn't end there, because she had a husband, who would want to be with her, and the baby, and needed a job. There were legal problems connected with all of it. It was reasonable to assume, that I would soon have three people to help instead of one. It was a big responsibility to take on.

Yet, when I think of her working up there pregnant, and being pawed at by people who didn't even speak her language, with that broken strap rubbing her heel, and her husband deported, I felt a certain respect for a brave woman. I decided to help, whatever it took.

"You're crazy and you'll live to regret it." For some reason, Sam thought the idea of me taking on Alicia, and her problems humorous enough to evoke a chuckle. "I'm going to give you the number of my attorney. If you find her, call him, and he will help with the legal problems. It won't cost you anything. Give this number to Mei Ling, too. I saw her yesterday, but I talked to him after she left, and I don't want to call her right now. She was upset. I'm afraid to wait until she comes, or calls back, I might not be here."

I struggled with tears. They won, but we went on talking with the unacknowledged tears dripping off the tip of my nose. I held Sam's hand for a while. I stroked it until he went to sleep, and even then, I stayed for a long time, watching the shadows lengthen. I stayed because I didn't want him to feel alone. Okay, it was partly for him, and partly for me.

I held his hand because I was afraid. I was standing at the edge of life and watching my friend slip away into eternity. I didn't want to be alone any more than I wanted him to be alone.

I went home to change and get ready for the night. I was afraid of Tony. I didn't know for sure whether his friends were out of commission, but I knew that he would hurt me, maybe kill me if he got the chance.

When I got back to my house, I thought, I would have plenty of time to pull something out of the freezer or just make a salad. A couple of gowns were beginning to feel tight around the middle. I was thinking about things like that, trying to avoid thinking about things like Sam, Alicia, Tony, or George, and all of the other major things going on. I put my key in the lock, and the door opened. Then, I noticed that the door frame was damaged when the lock had been broken.

The scent was there with me as I walked through the open door. I couldn't believe what greeted me. The place was all torn up. Things were all over. I wondered about my jewelry. I stepped inside the bedroom, but they had not found my little safe. The drawers were open, and things were scattered, and some things were smashed. They had been looking for something, but a lot of it looked like pure vandalism. I had been trashed.

I was angry and scared.

Who? Did Tony step out of the hall and do this to me? The guys, Spider and friend were incapacitated. They wouldn't know where I lived, but they could have gotten that from Tony and my work files. Tony would have been glad to give them my address. It couldn't be them. As far as I knew they were in the hospital or dead. Could it be an ex-lover? Toshi wouldn't do anything like this, even to an enemy. George had never been to my house, except when he followed me, or he could have gotten my address from someone else.

My mind went around and around.

I had the license number of the Mercedes. I could find out who the car was registered to, and the address. I didn't know the real names of Barbazul or Spider. That would be a place to start.

This assault on my privacy was hard to handle. It had already been an emotional day. I couldn't figure it out. The only person who wanted to hurt me, and maybe even wanted me dead was Tony. I was scared. I didn't call the police. I couldn't prove anything, and I had nothing missing. I thought about Tony's buddy Brian, the vice-cop. Vandalism was against the law, so was breaking and entering. If I were Elizabeth Taylor, they might have been concerned. For a dancehall girl in L.A., they would probably have a good laugh and advise me to change the lock.

Speaking of, I picked up the phone and called a locksmith. The second call was to a customer, Charlie who worked for the DMV. He was the kind of guy who would give me information instead of a tip. He ran the car license, and I had a name and address.

"Will this do it for you, Hollywood?" He was a middle-aged guy who thought he was cool.

"You bet, Charlie." He was an almost nice guy. A little too free with his hands and as a dancer, he was the master of the businessman's shuffle. "Thanks. I appreciate your help."

"Think nothing of it. Nice to hear from you," he said. "Long time no see, maybe I'll come in and say hi for a while tonight. We can catch up."

"Sounds great. I'll look forward to it." He was good for thirty tickets, and no tip. I always try to remember that every minute counts.

Then I began to clean the place up. I had to hurry; I didn't want to be late for work. Things were heating up. Who knew what would happen? I was scared stiff, but I wanted to be there. I didn't want whoever had trashed me; to think that they could scare me off.

Facing something difficult, I got dressed up. That night I decided to wear a long sleeved, black velvet dress, with black mesh hose and four-inch heels. It was a high necked mini, of my own design, with a low cut back, crisscrossed with velvet straps. Huge clusters of rhinestones adorned my ears. I had a wide rhinestone bracelet on my wrist and my hair pulled back on one side with a rhinestone clip to complete the effect. I looked like a million bucks. With any luck, no one could tell that I was nearly scared to death.

CHAPTER TWENTY-ONE

GEORGE, MEI LING, AND EVERYTHING

The dingy downstairs lobby of the Musicland looked even dingier that night, after my visit with Sam, and finding the damage done to my place. I felt so lousy about going to work that night, that when I saw No-nose, I could barely be polite. It was all I could do to sign in, and put my things in my locker. My churlish attitude, resulted in my having to stay on the line, without passing go, and without collecting any tickets.

Nobody wants to pay to dance or sit with a grouch.

Annie Fannie was in early and sitting alone on the line when I sat down.

"I wanted to talk to you," she said. "I was gonna call you, and then I thought no. I want to tell you something, and I want to see what you think. Face to face, not over the phone." She looked upset and frazzled. Her nerves were bad for an expectant mother to be. I wanted to find out what was on her mind.

"I'm listening." I reached over to pat her on the arm. She jumped.

"I wanted to talk to someone. I wanted to talk to you, but I don't want to have Tony sneak up on me and hear me."

"You talk and I'll keep my eyes open." I wanted to hug her; she looked so in need of warmth. She looked like an orphan sparrow.

"Tony is the father of my baby." She puffed on a cigarette and avoided my eyes.

"God, Annie. Of all people! I didn't know that you, and Tony were having a thing. I always thought you couldn't stand him." This was news, but not the kind she would want me to share with anyone.

"I can't. It wasn't like that. He caught me one night, as everyone was leaving. He locked the office door, and he forgot his guitar. He forced me. He raped me."

She gasped with pain or anger or both.

I knew that what she was saying was the unvarnished truth. There are some things you know about a person instinctively. I knew that what she said that Tony had done, fitted perfectly well with what I knew about him. "It's not the end of the world. You couldn't tell anyone?"

"Who? Tell me who should I have told?" She puffed on her cigarette. The police are not famous for their sensitivity to dancehall girls. I would have been a joke if I had tried to tell them. I could have told Sam, but then he was sick. I considered it, but Tony said, that he would kill me, or he would have me killed if I told anyone."

Annie was right. Who could she have told? Who would have cared? Even up there, it would have been a joke. They would have laughed at her.

They would have considered her stupid, for not seeing it coming. "I see what you mean. Sometimes a girl is really on her own. What are you going to do?"

"I'm going to keep it, Frankie. That's not a problem. A baby can't help who its father is. I didn't tell Tony that I'm pregnant. I just don't want the baby to ever know that Tony had anything to do with its genes. I'm more worried about you." Now she did turn her head to look around, and make sure that no one could hear us. "Tony asked me what we've been talking about. I said nothing, just tickets and stuff. He asked me if you'd said anything about the illegals or Linda."

"He mentioned Linda?" Something clicked. Just the wisp of an idea.

"Yeah. He asked, and I said, 'I haven't heard anything.' What's there to hear? He told me that if he caught me hanging around you, that I might get the same thing he has planned for you. Frankie, I think he means to kill you."

"Oh that!" I laughed with what I hoped looked like a certain nonchalance. "Tell me, something I don't know. Really, we should talk more often. He's been trying for the last couple of days. Don't worry. I can take care of myself."

"Don't be so flip, Frankie. I'm so scared, and so alone. Nothing in my life ever works out. You're the best friend I have. He's a dangerous guy. I don't want to lose a friend because she didn't take things seriously."

"Thanks, Annie. You're going to be ok and so am I. Stay away from him. OK?" I was touched that she cared. God! Imagine being raped by that asshole. "I don't know what to say. If you need anything I'm here."

"Sure. Just don't let anyone else know. I couldn't handle being the butt of jokes on the subject. I'll tell you something ironic. I don't even have a boyfriend. That's how I can be so sure, that it's Tony's. All the stuff downstairs never includes . . ."

"You don't have to tell me that. It's nobody's business." I silently wished her luck as a customer retrieved her from the line leaving me alone to reflect on my own situation.

The next thing I knew this good looking, man with extremely white teeth blazing out of tan skin came over and asked me to dance. He was about five-foot-ten and looked terrific in a navy blazer with a polo shirt, and white slacks. At the table he told me his name was Narin. From India, he was only going to be in L.A. for a day or two on his way to Ohio, where a very good engineering position waited for him. I listened and tried to enter into the spirit of the thing.

He talked about his country and how exciting it was to be here, and his plans for the future. The kind of things men, especially foreign men, talked about. I half listened, and then because so many other things were on my mine, for instance, crazy Lonesome George, that I finally looked into his eyes, and said, "Listen to this song, it's one of my favorites."

He closed his eyes; I can't remember which song it was now except that it had nothing to do with lonesome whippoorwills.

"Yes," he said, "it is just right. I'll always think of you when I hear this song."

I touched his hand and his larger hand covered mine. It was lovely that for just that moment in time, we were in love. It was a quickly blooming flower, which would wither under the scrutiny of any kind of reality testing, but for the next two hours, which was the only time I ever in my life saw Narin, we were in love. Truly in love; but only for that night and only in Musicland.

When he left, reality intruded as it has been known to do, and I was faced with the sight of George waiting in the bullpen, with a sullen look on his face. I wondered how long he had been watching me with Narin. I felt a pang for him.

He motioned for me to check in. He was very subdued, even for George. I didn't try to talk. I could wait until he shared what was on his mind. Meanwhile, the many-faceted ball turned, the music played, and the mirrors along the wall reflected us. Amongst the other dancers we stood out, he was tall, I had red hair. We glided in an endless two-step and the ball turned, and we turned, the mirrors catching all the reflections of light and the romantic vision. On and on we danced. We were dancers on top of a music box whirling around and around. Each of us was silent;

each of us had reasons for being unwilling to break the spell. For that period of time, I confess that I pretended to myself. I could almost believe that I loved George, and that we could exist somewhere together, in a happy married space. I pretended, but we both knew it was a lie. I knew that it was only a matter of time, until each of us would be faced with the reality, which would eventually intrude. Reality always eventually intruded in the dancehall, the dream place where fantasies, were the main coin. Everyone who didn't know, assumed that the dancehall was a sleazy trade in sex, or an Annie Fannie's reasonable facsimile thereof.

For me, the dancehall was always a fantasy dream world, where romantic daydreams were almost realities for whatever brief moment in time. It was a fantasy world, where less than perfect men, and women fantasized about perfect love, exciting adventure, and forever-after happy endings. George was for me, the perfect example, the hopeless romantic, the doomed lover who yearned as much for the drama of love, as for the love itself. There were times when I looked at all of us around the room, the women playing dress up, and the men playing courtship. We were all innocent, greedy children. I was one of them, and I was not so innocently playing a game too. Poor George.

I was the first to break the spell. "Are you ok, George? You're very quiet."

"Tony told me about Toshi, and Ed and the others." That's all he said, but I could hear a world blown away. I felt sick.

Toshi was over, Ed was a friend certainly not someone to hurt George with. Tony was being a bastard. I would tell Sam about this. It was strictly a no-no to ever tell a customer that a girl was dating someone else, or that she was married. I wasn't even dating Ed.

What a nerve! Even rival girls watched it about giving out information, if not out of loyalty at least out of concern, that your turn would be next.

Up there we all had something, we didn't want generally known. He had violated a cardinal rule.

"Tony would say anything to make me unhappy." It was major damage, but I would try to repair it. "Don't believe what Tony tells you. He hates me."

"I asked Toshi, he told me, yes, he sleeps with you, but he is more interested in somebody else now, so I can have you if I want you. I don wan you. I hate your kind of woman."

This was a powerful long speech for George, and it had a stunning impact on me. Talk about a strike-out! Wow! Toshi? Saying a thing like that? What did I do to him?

The next thing I noticed stinging my nose, was the pungent overpowering odor that announced my unseen friend. She was here. I felt and smelled a warning. When I looked into George's eyes, I could see madness staring back.

"I wait for you tonight. After work I'll go to your house like Toshi, and I'll make sex with you. Don' worry, I pay the same as Toshi.

"George," I was anguished for him and for me. "Please listen to me. You can't make somebody love you. I'm sorry for everything. I'm sorry. Don't make trouble for yourself this way. Forget it and I'll leave you alone. You can leave me alone. You can have your ring back."

"I don wan it. You keep it. I will see you after work. I have to go."

He stood up with great dignity and checked me out. I felt like I had the sword of Damocles hanging over my head. Oh George!

I was chilled to a tooth chattering; eye twitching, gibbering, by the time Henry showed up, and checked me in. Then I told him everything that had happened, about George and Tony, Sam in the hospital, his son, and Choug, and me, and the two guys, and the accident. He tried to slow me down.

"Pulease!" He held up his hand and made a little cross of the index fingers of both hands as if warding off Dracula. "Slow down, slow down. All of this couldn't have happened in the two days since I saw you. It's too much!" He made me stop and take a cup of tea.

He was right; I was very close to overload.

"Henry, do you know what these guys are into?"

"There's a rumor about something really heavy, and something very illegal. Tony is mixed up in it. I'm pretty sure that Brian is too. I don't know everything, but I know it's nasty stuff. The two guys make very bad kinky porno movies. I think it is S and M stuff. Very expensive and bad enough for you to stay out of it. Nobody likes to talk about something that could cause them trouble. You know what I mean?"

"Sure. Got it! I wish the night were over. I'd feel better about things. I feel like nothing is going right since Stan got arrested. I really feel alone. Sometimes, I wonder if I can handle it."

S and M, the thought of it made me sick. The women that they had found dead were tortured.

"When you get sick of this place, remember I've always got room for one more good-looking redhead. I take care of my ladies."

"I'm so sure. Thanks, but no thanks."

"Well, my pretty, we'll see. I'm going to check you out and try to find George and talk to him. I don't understand why a guy wants to buy a cow when milk is so cheap."

I didn't respond to Henry's standing remark. He'd said those same words to me at parting nearly every time I danced with him for all the time I'd been working at the hall.

He was wrong, at least a little wrong. His girls supplied sex, but the customers came here for something else. Henry, himself spent a great deal of the money he made on his girls, up there on me. I never gave him any sex, but he wanted to make people believe that I was his romantic interest. It was sex plus romance and sometimes, especially the foreign customers, dreamed of happy endings. They were looking for wives, families or sometimes, just an American citizen to marry, who would be easy to dump once they had their green cards.

That year the going rate for getting a girl to marry you for a green card, would cost fifteen hundred dollars, and the promise of a quick divorce. The Japanese men were not making deals but the Chinese and Filipino, and other Asians, Cambodian, and Thai's, were. The only group who insisted that sleeping with them was part of the deal was the Chinese. The rest either lied or tried to make romance part of the bargain. None of them really believed that dancehall girls, no matter how pretty, would be good long-term wives. Most of the guys who wanted to get their green card were educated, and knew that their skills were worth more, financially, here than in their own country. None of these marriages, to my knowledge, ever worked out, but they were entered into by so many.

Henry had just checked me out when Mei Ling pulled my arm. "I've got to talk to you. I'm in trouble. I'll go upstairs, and you come up for a minute if Tony isn't watching."

Tony again, the curse of the dancehall girl. I went to the snack bar and ordered a cup of tea. I listened to him put the make on the new waitress. He stroked his sideburns and did his Elvis accent. She seemed unimpressed. I liked her for that.

"On a vacation?" He never missed an opportunity. "Waiting for a bus? Get your ass over to the line, you know the rule. If there's less than five, you can't take a break. Hurry up, I'm gonna call free tickets in a couple of minutes."

"I'm waiting for someone," I lied. "I gotta comb my hair." I took my tea and climbed the stairs. I could feel him watching my back.

Shit!

I would have to tell Mei Ling that we could expect him to prance in and interrupt any second. There was no corner in the whole place that he would think twice about barging into, including the stalls in the john.

She was waiting by her locker, which was next to mine, and from which we could watch the stairs, and the approach of anybody. It was across the room in the corner and probably was the best place to have a conversation without sharing it with unnoticed listeners. Mei Ling looked so upset; I felt a pang for her.

"Tony found out about me. He's going to tell Sam. I'm fired, but he said I could finish the evening. I'm scared of him. I want to get out of here before he expects me to leave. Big Louie said he'll see that I get to my car. Sam is going to be so hurt. I never wanted to hurt him, honest Frankie."

"I believe you. He's been nice to you and he's a sweet guy. What could be so bad? Another guy? I think he would understand. He's a good guy, but he's been around. You could tell him just about anything."

"I know. What do you think about me?"

I had to think for a minute. I didn't know what she was leading up to. "I think you're a classy lady. I never heard anything bad about you, except that you don't date the customers. That actually shows that you're a woman of taste and discernment, as far as I can see. I know that you are kind of a loner, no special friends, no boyfriend, no lover except Sam, and I have a hunch nothing physical has ever really taken place between you, although that's none of my business. I think you're a nice person, a real lady."

"Well, that's very nice Frankie, except that I'm not a lady. I'm not even a woman. I'm a man. That's what it says on my birth certificate, and that's what I've been living with all of my life." She burst into tears. "Sam doesn't know. I've tried to tell him, and he stops me. He thinks my secret is my past. I wanted to tell him that I'm trapped in a body that isn't me. I'm a woman trapped in the body of a man. I don't even look like a man in a man's clothes. I look like a girl."

She held her hands over her eyes and sobbed. I put my arms around her.

God, life can be a bitch. Mei Ling was the most feminine, the most ladylike girl, I ever worked with, and she wasn't even a woman. I felt like Alice in Wonderland. Everything was slipping around so that I couldn't find a place to tack a tag on reality. I really didn't have much to say in the way of comforting. "I will always think of you as a beautiful sensitive woman. Please don't cry. How is Tony mixed up in this?"

"Tony found out!" She choked back a sob. "He tried something, and that's how he found out. He said he couldn't wait to tell Sam. He tried to blackmail me into doing some vile porno movie with his friends. I pretended to go along with him, but I know something about him, and his friends. I can't be blackmailed. The only person I care about is Sam." She paused and pulled her head up. "He's dying, Frankie. I don't want to tell him now. It's not fair."

A detail like ruining somebody's life, would not seem very important to Tony. Why would ruining someone's death, mean anything to him? I wished to help, but I honestly couldn't think of what to do. I loaned her some tissues. Porno movies and Tony's involvement mentioned twice in one evening.

"Do you want me to talk to Sam? I will, but I think it would be better if you tell him yourself before Tony does."

"There's something else. There's a guy, he's danced with you."

"What about him?"

"He's got connections to big time gambling, drugs, and something bigger. You need to know. It's the guy they call Danny, he's a friend of George. He's dangerous, watch yourself around him. As for Sam, you're right, I've already decided. I'm going to see him first thing in the morning." She paused; her eyes had a long distance, look. "I'm going to San Francisco. I'm not even going to wait for my paycheck. I have some friends, and a job there. My family's there. That's why I came here. There's one more thing. I found something in Tony's office last night when he tried to . . . when he attacked me. It was a film reel. I only got to see a few inches of the beginning before he caught me in his office. The girl in the film was familiar. She had a birth mark on her thigh. It was that illegal that worked here for a while around New Years. Her name was Val, Valenzuela, something like that. I recognized her. Remember? Tony fired her."

"Sort of. Wasn't she a friend of Linda?"

"Yes, French Linda. Well, I think they lived in the same building. Only I remember that Val was an illegal and was worried that someone would blow the whistle on her. Then Tony fired her, and Linda said she just disappeared without saying goodbye. I wonder if Linda ever heard from her again. She never said, but she left suddenly not too long after that."

"No, she never said. I guess that is around the time Linda left." I felt a chill on the back of my neck.

"I always meant to ask you if you ever heard from either of them, but you know how it is. Nobody seems to keep in touch."

"Did Tony see you looking at the film?"

"Yes, he caught me, but I only saw a little of the beginning. He was really furious. I think he could be dangerous."

"I could write a book. Was there anything unusual about the film?" I didn't bother to tell her all I knew about how dangerous Tony, our own little Elvis impersonator, could be.

"Like what? I'm sure not a connoisseur of porno films, but it seemed to start fairly ordinary. It was just Val allowing two guys; one of them looked like Stan, to tie her up. It was probably one of those bondage things. I don't know. I didn't see enough to know. I wouldn't know what was unusual."

"I guess I don't know either. I don't know why a porno film with people we recognize is such a big deal. There are a lot of sleazy people in this town making those kinds of things, and they're not that illegal or dangerous, unless there is something special going on that we're not aware of."

"I hear somebody coming. I want to get out of here, so I'll go down first. Maybe you can find something to chat with Tony about." Mei Ling's voice, his voice dropped to a husky whisper. I don't care what her birth certificate said, she was a beautiful, feminine woman and I'll never be able to think of her in any other way.

"Tony dear, what a nice surprise!" I tried to keep him off balance.

Mei Ling tried to slip past him, he reached for her, but he wasn't fast enough.

"Cut the crap, I know what you're up to. Get down to that line." He addressed this endearment to Mei Ling. He turned to me. "You too, get your buns down these stairs, and dump 'em on that line. There's nobody out there."

"Maybe if you didn't let so many people go, there'd be enough to keep the line filled. At least there might be enough to take up the slack."

"What's that supposed to mean?" I couldn't be sure, but his hair looked like it had been recently dyed. He wore his black suit bejeweled with white pearls tonight.

"I mean," I said, "it's kind of funny that people disappear around here just about the time you get to know them. A lot of illegals especially."

"What did Mei Ling tell you?"

"Nothing. My, aren't we touchy? I guess I'll go down to the line and ask her what she has to tell me that you don't want me to know. I'm sure that if she knew something that it would bother you to have me know, she'd tell me first."

"You know nothing. Stop waltzing around with me. You're going to regret it. I have friends who could give you some things to think about. I believe my friends could teach you some manners."

"How are your friends? You know, Spider and what's his face? The last time I saw them, an ambulance was waiting for their bodies to be pried out of a wrecked car."

"I have other friends, and they know what to do about smart ass broads, who poke their nose into things that are none of their business."

"Is that what happened to Val?"

I couldn't help it. I don't know what made me say it. It was stupid, and dangerous to let him know that much of what Mei Ling had told me. I didn't really know anything about the film, but I could see that I'd struck a chord.

His eyes narrowed to homicidal fury.

"What is that supposed to mean? Let's hear what you think you know." He didn't wait for my answer. "I've had just about enough of you. You're running out of luck, Hollywood. You're beginning to get on my nerves."

"I'm not afraid of you." I lied. "I never walked around here basking in the sunshine of your approval. You can't scare me. I'm warning you, if you threaten me again, I'll go to Sam and his son. They would probably be interested in what you told George if nothing else."

It was a good bluff, and I was really hoping that he wouldn't realize how little I really knew. "I don't think you'd want them to know everything I know." Maybe if he thought I held a high card he wouldn't have the guts to do anything to me.

Before this interview could get any heavier, Greek Helen popped up the stairs to tell me that there was someone downstairs asking for me. A paying customer was the best excuse, plus a witness, to get away from Terrible Tony. One minute more, and I might have had to expose my ignorance or let him know what Mei Ling had told which wasn't that much.

As I descended the stairs, I kept thinking about Mei Ling. How had he kept his secret for so long? Well, part of it had to be because customer, and girl alike knew that he had a special relationship with Sam. They weren't lovers or Sam would have known, but he was attracted to him/her and we all saw it. They'd often gone to breakfast together after work at the Olympic Café where everyone went. That probably discouraged customers from pushing her/him to go out with them. Still, it was a miraculous tribute to Mei Ling's chaste behavior that no one noticed in the whole year that she or he worked there. For goodness' sake! We had even changed clothes and fastened zippers for each other and I hadn't caught the tiniest hint.

Nobody was waiting for me but No-Nose Harry, with his fifteen minutes, of his free tickets. We had a cup of tea. Tony glared from the snack counter. It was late, and I still had to deal with George.

I counted my tickets, and Filipino Henry motioned to me to meet him downstairs. I nodded. I met Henry next to the elevator. "I didn't notice that perfume before, Frankie. I hate to say it, but that is pretty strong stuff." I took his arm, and we strode out to the lot in the general direction of my car.

I had my hand on the door handle when George stepped away from the building's shadow. I was by this time engulfed in the scent familiar. All the hairs on my body erect, I was covered with goose flesh. I looked him in the face, but all I saw was madness. We couldn't have ended any other way. He had written the script from the beginning, and given who I was, and how we each saw ourselves; it was inevitable.

"You come with me." He held a gun in his hands. It seemed enormous and it dominated my attention. This whole scene was really beginning to get on my nerves.

CHAPTER TWENTY-TWO

OVER THE EDGE

When I looked at the gun in George's hands, I knew that this might be my last few moments.

"Don't do it, George. You'll throw your life away too. It's not worth it. It's not that important." I saw his eyes narrow into slits. I stopped feeling sorry for him. I lost my patience, and I wasn't afraid. I pulled the door open. Linda's scent was all around me. Behind the open car door, I faced him.

"I wanna' marry you. I know what kind of a girl you are. I wanna' marry you anyway. You make a joke; everybody laughs at me. I don' care what happens. If you don' marry me, you don' marry anybody." He said all this while moving towards me with both hands around the gun pointed straight at my head.

"You, stupid jerk!" I don't know what came over me, but I was yelling.

George looked surprised. He might have expected a different reaction from me.

"Put that damned gun down before you hurt yourself, you moron. I hate you. I hate your face. I'll never marry you, and I don't care if you shoot that thing. Go ahead, shoot!" I was right up in his face, and I knew that something in me had snapped. I was as crazy as he was.

There was an electrifying glow beside me. A dark shadowy form reached for the gun.

George made a noise like an animal in pain, and I think it was Henry who grabbed the gun, while somebody pushed me into the open car. I heard the shot, and felt a bullet pass very close to the top of my head on my way down. I fell across the front seat as the gun went off. Everything happened at once. That idiot had actually pulled the trigger.

If I hadn't guessed before, this the perfumed interior of my car was enough to let me know that I wasn't alone. Not that she was any good for anything, but she was there. I lay across the sea with my face down, in a humiliating and vulnerable position, for what seemed like a long time, but which might have been only a couple of minutes. There was something more than a little embarrassing about the posture I found myself in; especially in that dress. I could feel the night air on the back of my legs, my exposed thighs and that opened low back of my dress. I was angry, terrified, and indignant. He had actually pulled the trigger George had meant to kill me!

Henry tapped me on the back to let me know that it was okay. He and some of the other guys had gotten the gun away from George who was in the back seat of Henry's car, between two of Henry's friends.

"It's over. George is in my car. We got his gun away from him."

"He tried to kill me!" I was more than a little indignant.

"Get out of here! The police may be asking questions." Henry wanted me to leave before the police got there. Did that make any sense?

"George? Are you just going to let him try again?" I was a little upset because I understood that they expected me not to tell the police. I had just been shot at, and I felt some little concern that he might try it again.

"George is going with me, and my girls for a few days. He'll be all right before you see him again in a couple of days."

A couple of days? He tried to kill me. I understood that I didn't have much to say about it. The guys had decided to keep George from killing me. They expected me not to make a police issue out of it. They were going to use their brand of street psychology, to calm his psychosis. It had been taken care of. Henry would snap him out of it, and there would be nothing official.

I didn't like it, but I could live with it as long as I could be sure that he wouldn't do it again. It didn't seem fair that I got shot at, and George got a few days of vacation surrounded by sympathetic women. Go figure.

That was something to take care of some other time. I started my car and was out of the lot, headed for home when I heard the police siren. Henry's car had left before me. Most of the onlookers were gone and nobody would tell the police anything. It was the accidental discharge of a firearm by person or persons unknown.

There were so many questions and no one to ask. Where did George get a gun? There was also something about Henry. Not that I wasn't grateful. Saving my life was something that didn't happen every day. I was lucky that he was there. He seemed to always be there at the right time. Maybe that was what was making me so uneasy. It was something about Henry, my friend and protector, the world's oldest living pimp. Johnny on the spot.

It was over, for the moment. George was not a murderer, and I was still alive. If the psychic, and Linda were correct, then this was, at least, the second attempt on my life. What next? Where was Elena? What was Tony so worried about? Why did everyone want to kill me? How did the porno movies fit in? I felt like having a drink.

Once I reached the security of my little house, I felt like all the rubber bands that held me together came undone at once. I was like a puppet with the strings loosened, limp. I didn't sleep well either. I had all the lights on, and I tried to read, but all that passed through my mind was the tableau over, and over again. That was the second time that someone had tried to kill me in a week. I wasn't exactly happy with where my life was taking me. Ed was right about one thing. The dancehall was beginning to seem like a fairly dangerous place to earn a living. I felt sleazy, grungy, and more than a little scared. The shine was definitely off.

For a long time, things had been more or less the way I wanted. I liked my house. It had seemed perfect for me, just like the dancehall had been perfect for my needs. Now it seemed that things were moving in a direction that I had not foreseen. I might have to leave. Sam was dying. God, just thinking about that gave me serious pain. When he was gone, I would really be on my own. If I found Elena, I might have more mouths to feed. I would need a larger place, and more money. My career as an actress brought in very little. I hated to admit that it was a long time between the small bit things that had constituted my hope of really making it.

Maybe Ed was right.

Maybe Real Estate was something to think about. I decided to call him, and make an appointment with his partner, his mother.

There was so much that I wanted to know, things that probably wouldn't be known for sure. Why did Linda go with Filipino Henry, even for a little while? Why did Tony tell Stan where to find her? How did Tony know? Did Tony want her dead? Did he know that Stan was a killer? Why would anyone want to kill Linda? So many questions unanswered. Could I have helped her? Was it the dance hall that ultimately killed her?

There had been plenty of women during my time there who couldn't cope with it. Some had disappeared down the tubes, some with alcohol or drugs, or those who found their way into somebody's stable.

There were all kinds of women who worked there, and I was one of the survivors, which proved nothing. The truth was that even without getting shot at, I was getting just a little tired of the game. I felt like a big game hunter who had done it all. I was sick of having to resort to getting money out of men. I was tired of it, in a way. When it was a challenge, it still left a bad taste in my mouth. When it was easy, too easy sometimes, I was a little ashamed of myself. I didn't feel sorry for them exactly, but I wasn't always proud of my survival techniques either.

The phone rang. It couldn't be George. I didn't answer it. Whoever wanted to talk to me could wait until tomorrow. The only person I wanted to talk to was Elena, and she didn't speak English.

Right then I knew that I could do anything if I wanted to. The dancehall had been fun, but maybe it was getting time for me to think about earning my way in another field. I never saw any really old dancehall girls. What happened to retired dancehall girls anyway?

I fell asleep with the image of L.A.'s bag ladies marching down the street pushing their supermarket shopping carts and talking to themselves. It was an image that came to my mind too easily, and I clutched my pillow, and tried to imagine a prosperous old age surrounded by friends and family.

A picture of Sam, gray and pale, in the hospital, came to me. Not the vibrantly, hilariously alive Sam as I'd known him, but lying there, vulnerable, and damn it, helpless. I hate that word. He had money. He wasn't a bag lady, but I didn't envy him. I wanted to scream. It was so unfair. With all of this on my mind I was prepared for insomnia, but I did fall asleep.

I am somewhat insensitive that way. No matter what happens, I hardly ever miss a meal or a night's sleep. Tomorrow is always another day. I am so practical, that I will face anything, including the end of the world (should I happen to be around), with a good night's sleep, and a reasonably full stomach.

Disappointment was nothing to me but a speed bump in the road. I once danced with a psychologist who told me that I had "all the resiliency of a rubber ball." It's a good thing. I think it comes from my genetic mix, and more importantly, from my solid mid-west upbringing with two lovely old maid aunts. They were a special no-nonsense kind of practical team who worked on solutions, and never counted themselves as victims of any kind. They gave me a solid sense of reality and some warm memories. My dad was an army man who died young before I was old enough to remember much about him. My half-Japanese mom died in childbirth. I was lucky to have my aunts, who gave me a loving home and a good education.

The next day was not the end of the world, or the second coming. It was a day where hopes were crushed, and fears realized. The next day Alicia was found.

CHAPTER TWENTY-THREE

SAM'S GOODBYE

After realizing that I had worn exactly the wrong dress the night before, I spent some time figuring out what to wear the next night. A mini skirt with a low cut back, had proven the wrong thing to wear for being draped face down over a front car seat for any length of time. It had been poor planning on my part. There's nothing like mixing terror with the indignity. The next time, if there was a next time, would be different. I wanted to wear something long and wide enough to run in. Maybe tennis shoes under the gown would be good.

While I was sorting through my options, the phone rang.

It was Choug. "Did you see the paper this morning?" She was in a state.

"No hello Frankie, how are you? Nothing? No, I haven't read the paper. Did you hear about last night?" I knew that it wouldn't be on the front page, but possibly gossip would have gotten to her by now. It was almost noon.

"It's Alicia! They found her." Her voice was serious. "I tried to phone you last night, but I figured you thought it was a customer, and didn't answer so I waited till I thought you would be up."

"They found her. Is she okay? Where was she?" There was so much to ask. "Who found her? Who are they?"

"They, the police, found her body. She's been murdered."

I couldn't say anything. The blood in my body all rushed to my stomach, and I could hear my ears buzzing. I had to sit down. I knew that she was in danger, but I hadn't expected to hear this. A different "they" had gotten to her first. She had been so young and so alone.

"Are you okay? Did you hear me? I know those guys had something to do with it. I just don't know why." She was quiet for a minute too. "Frankie, say something."

"George tried to shoot me last night. Tony told him some things." It didn't have anything to do with Alicia. It just seemed like some kind of nasty coincidence.

"I think Tony has a lot to do with all of this. He's a bad actor." Choug was making me feel like it wasn't just a coincidence. "I want to prove it. I'm thinking of calling the police, but my brothers are against it. I don't have any proof to share with them, the police that is."

"That's it, Choug! Until we know something for sure we don't have anything to say. Those two guys, Spider and Barbazul, are still in the hospital, I think. Does the paper say when she was killed?"

"It's in the paper, under "Body of Pregnant Teenager Found." They found her tortured, and mutilated. They don't know her name. I could call them and tell them her name." Choug sounded so angry.

"If we knew it." I told her about the different name in the file that I'd found.

"She probably used somebody's driver's license to get the job." Choug was crying.

What could I say? I didn't know what to tell her. I wanted to know who did it, and why.

Why? She was just a kid.

I had a lump in my throat. I understood why Choug wanted to turn the bastards in.

"Go ahead. You could tell them where she worked. You can't tell them anything else. You don't know for sure." I had an idea. "Maybe one more thing first, I have the name and address that goes with the Mercedes. It's out in the desert, out past Pearblossom. I wanted to drive out there, but I have to go to the hospital to see Sam, and I wouldn't miss work tonight for anything."

"Give me the address and the name. I'll take my brother with me, and we'll nose around."

"Thanks. If you could just check out the general stuff, like where it is, and if there is anybody else there. Don't take any chances, these guys aren't screwing around."

"Sure. Leave it to me. My brother knows how to case a place. So, what happened to George? Did they arrest him?" She had been away from the hall long enough to miss a couple of chapters of the ongoing saga.

"Arrested? For merely aiming a gun, and pulling the trigger on a dirty old dance hall girl? Surely, you jest. Filipino Henry took him home to stay with his girls for a few days so that he can cool off. The police have not been informed, and God knows I'm not saying anything."

"Cabrones! What a life! Did you ever think about earning a living in some other way?"

"Really Choug? What did you have in mind?" I had given considerable thought to becoming a movie star. Needless to say, that probably wasn't going to come to fruition this week.

"Well, if this keeps up, I'm joining the army."

She made me laugh. Of course, she would say that. Although, with Choug, the idea was not entirely outside the realm of possibility.

"If you join the army, friend, then I'm joining a convent."

"This is serious, Frankie. How do we find out who did this, and why?"

"I'm going to the hospital, and see what Sam says. Maybe he'll give me the keys, so I can get into Tony's office. Maybe there is something in there. Maybe if you go in to work tonight, after work, we could get into his office. Maybe that film is still there." She had not been in to work since the adventure with Spider and friend. "How's your hand?"

"Okay. I still have a bandage, but I don't dance with my hand. My legs are okay, and my feet don't hurt. If you think you are going to find out what Tony is up to, then I want to be there. Besides, I might have some important stuff to tell you after we see where those guys live."

So, we set it up. We would not go out after work; we would just go have some coffee. Then we would wait until the place was empty, and closed, and then we would come back. It sounded like a plan to me. I wanted to find out, if not for my own sake, then for Alicia, Lupe, and Linda. Maybe there were others. It felt like all of this was connected and Tony was the connection. Maybe, Tony's office held the key. I wanted more than anything to see that film.

I went to the hospital. Sam was propped up on his pillows looking pale, but more alive than the last time that I'd seen him. I brought another bouquet of daisies with me.

"You're my second visitor today. Mei Ling left a little while ago. She left before I had a chance to do something."

"She told you."

"She should have told me before, but I knew there was something. I thought it was her health. I knew it was something physical."

"You still say she, me too. I can't think of her any other way."

"Frankie, you gotta do something for me. Try to find her, try to catch her before she leaves town. I'll give you her phone number. Give her this." He removed his pinkie ring, a huge diamond, at least five karats. "This could help her if she ever needs money. Tell her to think about Christine

Jorgenson. Maybe she can get the treatments. Besides, I'd like her to remember me. I care about her. Tell her that."

He beamed like the sweetie he was.

"That's a pretty big rock to trust to a gold-digging dancehall girl like me."

"I trust you. Besides, if you screw up, I'll haunt you."

Not funny, but he didn't know about Linda. I told him about her then. I told him everything I knew about Terrible Tony, including Annie and the baby. Everything, from Tony telling George about Toshi to the reel, with the porno flick. I left out nothing, including my personal experiences with him and his threats, even though I risked having Sam think it was a personal thing with me. I told him all I knew about Val, Alicia and all the disappearing illegals. When I was finished, he was quiet for a while.

I felt like a jerk, but I waited for what he would say.

"I wasn't going to tell anyone until I was sure, but my son, Carl, already spoke to me and we decided to replace Tony. We're talking to Big Louie today. We think he would be better for the job. I trust him. What do you think?"

"Big Louie as manager? I think it would be terrific. Tony is going to be furious. I don't think he is going to like getting the axe one bit."

"Carl can deal with Tony. He's so stupid that he's been fooling around with the books. Carl caught it right away. He also doesn't take crap from anybody any more than his old man."

We sat holding hands for a while. This was good news and it solved some of the problems.

"Tell me about the séance," he said. I told him about the perfume and the group. He laughed.

"Do you believe there is life after death, Frankie?" I wouldn't have known how to answer if I didn't have a constant reminder.

"Too much of it for me. I'm sick of an invisible roommate, and her rotten taste in perfume." I looked at his face, so tired, and I wanted to hug him and protect him. "I believe there is more than we know or will ever know. I think there is more to us than the bodies we wear." I pictured my invisible roommate hanging around forever.

"Frankie, I have the keys to the hall. If you want to get in when no one is around, as you said, maybe you can find something. I'd like to help find out what all this stuff about the illegals has to do with the hall. You have my permission. It wouldn't be breaking and entering. If you get caught, I'll vouch for you."

"What an offer! Choug, and I were thinking of trying to get in tonight, after work. Thanks. I think."

"Go in and look around but be careful. Maybe Tony left the film around or something in his desk. Carl doesn't know him well enough, or the whole situation well enough to explain it to him before tonight. Besides, Carl already thinks we're sleazy. Maybe we could find out what is so special about this film to make it so important to Tony. He has probably removed it, but if you get in there, and have time to look undisturbed, maybe you'll find that or something else. By tomorrow, if Louie says yes, he'll be packing everything up and getting it out of there."

He was quiet.

"What's wrong?" I said.

"I wish I hadn't been so blind about what he was doing up there. I was kind of wrapped up in my own stuff."

"Sam! Don't do that. Everything seems so clear, looking back. You couldn't know what he was up to, and we couldn't snitch. It's over."

He shrugged. Sam didn't look happy. "The cleaning people don't come in before ten a.m. Don't go alone. Take Choug with you. Be careful. I want a report tomorrow."

There it was, I could let the police solve it, or do it myself. I knew I had to. "Give me the keys, and Mei Ling's number. Then I'll get out of here, and you can get some rest. I'll call you and let you in on what I find before I tell anyone else. Okay?"

"Thanks, honey. I'll call Mei Ling myself and tell her myself. Just take the ring to her, I think she's packing."

"You don't have to." It was Mei Ling. She was wearing a dark violet pantsuit and never looked more elegant. "I had to come back. I wanted to see you again. I'm sorry I ran out of here without saying goodbye." She had been crying.

Sam opened his arms, and she leaned down, and put her cheek against his.

I was so touched. I'll wait outside for a minute." I handed the ring over to her before I left the room, so that they could be alone.

I was out there thinking about true love, and how rare and strange it is, when Mei Ling came out and got me.

Sam was smiling from ear to ear. "The keys are on the ring in that little drawer." He pointed to the table that swung over his bed. "That's the front door, that's the office, and that's the alarm. Don't forget to shut it off before you go in and turn it back on when you leave."

I took them and kissed him on the cheek. "If I can come back," he said, "you'll smell a good cigar." I didn't want him to leave. "If you can wait for Mei Ling, I would appreciate it if you would take her home. She doesn't have a car. Visiting hours are almost over. I want a few minutes with her, and then I think I can rest."

His head was flat against the pillow and as pale as the sheet, but his eyes were shining.

"Goodbye Sam. I wish I could tell you that you're wrong, that you'll be here longer than you think you will, but maybe you know something. If you're right, and I don't see you again, I want you to know that it won't be the same without you. You are missed right now. Is there something I can do?"

"Do what I asked you. Find out what this is all about. Take care of yourself, and help Annie, if you can. I love you, Frankie. You've been a good friend."

I was going to sob all over him if I didn't get out of there quick. I squeezed his hand. Mei Ling looked like a young girl. She looked open and vulnerable.

I left them to talk again. I hated this hospital. I wondered which rooms Spider and Barbazul were in. I didn't want to visit unless I could drop something on a cast or cut off and IV. I made myself smile by thinking of all the mean things you could do to someone in traction. Then I took a white-faced Mei Ling home. She was wearing that huge diamond that fit on her left hand.

"I'll probably never see him again." She looked so forlorn.

"None of us are going to see him very many times again," I said. We both broke down and cried.

I stayed longer than I had intended. I noticed that her apartment was just like her. It was beautifully done. Her rugs were blue and white, and her furniture antique black lacquer. It was lovely and graceful, in good taste, just like Mei Ling. She was every inch beautiful, and every inch a lady. I will always think of her as I saw her last. I wish her well wherever she is.

I had to hurry home to get ready for the night. I wondered how Choug was doing on her mission. There was much to do. It promised to be an interesting night, at least, and if the last few nights were any indication, it might be exciting and certainly dangerous.

CHAPTER TWENTY-FOUR

READY OR NOT

That night I got to work wearing a long sea green gown cut low and slit up the side with copper jewelry to go with my hair. I didn't wear tennis shoes under it, but I had some in my bag, and a tee-shirt and a pair of Levi's.

Choug was already there when I got there. As usual she was cool and detached. Right. Leaning forward from where she was sitting on the line when she saw me, she got up, and followed me around while I got my timecard clocked in, and I signed the worksheet with my number. She even followed me to my locker, talking fast all the time.

"Did you bring the flashlight? What if they catch us? I brought something to change into and put it in my locker. Do you think we'll find anything?"

"Choug! If you keep this up somebody will hear. Do you want Tony here waiting for us? No? I didn't think so. I don't, so shut up. Okay?" It was still early, and she was getting on my nerves already. "Do me a favor, don't drink any more coffee."

"Don't you want to know what I saw today? My brother and I drove out to the desert and saw the house. We checked it out." Choug was almost pacing in place; it was obvious that she was having trouble standing still.

"Relax," I said. "You checked out the address and . . . ?"

"And nothing! It was empty. I had a bad feeling about it, but there was nothing there, just a shack in the desert. We looked in the window and saw a chair, a mattress. Nothing."

"Nobody was living there?" I could not figure out why the Mercedes was registered to a vacant shack in the desert.

"How can you be so cool? This place is driving me crazy." It was obvious that Choug was under stress. I talked her into drinking milk instead of coffee. The woman was wired.

There was very little time to think about it because the evening started off with a bang. I had just settled myself down on the couch when I was tapped on the shoulder. I turned and was more than a little surprised to see Toshi.

Then I checked the waitress, it was the new one. How interesting, I thought.

I didn't refuse to dance with him. Once we were on the dance floor, I became aware that his dancing hadn't improved since the last time I'd endured it, and I had less incentive to pretend.

I must have been quiet, and maybe he interpreted my silence as hostility.

"I hope that you are not still angry. I wanted to talk to you for a long time. Well ever since what happened"

"I'm not angry, anymore. I am surprised. I thought you had somebody new to dance with or talk to or whatever." I was glad that I had dressed carefully. For some reason I felt exposed.

"I like to come here. All my friends come in here." He shuffled his feet around like a large awkward bear.

"I noticed," I said. He looked good, but I wasn't in the mood for this. If he wanted to say he was sorry, I wasn't going to make it easy for him. I was a little disgusted with men right at that particular moment, and he was at the top of my list, right under George, Tony, Brian, and minions. Then, I remembered that he had been in the hospital for a couple of days.

The new waitress came over to our table. She was lovely, I'm pretty sure that she was a Native American. I ordered tea, and Toshi ordered coffee. For some reason that gave her the giggles. We laughed too, once we figured out what she was laughing about. It broke the ice.

"I just wanted to say I was sorry for being so stupid, and so bad, Frankie."

"Why did you tell George that he could have me, you were not interested?" I couldn't help myself. I was hurt by that more than anything else.

"I didn't. I don't get it. George asked me if you were my girlfriend. I told him that we were not together, but that's all I said. I think he improved my answer." He was looking me in the eye, and I believed him. "I just want to be friends. Could you?"

"Why not?" I couldn't stay angry with him. "A person can never have too many friends."

"You are nice and the best-looking girl working here."

"For all the good that does me. What about Ms. Goulash? What happened to the Hungarian dish?" He wasn't off the hook entirely.

"She doesn't work here anymore. She decided to return to her husband after the accident."

"How sad for you."

"Not really. Please, no argument. I just want to be friends. If you want to go out after work tonight, I'll come back for you."

"No thanks." What a nerve! I suppose he expected the same kind of response he received on our last date. A night that shall live in infamy forever.

"I see. You have somebody else."

"No, I don't. After George tried to shoot me, I decided to be alone for a while. Maybe I'll turn to religion." I didn't want him to see my eyes, so I examined my nails, carefully.

"I see. I didn't hear about that. I'm glad you are okay. Maybe, after some time has passed you will understand that I am really your friend." Maybe after ten or twenty years have passed, I thought. I resisted the urge to kick him in the leg.

I could see that my lack of enthusiasm had saddened him. He didn't ask any questions about George.

"The truth is, I don't trust you anymore. You knew that I cared about you, and you hurt me. Why?"

It was a good question.

"I didn't think clearly. I can't marry anybody here. When I finish my education, I have to go back to Japan. I'll marry a Japanese girl, and my family will send me to work in South America, in the business. I have to work in the family business. The family already knows the girl. No choice."

"We never talked about marriage. I don't want to get married." My face was hot, flushed and I wanted to rip his face off before I ran away to hide.

"I never told you how I felt," he said. "It was time to stop our relationship, and date someone else. I was thinking I was in love with you. I ruined everything because I did the right thing." He looked so muddled. From his point of view that ludicrous statement made some kind of sense.

He wasn't prepared for my breakup. I laughed until it hurt. My sides ached, my bladder begged for mercy, and when I was sure that I had a permanent injury, it began in earnest. I really couldn't stop, and he finally joined me. We were hysterical, but it was cathartic. We were so lunatic, that Tony shopped by the table to try, and find out what was going on. It would be impossible to tell anyone as thick as Tony something as personal, and silly as this.

"I want to see you in my office after your customer leaves, Hollywood. Don't make me wait." He was wearing the other white suit decorated with rhinestones.

Toshi was concerned. "Are you in trouble? Is it my fault?"

"Not your fault at all. I can't explain everything, but Tony is my enemy. I can take care of it." I didn't trust Tony any farther than I could throw him, but I couldn't involve Toshi. It wasn't his problem.

Later, when we had recovered, we danced, and then shot some pool. I beat him two games out of three. I had forgotten how much fun it was to be with him. It was nice to see him, and he was making me forget all the things that had happened in the last few days. We could be friends if nothing more, I thought. I sure had missed his body. Well, it was nice to know that I didn't have to. Anyway, there was no hurry. He'd explained why I couldn't trust him. I'm sure that he was being honest, Asian style. I didn't feel any confidence about getting involved with him again. In my heart I cut him loose and decided to be friends. He can dance, and court anybody he wants to, I decided. I don't want to depend on him. He was a hunk, but not worth the pain.

The funny thing is, that once I had decided definitely that I didn't want him, he became sweet and attentive. Men are really hard to fathom. I don't think Asian are especially inscrutable. I think men, in general, are hopelessly inscrutable. Every time I thought I knew something about a man, I'd find out what a pitiful tiny bit I'd plumbed the depths.

After Toshi left, saying he would be back in a couple of hours, I knocked on Tony's office door. When I was admitted, the first thing I noticed was the man in Sam's chair at Sam's desk. I walked directly to him with my hand out to shake his.

He rose behind the desk to shake mine. I could see Tony twitching uncomfortably out of the corner of my eye. He was a tall almost middle-aged man, impeccably dressed, who looked like a successful attorney would look.

"You must be Sam's son, Carl. I'm Frankie Hollingsworth. It's possible your father might have mentioned me."

"As a matter of fact, I've been wondering which one you were. I think that I might have seen you on a brief office visit before. He had mentioned you to me, more than once. I'm pleased to meet you."

Tony writhed in his chair like someone had sprinkled his underwear with itch powder. I'm sure he'd had something different in mind when he'd called me in to the office.

"I saw your father this afternoon. He told me to expect you. I'm glad you could make it. Welcome aboard."

"I called right after you left. He isn't doing very well. It's just about the way the doctors predicted. He appreciates your visits; he told me so. You're the only one he wants to see now. He doesn't want any of the other girls or customers to visit. I think it's because he's not strong."

"He's a nice man, a good friend. I haven't seen you here before. Are you getting acquainted with everything?"

"I'm here because he asked me to come. I'm not particularly interested in this business, and he knows it. This was his toy."

"I'm sorry." That was all I could think of to say. It was none of my business and he had a perfect right not to be thrilled with being saddled with this shabby, sleazy taxi-dance establishment. Still, it wasn't very gracious of him to let it out like that, after all, I was connected to that shabby, sleazy place too. I could see how different the two men, father, and son, were. I felt a little sorry for both of them. He was a son that Sam could be proud of. He was smooth, classy, well educated, and Sam was rough around the edges, the way a lot of self-made men were. Carl was about to own a business that was not a social asset.

Sam probably thought his son was a bit of a snob and his son probably thought his father was a little disreputable. That could get in the way of genuine affection.

I'd lay odds that any son of Sam had good stuff, and that he was probably a good decent man.

I held out my hand again. "Let me know if there's anything I can do. I'd like to help you or your father if there is anything. Any son of his can consider himself a friend of mine."

"I'm so sure." Tony had been silent until he spewed this little bit of venom. He surprised me, but not a lot. "It will be "a cold day in hell," when he needs your help. What are you going to do for him, teach him how to grind?"

"Maybe I'll help him figure out who he can trust, and who he'd better watch out for around here." I didn't like lowering myself to Tony's level, but that man brought a new dimension to the meaning of rude.

"Maybe you'd better get your big ass out to the line before your tickets drop, and I have to pay you the minimum."

"I'm confused. I thought you wanted to see me." I turned to Carl. "Nice meeting you. Thank goodness everyone around here isn't as low as this." Obviously, Tony hadn't been told that his days, maybe hours, were numbered.

I stepped out of the office in time to see Ed Wong getting off the elevator followed by a sullen George, who glowered at me, and then went to sit in the bullpen, without talking to anyone. I wondered where Filipino Henry was.

Ed motioned to me, and I checked in. Mr. Wong was excited about a big deal he was putting together. He needed to do a little bragging. I listened with half an ear; I was thinking about a lot of other things. It had been one hell of a week.

"I think you should get your license. I'll pay for the school. Get your license, and come to work for us, Frankie. I talked to my mother about it, and she said to come and talk to her. She'd like to meet you."

"What?" Like I said, I'd been thinking about a lot of things, and something had gotten by me. "What about your mother? I'm sorry, but I think I missed something. I had thought about making an appointment with her. I had some questions. I think sometimes think you can read my mind."

"I was just saying that I think you should get your Real Estate license, and come to work for my mother and me, we're partners. It's a good field for women. You've got a lot of personality and you're smart. I talked to my mother, and she said she'd like to talk to you. We have a couple of people, working in the office, that I recruited, and they're doing really well. We could honestly use more good salespeople."

"What made you think of making this offer tonight?"

"I've been thinking of recruiting you for our office for a long time. I've even mentioned it to you, but you never take me seriously, Frankie. You're very likeable, even the other women up here like you. You have a way of making people trust you."

"Gee Ed, I'm overwhelmed. You did mention this to me before and I was thinking, just yesterday, about calling to make an appointment to talk about this very thing." After the encounter with Tony and Carl I was grateful for this. "I've never thought about a career except as an actress."

"Well, maybe it's time. You're wasting yourself up here. I know you talk about acting but think about it. How many acting jobs have you had in the last six months? How much acting are you really doing? Are you in a class? I think it's a habit to think of yourself as an actress, but I don't think that you're all that dedicated."

He waved to get the waitress' attention. "When we've talked about this before, you just never took me seriously." His face had reddened as he talked. "I could be wrong."

He looked embarrassed. I think he was worried that he had offended me. I wasn't offended. In fact, I had to admit that a lot of what he'd said made sense.

I reached over and took his hand. "Thanks, friend. You are probably right. To tell the truth, I've been thinking along some similar lines myself."

"Listen, Frankie. Real Estate agents don't punch a time clock. You could still go to auditions and do the acting. It is a very flexible kind of work."

"Tell your mother, thank you. I'll give her a call, and maybe we can get together next week. Maybe you're right, and this is a good time to give my future some thought. I guess the flexible hours, and erratic pay are similar to this. I don't know. I am giving it some serious thought. I appreciate your offer. Thanks for thinking of me."

He beamed.

I wondered about how long he had thought about my future before tonight. He had mentioned it before, I just never felt any urgency about it. I never took him seriously enough to act on it. I liked the fact that he was a business partner with his mother.

Things were moving quickly. I felt like the bottom of everything was being pulled out from under me. I needed more time. I had to find out what Tony was hiding and why he wanted to get me. I thought about dope. That was the most illegal thing, I could think of, but why would porno people be mixed up in it? The most illegal porno that I knew about would be kiddie porn, but that wouldn't make sense with the illegals. Maybe bondage, S and M. Well, then what? Bondage wasn't that big, there was a girl on the line taking a break from one of the parlors, she was into domination. She even maintained a couple of hapless slaves. It was all a kind of silly fantasy where hardly anybody ever got hurt, according to her. You hear things once in a while, but that was isolated. I could only speculate, but the whole thing was giving me the whim whams. I had to find out. I was still thinking about it when Ed left.

I was watching him get on the elevator when James Chang tapped me on the arm and motioned to the time clock. We'd danced together before, and I was pretty sure that he'd had a crush on me. He was the one that really started George's insanity. James was very shy, but he drove me crazy with his gently expressed lust. I had never dated him, but I enjoyed his attention.

Dancing with him, was a very sexy experience. He didn't say very much. I was dancing in a conventional way with my left hand on his shoulder. His right hand over mine guided us. Now we danced to the ballad. I think he'd had lessons because he was so expert at the steps and turns. People were watching us, and when we and the music ended, it was in a low dip, and I was bent over backwards. We had been dancing awfully close together even with the intricate steps and turns.

Then his eyelashes brushed my cheek, his head rested against mine, and his whole body began a light tremble. God, he turned me on. Without doing anything really obscene, this shy sweet man was making me orgasmic right there on that crummy dance floor.

We danced to the next tune, and it was a waltz, and I loved it. Moments like that could make Taoist out of me. It was like a gift from life, right in the middle of all the crap that life piles in heaps, in our lives. It is the wonder and rhythm of life. I'm not sorry to say that I have always enjoyed those mysteriously unconnected moments of life and joy. Sex is wonderful! Life is wonderful! It's great to be warm, alive, and in lust.

The music stopped, and I reached up and kissed him on the cheek.

He leaned down to really kiss me, which was a no, no, and Tony rushed right over to tell us the rules, thereby humiliating him. He was so shy that he would usually carry on a conversation, about the other girls, and if they might be interested. He found an excuse to leave shortly after. I knew that we would never date, never see each other away from this place, but that moment was sweet, and wonderful. It was something I would carry with me.

After James left, I shook hands with him at the elevator, I made my way back to the line. Annie Fannie was sitting there alone. That was a pleasant surprise, because once the evening got under way she seldom sat down anywhere. She said that it was hard for her to get a guy who would let her sit down and have a coke. They made her earn her money on the floor, working it off for them. Damned animals. Annie didn't seem to mind too much, and hardly ever complained. She was the best sport up there.

"I heard about George. Good that he missed."

"Likewise, I'm sure. I haven't seen you sit down all night. Are all your regulars out of town on vacation or something?"

"Or something. You won't believe this, but see that nice little old man talking to the cashier? I was dancing with him, and he had some phone calls to make, and some business with Tony. He's the accountant for this place. Anyway, he bought me three hundred tickets, and returned me to the line, so I'm taking a break. Look, he even tipped me." She pulled a twenty off her ticket stack and attached it to her finger by a rubber band as she showed it to me. Her eyes glowed with this show of extra kindness. Poor baby thing, what she thought of as excessive kindness, some of us got all the time. Nobody was this nice to Annie, hardly ever.

I naturally congratulated her on her good fortune.

"Oh Annie, that's so nice. How are you doing? I mean physically." I didn't want to mention the pregnancy, not up there. If it got out before she wanted it to, it could cause her a drop, in business.

"Oh that, I'm okay. You know, a little queasy when I get up. I've lost a little weight. I'm going to see a doctor next Tuesday. I guess I'll be okay. My sister, and I are going to share a house, she needs help with the kids. She's got a job. I can get welfare. We'll be all right."

Welfare! A fate worse than death. I wouldn't say anything because it was, after all, her life and her decision. "Maybe you should let Tony know or at least talk to a lawyer. Even people who are crud otherwise can be nice about a little one."

"Never!" Her answer was fast. "I don't want him to even suspect it. When I get away from him, I want a clean break, so that he has no reason to look me up ever. I'll make up a name for the birth certificate."

The look on her face made me feel protective. He was a real asshole to get this kind of reaction from Annie. She put up with a lot before she ever complained. Her first husband was an alcoholic who beat her up twice a week, and robbed her purse, while she supported him. She didn't actually complain until he ran off with her younger sister, one night while she was at work. Annie had a forgiving nature though. When he left her sister with two kids, Annie made it up with her, and even babysat the kids. This would be Annie's second child out of wedlock. I don't think I've ever known anyone as good as Annie, or anyone with her Christlike ability to forgive, and to turn the other cheek.

"If you need something like a godmother, or anything, let me know." I squeezed her hand. The grinders were what everyone pointed to, as the sleaze element of the dancehall. I thought that they earned every penny they made. I also wished for Annie something better, I just couldn't think what it might be. Maybe this baby would be something wonderful, instead of the added burden, it seemed to a selfish observer like me.

Our conversation was interrupted, when a customer came over to claim the lady, leaving me alone on the bench. It wasn't the first time, but I didn't spend all that much time on the line. Usually, I had my own group of regulars, but I didn't see anyone I knew for the moment, so I leaned back to relax and think good thoughts. Tony decided to call tickets.

Now, several times during the evening, to keep too many girls from sitting down too long, the management would get on the microphone, and offer customers, who were milling around like lost sheep, the fabulous bargain of fifteen free minutes, in the arms of one of the one hundred beautiful girls. Then, all of the girls would dutifully hoist their tired carcasses to a standing position, so that these charming gentlemen could get a better look at the merchandise.

Well, I was the only lovely gracing the couch, so it was pure maliciousness, that caused him to grab the mic and intone, "Fifteen free minutes for some lucky customer. Stand up, Hollywood, show them what they're missing. Come on gentlemen, doesn't anybody want to dance with this slightly used, almost luscious red head? Get up Frankie, got off your ass, and take a deep breath, so the guys can get a good look at what I'm offering here. Check the goods out, guys. Fifteen free minutes, no takers? Well, going once, going twice, going third and last time. Too bad you missed your chance. See you in my office, Frankie."

Tony had finally gone too far. I couldn't endure it. It was a public insult and humiliation, not only that, but my Asian friends would understand it as a loss of face. I would lose their respect; I would be contemptible. As long as I was popular, a top girl, a friend of the owner, I had face. Now, I was finished. I couldn't keep working here, where I got this kind of public mistreatment.

If only Sam was here.

He would never allow this, but who could I appeal to? It was too late I could barely control my tears.

I stood up. I didn't stand during that assault on my dignity, but when it was finished, and I knew that I was finished, I stood up and began walking toward Tony's office. I wondered if Carl was still there, and what he must think. Someone tapped me on the shoulder.

It was Filipino Henry. He handed me his free entrance tickets. It was a sympathetic gesture, he looked away in embarrassment.

I turned toward the office, and someone took my arm.

"Could we dance?" It was Toshi. "You can talk to that asshole later."

I looked up into his grinning face, he was a knight in shining armor. I looked around and there were several people I knew standing around looking, and not looking. "Actually," he said. "I'm free for the rest of the night. Maybe I'll just buy your tickets till two, and you'll have to talk to him some other night."

My face was saved, as simply, and as nicely as that. We were no longer lovers, but we were friends and it counted. He made me laugh, and Tony became, for a moment, less of a menace. A gentleman is a gentleman, and I will always be grateful for that whenever I find one.

The rest of the evening was almost fun. I forgot to be afraid. I stopped worrying about what was coming when work was over for the night. I forgot to think about what I needed to know; I just basked in that protected state. It's so hard to be a grownup independent woman, and independent of men. It's hard to give up that Cinderella legend, where the knight on a white horse, prince charming, saves you from the dragon or just a bad Elvis impersonator.

Sometimes I can be so easy.

I know that it was fantasy like everything else up there, but it worked for a couple of hours, and then it was closing time.

Choug and I met upstairs. We were both in a hurry to get out before Tony could stop us.

"How are we going to work this?" Choug was nervous.

"You can back out if you want to. I won't hold you to it." I didn't want anything else to happen to her. She was still wearing the bandage on her hand.

"Don't be stupid. I'm in. Let's go out and get some coffee. I don't want to change up here. We'll change at the coffee shop. Let's go. Andalay!"

CHAPTER TWENTY-FIVE

BREAK IN

Choug and I each took our cars to the coffee shop. When we got back to Musicland, we parked them around the block. We did not want them spotted in the hall's parking lot. Armed with the keys, a flashlight, and wearing more appropriate clothes, I felt like we would be stopped, and hauled off downtown any minute. This despite Sam's assurances. The life of a cat burglar was not in my future. If I was nervous; Choug was demented.

The key was inserted in the lock, and then I turned off the alarm, the way Sam had told me. I slid inside with Choug right behind me. Then I locked the outer door again, so that no one could sneak in just by trying the door. They'd have to use a key. I turned the alarm back on. It was dark and gloomy inside with all the lights off. I looked at my watch, it said three thirty.

My unseen friend, Linda, and her rotten perfume, was with us as we climbed the stairs. The elevator was closed, and I didn't have the key for that. The snack bar was clean and empty just beyond the cashier's desk. The line couch, empty of any of the 100 Beautiful Girls, was torn on one corner and sagging in the middle. The flaking paint was clearly visible, on the mural that graced the wall. The worn, neglected interior was all revealed in the beam of the flashlight.

Choug had been quiet. "Jesus y Maria, this place gives me the creeps. Let's get in and get out." She whispered. I knew why. It was awful how much it felt like we shouldn't be there.

Sam's office was in the back. Tony had been using it, while Sam was ill. Before that, Tony had the outside office, where he had kept a desk, and the personnel files. Most of the filing was in the outer office, still, except for the ledgers which Sam had always kept in his office with the bank statements, and his correspondence. The old tickets, and the unused tickets, the employee records, and the payroll checks and information, had been stored in the files in the outer office where Tony's desk used to be. It had always been tidy, when Sam was there. The first thing I noticed, when I opened the door with the key to the outer office, was the mess. It hadn't been like this when I met Carl just a few hours ago.

So, it seemed that Tony had gotten the news about his imminent retirement. The second thing I noticed was the shotgun under Tony's desk, formerly Sam's desk. A shotgun. Maybe, it was standard equipment. After the stimulating experience with George, a little more than twenty-four hours ago, I had a good reason to be nervous about firearms. Still, it was a small part of what we were looking for. I didn't see any film canisters. We were just getting the desk drawer open when we heard some voices. We froze.

Choug motioned me to the closet, and I saw her get under the bookkeeper's desk.

The door to the outer office opened, we were in the back. In the closet with me were some of Sam's old clothes, a raincoat, and a couple of sport jackets and even a couple of pairs of pants. I had to be careful not to stumble on the old shoes, and a stack of printed material that cluttered the floor. I wanted to hear what they were saying, but I didn't want to be found. I pushed as far back in the closet as I could. I didn't close the door completely.

"What did you expect? I got the axe tonight. I wanted to finish cleaning things up before Carl gets back in here tomorrow. Can you believe they're making Big Louie the new manager? Those broads will run amuck. Well, it's not my problem."

That voice I recognized as Tony's. He was fired. He probably did have things he wouldn't want anyone else to know about. I would have been a lot happier to know this, if I weren't crammed into that little space, and worried that he would find Choug and me.

"I don't want to carry this around. George said he got it from you." That was Filipino Henry. "Why would you give him this? He could have killed her."

"I was hoping." Tony laughed. "What a dumb ass! Well, it almost worked. What the hell. If he didn't, I will. It'll look like he did it. Everybody knows he already tried it once." I heard stuff being slammed around in the outer office. I was sweating. I wondered if Choug was as scared as I was. "Anyway, with his connections he would probably skate."

"What's the matter with your head?" My good friend Henry's voice rose. "The last two guys who tried to get Frankie are still in the hospital, with some tubes going in and tubes coming out. Why don't you just forget about her? She doesn't know anything. Brian told me to give it up, he would take care of her, we should just leave her alone."

"I don't take orders from Brian. Didn't you hear? He's got a Grand Jury summons. She's nosy, and this is personal. I hate that cunt." Tony said this in an offhand way, like he was talking about spinach.

"Besides, things are heating up. I don't need the aggravation." Was Henry talking about Alicia?

"What are you talking about? You stepped in and saved her ass. Your nose is clean." Tony was probably the one rattling the papers. I yearned to see what he was collecting.

"If George killed her with your gun, you might have to explain how he got it, and why. The other thing is they found Alicia. Somebody identified her. "Body of Pregnant Teenager Found," Henry quoted. What the hell, what was he so cozy with Tony about? Was he in on killing Alicia? It sounded like they were both involved.

"She's not my problem." I heard Tony's chair creak. I could picture him with his feet on the desk. Thank God, it wasn't the desk that Choug was crouched behind. He could start going through those drawers any minute and find her. They had at least two guns. There was the shotgun on the floor and the gun that George had tried to shoot me with. I was more than a little nervous.

"Maybe they'll find out she was one of mine. I wish she'd stayed." Henry actually let a little regret creep into his voice.

One of Henry's girls? He knew that I was looking for her. That no-good rotten little creep! I was letting the tears come. I couldn't help her or the baby now.

Nobody could.

The phone rang, and the chair legs slammed to the floor. "Yeah, Carl. I just came back to get some of my stuff."

There was a long pause. It was beginning to get stuffy in the closet, even with the door open a crack. I could swear that I smelled cigar smoke, maybe lingering from Sam's last visit up here.

"I'm sorry to hear that. I'll be in to see you tonight before it opens. You can give me my last check." I heard the phone replaced in its cradle.

"I gotta go. Phone calls at four a.m.? Whew, this business is as bad as mine." Pimp Henry's idea of wit.

"That was Carl, Sam's son. He had something to tell me," Tony leaned back in his chair. "Sam died tonight. The old geezer finally croaked. I think he was just checking up on me. He tried my place and had a hunch I was in here. Out with the old, and in with the new. Maybe he's afraid I'll pack up the family jewels and take them with me."

Sam was gone. Another minute, and I would be screaming. I was expecting it, but it wasn't any easier. I said a little prayer. Rest in peace, dear friend. I tried not to think any more about it. The grieving would have to wait.

"What are you going to do? Henry didn't sound worried or anything. He was just conversational. I had no idea that these guys were that close.

"Help me carry this down. Here, you take the box." Tony told Henry. I heard more scraping and their footsteps. A door closed. I waited for a little while, my heart pounding. I stood up and lurched out of the closet.

Choug was trying to get the window open with both hands, one of them still bandaged.

"We've gotta get outta here without getting caught." She got it open and was hanging out of it. Was she planning to leave from the second floor?

"What are you going to do, jump?" She started over the edge of the window. I moved to grab her legs.

"Let go, Frankie. There's a fire escape." She pushed me aside and was on it.

Then, I heard footsteps.

"I'll give you a lift. I've got to put something away." It was Tony.

I stuffed myself back into the closet behind Sam's trench coat, holding my breath. The closet door opened, and Tony was less than two feet from me.

He had something large that he was taking down, and then he rearranged the shelf. I was afraid to try to get a better look. I was sure that if I moved an eyelash he would notice.

"Jeez, this place smells like women."

The closet door slammed, and I let out my breath. That was close.

I knew that he was referring to the odor that I had almost become used to.

"Frankie, come on!" Choug didn't know that he'd come back. She was calling to me from the fire escape.

"What the hell?"

Tony was still in the office. I opened the closet door in time to see him leaning out the window. He had the gun, and I heard him shoot. He was shooting at Choug! I couldn't do anything, but I hoped that she got away. I hoped he missed. I looked for something to hit him with. He fired again.

CHAPTER TWENTY-SIX

DO SOMETHING!

I could smell the perfume. "Do something, don't just hang around!" I said. I know that she heard me. I saw the gun recoil from the explosion. It made enough noise to make me think of cannons. While he was still leaning out of the window, I pushed myself out of the closet, and ran to the hall door. He saw me. I know because I could hear his footsteps behind mine.

Near the elevator, I remembered that it was off. The exit door to the downstairs was next to it, but I ran past that, and up the stairs to the lockers. I don't know what I was thinking. I was just afraid of going down to that dark parking lot where Henry, good old Henry, waited. I didn't trust him now. I ran upstairs, and I found the stairs that went to the roof next to the girl's bathroom. I kept running. For a minute I didn't hear him, but I kept on running. Maybe I could find a place to hide on the roof.

Not a chance! When I reached what I hoped would be safety, I found myself trapped. There were only the vents, and the large air-conditioning unit. I tried to get behind it, but I knew that it wouldn't fool a two-year-old. I counted the seconds and held my breath. I was waiting for my next opportunity to look down the barrel of a gun pointed at me by someone who would like to see me dead. While I waited, I looked around for something blunt, and heavy or sharp, and pointed. There was nothing. Where was Choug?

Tony opened the door to the roof looking like he was having a good time. He was not threatened by either of us. Where was she? Maybe she got away and was at this very minute calling the cops. I wanted Tony caught. I didn't really believe that I was going to get away from him, but I didn't want to just be another body. Besides, Carl knew that Tony was here. He would know that Tony didn't like me. Please, I thought, don't let me be just another dead dancehall girl.

"Come on out, Hollywood. Be cool, I want to talk to you. Don't kid around with me. You'll spoil the fun." He was walking toward the place where I was hiding.

I moved around the vent away from him, but there was no place to go.

"You heard about Alicia. You probably think you know something about it. Am I right?"

"When you're right, you're right." I stepped out into the shadowed area next to the vent. I don't think that Tony could see me clearly.

"That's better. Why don't we cut the crap; let's put our cards on the table. You have nothing more to lose, and I'm tired of pussy footing around." He walked closer, the gun held chest high in front of him. He looked like he wasn't that familiar with it. I wouldn't want to swear to it.

"Anything you say, Tony. I guess you hold the high card." I held my hands up a little, but I was watching for any way to get out of his sights. "Why don't you explain what was so bad about the movie, that you would want to get rid of anybody that found out about it."

"See! It's that kind of nosy punk attitude that got you into trouble in the first place, honey." He had lapsed into his fake Elvis southern drawl while he closed the gap between us. Now, I could feel his breath, and the gun touched my chest.

My heart was pounding, but my brain was working.

"You misunderstood me sugar. I always thought you had a great ass. I wouldn't mind knocking off a piece before I take you outta here once and forever."

"Give it a rest, Elvis. You don't want them to find that kind of evidence when they find the body."

I was having trouble breathing, but I wouldn't let him know how terrified I was.

Then I heard a little noise, a kind of scraping. Choug was on the fire escape twenty feet away from where we were standing. Her head popped up and then back down. She was alive and right there.

"On the other hand," this better work, I thought, "Maybe a last moment of ecstasy with you would be a good thing to take with me. Is it okay if I move over here a little bit? Now, I can see your good lookin' face a little better."

"Don't get cute. You know what my face looks like." He reached out and grabbed my wrist, pulling me away from the vent. Now my back was turned toward Choug. I pulled away from him and turned to walk over to the edge of the roof. I sat down next to the fire escape. I hoped that he didn't remember that she was out there.

"You're lucky I haven't killed you already. Yeah, you think you're pretty smart, Hollywood. I'd like to give you the chance to star in a movie." Whatever nasty thought crossed him mind, it made him smile. "Come on, we're leaving now. Fun's over."

I stood up. It was nine stories down, but I considered jumping instead of allowing him to do anything he thought of as fun to me.

"Where did she come from?" He was looking at something to the side of me. It wasn't Choug. It wasn't anything that I could see, but the smell was overpowering.

"Who Tony, one of your victims? Can you see her? Is it Linda? She's with me a lot lately. Can you smell her perfume?"

I couldn't believe how scared he looked. Well, he was sure that she was dead. He was so engaged with his vision that he didn't seem to notice Choug. She climbed up on the roof and slid along the side while Tony seemed to be in another place.

"Stay out of this, Hollywood! I'm not afraid of any little two-bit cunt. She got what she deserved. You're next." He turned back to me, but I was close to the fire escape, and Choug had moved to the vent he was standing in front of.

He waved his gun at me. "Get back."

I couldn't go very far back. One more step and it was a long way down. I wished that I could see her. "I thought you wanted to party." I was grasping at straws.

"Move!" He waved the gun, and then he turned. "I said get back! Get away from me!" He was waving the gun around like there was more than one of us on the roof with him. Technically, I wouldn't like to have to swear how many. He wasn't looking at Choug, she was behind him. He moved toward me. I wanted to back away, but there was nowhere to go.

"Take it easy, Tony. You said you wanted to talk. You still haven't told me what the big scam was. Why the illegals?"

He stopped and looked around. He seemed dazed. "That's right. Why not tell you? I know that you'll understand. You always wanted to make movies. I used to think about that and laugh. I couldn't use you because so many people might miss you. Also, you were good, your tickets were high. We used the losers." He wiped his forehead with his sleeve, the gun still in his hand.

"We made movies. Special movies. Each one was a little different, but basically, we took a cunt and had fun with her. Sometimes, it lasted for days." I didn't want to hear the rest. I was physically ill. "We let them think they were going to a job, and they were all girls who knew the score.

In the beginning, none of them minded being tied up too much. Sometimes, we didn't tie them up at first, then things got rough." He shrugged his shoulders. "I like the last one we did. It looked real. It was a real Elvis movie, but he killed her in the end."

He was a psychopath, and he had a gun. I cared that he was going to kill me, but there was something else I cared about. I wanted justice.

Choug was behind him but, without a weapon. The other person there apparently couldn't do anything to him either. He came closer to me and closer to the edge.

"Stan helped. In fact, he was important at first. He did most of them on his own. He had a specialty act, he liked taking them apart. We even had a guy that acted the part of a vamp. There was a lot of money from the right collectors. We had some good connections. Your buddy, George is a big one, especially with the guys in Hong Kong. He's a big deal in the Triads. You thought he was just another dancehall Johnny. He was a sucker for you." It was awful to hear this and he wasn't finished. "You would be surprised at the rich, and famous people who are really into these." He smiled. The effect was horrible. "I made, well, we made, a lot of money. The trouble was that Stan wasn't very dependable."

He was three feet away from me or three and a half feet from the edge. Choug was sliding up behind him.

He turned and saw her. "I thought I got you the first time." He let off a shot. Then he turned and shot at the dark shadow next to me. I pushed him toward the edge. He knocked me away.

Choug was down. I couldn't tell how badly she was hurt; I could see blood. It was my fault for getting her into this. I was down.

He was standing over me. I expected the gun to go off any second. "You had your chance, Hollywood. I guess you are going to die without getting your big break." He had both hands on the gun which seemed to be aimed at my face.

I took a deep breath, closed my eyes, and prepared to join my late friends.

Nothing happened. Nothing. Not even a click. I looked up.

Tony was watching something that I couldn't see. The gun was pointed away from me, at whatever he was watching.

I started to get up. It didn't matter, he didn't notice me. Choug was crawling closer. If he turned, he could shoot her again or shoot me.

I got up to a crouch, then I lunged at him.

He tried to grab the rail of the fire escape. He was off balance, with the gun in his hand, he couldn't save himself.

It was too late.

I saw her then, with her arms out as if she had pushed with me. That was the last time I ever saw her.

Tony screamed once during his three-story drop. It seemed to last forever.

The next thing I heard was Henry. I couldn't figure out where he came from, or how he got there so fast.

Henry was beside me clutching his chest. "I heard the gun shots, Frankie. I thought he killed you." He tried to catch his breath. There wasn't much room for him to sit on except the curb of the roof, and I was afraid he would topple over and join Tony.

I helped him lean against the large vent. He was almost in my arms. "I called the police. I didn't know. I swear that I didn't know." I was so shocked that I must have looked like I didn't believe him. "Honestly, at least, not at first."

Then Henry told me about the girls that Tony sent him, and when they were not happy, he sent them to Tony's other friends.

Vice-Cop Brian was an inside guy who could tip them off about any interest at the Police Department that Tony or the people he worked with needed to hear about. He was involved in the undertaking. He helped them get the fake documentation for working in Musicland. They were able to find who they needed, and he kept it quiet.

"Tony said that George was involved." I had to know.

"He was part of the money people and the Triads. His uncle is big in Chinatown. Not just him, Danny was part of the money side of it too." Henry was in a bad way. His voice was weak and shaky.

Tony's friends were in the lucrative business of making snuff films. They tortured and killed women, with the cameras rolling, for very sick, and very rich weirdoes. He said Danny was a big part of it. Danny was from a very wealthy family, but he had sick fantasies. He made a reputation by producing, and sometimes directing these films. Tony would joke to Henry that Danny might even be the guy that put salt on the victims' wounds and even wore a mask as a vampire. Danny wanted to make a film with Mei Ling.

I don't know much about medicine, but even I could see that Henry was in trouble. The world's oldest living pimp appeared to be having a heart attack.

I didn't know how to help him.

I also didn't know if I would have helped him, even if I'd known what to do. He knew what he was sending Alicia to. He knew, and he knew that I was looking for her.

Women were meat to Henry, Tony, Stan, and Brian and the rest of them. We didn't matter.

Was Henry better than the others? I don't think so. He lied to himself better. Was anyone who I thought they were? Choug got to the phone and called 911.

By the time the ambulance got there, Henry wasn't breathing anymore. He died with his head on my shoulder. Tony was dead; they were both gone. When the police traced everything down, they found the place out in the desert where they had been doing the filming. The empty shack that Choug and her brother had puzzled over, was their studio. They also found some bones and remains of women who were unreported missing, probably illegals. Spider and Barbazul were all that was left of the people that I knew of, that were involved, except for Brian. There was a chain of people connected to it, and the investigation continues. I will, probably, never know all of it.

Maybe I know enough, even more than enough about what happened. I can't imagine people who are ordinary enough to not be in jail or an institution, who would enjoy the dismemberment of a woman, as some kind of entertaining sexual fantasy.

The revolting thought that strikes me in the middle of anything I'm doing, is that they probably look like anyone else. I might run into one of them and not know. I guess something like knowing that there are men out there who enjoy snuff movies, makes strangers even more strange. It makes me wonder if any more of the men I've met, have a taste for that kind of evil. I've danced with some of the guys involved in that.

The part that George played sickened me. I had even felt sorry for him. That despicable creep had the nerve to court me. That's not a stranger. That's too close, and too personal. I couldn't stop crying. It was all too much, but I couldn't run from it. There was still unfinished business, lots of it. I was part of it, and I had to see it through. It would be a long time before that night would stop haunting my sleep.

CHAPTER TWENTY-SEVEN

FINAL FAREWELLS AND NEW BEGINNINGS

Owner, Sam Weintraub's funeral was well attended by the people from both of his lives. There was his respectable middle-class family, his former business associates, and a few of the people from Musicland.

Big Louie, and I went together. Sam's son delivered a heartbreaking eulogy. Sam would have been proud. It was a nice service, but it was exactly as if he had been two different men. I knew him from the other life. As we were leaving the Chapel at the end of the service, I saw a slender dark-haired woman leaving ahead of us. I'm pretty sure that it was Mei Ling. Only the family had been invited to the graveside. I didn't want to go. I had my memories, and the place in his life where I fit. Big Louie and I stopped at a local bar, and toasted Sam on his way, before Louie took me home.

Big Louie attended Filipino Henry's funeral. He was a pallbearer. He told me about it. I didn't go. All the dudes and their ladies were there according to Louie. It was a Catholic mass. When it was time to roll the casket out of the church, one of the wheels stuck. It just wouldn't move. Somebody from the attendees whispered loud enough for the whole congregation to hear, "It looks like Henry ain't ready to go yet." They laughed at the fitness of the epitaph for Filipino Henry, formerly, the World's Oldest Living Pimp. He was nearly ninety years old, when the heart attack took him.

Were we friends?

He saved my life once. I don't condone his life's work. Was he better than some, and worse than others? I hold some things against him, like Alicia. He did turn her over to be killed. When did he find out what was going on? He was involved with the murders up to his armpits. Maybe I'll never know the whole truth. I believe he will be judged by a higher authority on the subject.

After all, what do I know?

If Tony had a funeral on one mentioned, it to me. This is one judgment not hard to make. He was bad news, and we are all better off without him. I never heard of anyone, man, woman, or child express regret at his passing.

If there is justice in the hereafter, I have confidence that he will get his. I think he has karma to deal with.

If there was a funeral for Alicia, I couldn't find out about it. I hope that she was reunited with her loved ones. She and all the others; I wish them peace.

Choug had only been grazed by the bullet. She sported a bandage on her thigh when she went for her physical. She said she thought she would be safer in the Army, than hanging around with me.

Ed Wong's mother was a surprise. We had lunch at Michael's on Los Feliz.

"Frankie," she said. "Sit down. You can call me Lillian. You're just as pretty as Ed said you were." The attractive woman in a designer suit might be over fifty, but she looked like a young forty. Ed had never mentioned that his mother was a Eurasian, like me. She was a fashionable, somewhat exotic woman.

"Your son had told me a lot about you." I couldn't remember anything specific except that they were partners and that she had raised him by herself. "I wasn't prepared for how young you are." I meant it.

"Don't believe half what he told you. I'm young enough. I still get around without any help." She smiled showing me the most perfect teeth. She reminded me of Mei Ling only in the perfection of her parts.

"He said that he likes working with you. I think Mom and son teams are unusual." I had a feeling about her. "He kept saying that he thought I should check into Real Estate."

"He's never wrong." She sipped her water from the goblet. "You are the first younger woman, that he has ever wanted to hire himself. He's been uncanny in the team he has helped me put together." She studied a jade ring and didn't look at me. "I wondered if he was involved with you personally."

"No. Don't worry." I was embarrassed.

"I think you would fit in with the team. We have some good people working in our office. The ones that he recruited have been doing very well." She looked at the menu. "I don't usually, especially for lunch, but I think today I will have a glass of wine. Maybe some white wine."

"Sounds good. I'll have the Lobster Salad. I've decided to start Real Estate School, so I guess you could say that he convinced me. You don't have to worry. We are just friends."

"If you come with us, I'll reimburse your tuition when you pass your license exam." She motioned to the waiter and gave the order.

"Now there's an offer. Don't you want to know what I've been doing for a living? No references?" I was so glad that I'd worn my best Channel copy. Having learned my lesson the hard way, my perfume was all refinement and restraint.

"References? I guess I didn't tell you how much I trust my son's intuition." I watched the waiter put the glasses on the table in front of us. It's a nice restaurant, cool and full of women on a weekday. "I trust Ed's judgment," she said. "Also, I used to work in a dancehall, years ago. That's where I met Ed's father. He was killed in World War II. I had two sons; it wasn't easy. I went back to the dancehall at night, and went to school, and finally sold Real Estate in the day. When things began to go well, I got to give up my night job."

"It couldn't have been easy." I was beginning to be extremely comfortable with her. "You have at least one nice son. I haven't met his brother, but Ed is special. You must be very proud. Let's make a toast to doing well."

I lifted my glass, and she clinked hers against mine.

"Now tell me about you and Ed. He won't answer anything I ask him."

I could feel my ears turning red. That's a thing typical of a redhead. "We are just friends, like I said. I've known him for about a year, and I always look forward to talking to him. That's the truth." Now my ears were burning.

"You haven't even gone out for coffee?" She arched her eyebrows and made me laugh. She really knew. I couldn't fool her; she was one of us.

"Not even!" My ears were really red. "I think he asked me once, and something else happened. I think I would have, but he didn't push it." This was his mother. How embarrassing. "I think he's shy."

It was her turn to laugh. "I don't think so. Anyway, that will make things easier when you come to work in the office. No complications to begin with. I like that." She grinned from ear to ear. "Could be that he's even smarter than I thought. I think you're going to spice things up around here, Frankie. Maybe by this time next year, you'll be the top salesperson."

Maybe Ed was right. It looked like it could be fun to work with Ed and his mom. I would be with people that I didn't need to hide anything from. It could work out. Just hearing that, made me feel good. The food was great, and I ate everything, but the tablecloth. I noticed that Lillian wasn't too dainty to enjoy a good feed either. I looked for, and found lots of things about her, that made me think of Ed. This was the best job interview, I'd ever had. I couldn't wait to find out if I could work this out. There was a lot more potential money in Real Estate, than the dancehall, and bigger challenges.

I looked at my watch.

"Please forgive me. I didn't realize it was so late. I really enjoyed meeting you, but I have an appointment. Thank you, Lillian." I held out my hand, and she held it in both of hers. I had the feeling that she wanted to hug me.

"Call me next week, and I'll show you the office, and some of our listings. Promise?"

"You bet. I can't wait!" I meant it. However, I had an appointment with Adriana.

"Frankie, in my office you won't date any clients. It's a rule, and no fringies." She smiled the most charming smile at me. I would have been offended if anyone else had said that.

I had a sudden picture in my mind of what she must have looked like at my age. I'll bet she was a top girl. I just smiled back and waved. It wasn't going to be easy to work with someone who knew so much, but I didn't think it would be impossible.

"A sensible rule," I said. "I'll call you Sunday at the office, and then maybe you can make some time for me next week." By the end of the lunch, I was so impressed with her, that I was glad that Ed had pushed me to this meeting. I walked out of the restaurant thinking that Real Estate could be just the thing for me. I had already signed up for a License class. It felt like my life had taken a dip and turn in a different direction. It felt good.

CHAPTER TWENTY-EIGHT

MOVING ON

Adriana and Teji were waiting for me. The cats looked like they hadn't moved, since I'd been there the last time.

"Frankie, how are things going? I invited Teji to sit in." She motioned to her sidekick who was still resplendent in turban and beads.

He was now sporting a beard. Cute, very cute, I thought.

"To tell the truth, I'm a little confused. Tony's dead. We found out about Henry, and the other guys. We know about the snuff films. Everything is solved. Right?" I wanted answers, and I wanted an end to the persistent perfumed guest at my place.

"Sit down, we'll do a little reading and decide what to do next." Adriana spread the cards, while I lifted one cat off a chair to make myself comfortable. He came right back into my lap. Adriana did have a different look, since she'd given up makeup. I loved her flowing caftan, beads, and head band. Her hair was reaching her waist. She looked like an ad for healthy hair, except for the bare feet. The last time I saw her she'd been wearing sandals, now she just had rings and bells, I swear it, on her toes. Her feet were black on the bottom, which showed when she walked.

The cards were in a pattern in front of me. The two of them conferred. I was the wise fool. I was also the fair queen. They huddled.

"It's fairly obvious. She's earthbound."

"Yeah," Teji added, "We're going to have to talk her out of it." They both looked serious. I would have laughed, but they were serious. It would have offended them. The truth was I didn't like the sound of it.

"What do you mean? What is earthbound?" I felt a certain panic. The whole thing was over. Linda would go now, wouldn't she?

"You need to have another séance. Linda likes the arrangement between the two of you. She doesn't want to leave. She isn't going to the light."

"She likes the arrangement? What arrangement? I haven't agreed to anything." I know it sounded churlish, but hell, she wasn't even paying rent.

"We're going to have to convince her that it's all over and time to go on." Teji looked serious. "Sometimes entities like it here. They become earthbound, and the longer they stay, the harder it is to convince them that it is better to go on to the light."

They had to be kidding.

After all this, I now had to find a way to evict a ghost. It was too much. After all I'd done for her. The ludicrous situation of my having a non-paying, invisible roommate with a taste for bad perfume, and an unhealthy interest in my sex life, was more than I was ready to cope with. I agreed to another séance. I would do anything; anything within reason to get rid of her. This time I would remember the dip; which gave me a great idea.

This time I was ready. Choug had helped me decorate my little house, and it was festive. I had invited as many of the one hundred beautiful girls as I thought would come. I thought that most of them would, but you can never tell. I wondered what they would think at the Musicland if everyone took the night off.

Actually, they were not taking the whole night off in the strictest sense of the word. They were invited for seven, and they would be free to go to work by nine, if all went well. Well, at least most of them. A few special people would stay for the second event planned for later.

They began arriving. First Helen, in a beautiful gown of dark wine velvet. She looked lovely. She had a creamy quality to her complexion, that I have never noticed anyone else having exactly the same. She was grumpy, but she brought a covered buffet dish that smelled delicious and was unpronounceable Greek. She wasn't a big fan of Annie's, but she brought a gift wrapped up, so that I knew that the spirit of the thing was pulling her along.

Two of the Latina women showed up with Choug. She would be going off to basic training in another week. One of the Latinas was an illegal. The new owner said that he wasn't going to hire any more, but sometimes, like this one for instance, he was a little soft. Especially when they had almost real I.D. Choug and the Latinas brought some packages wrapped too, and food so they disappeared into the kitchen while I got the door.

It was Beverly. I loved the black leather. Her skirt was two squares of material laced up the sides, same for the top, mesh hose and boots. Perfect for a baby shower. Big Bev had a large pink package adorned with a rattle. She also brought something to eat. I was hoping that it was from our home planet.

I didn't have time to speculate on this, because Adriana was at the door with Teji, and the guest of honor. Annie couldn't have been more surprised. It was, of course, a baby shower with at least twenty of the one hundred beautiful girls showing up to celebrate.

The séance would be later after the big crowd left.

Almost everyone brought something. This time I had enough dip, and lots of other things for a pot-luck buffet.

Annie was very quiet, that is, until she started opening the presents. Her little one was going to be the best dressed baby in town. I hoped that it would be a girl. The gifts were heavily weighted on the pink side.

Adriana, being a professional psychic, had reassured everyone that it would be a girl.

I saw Annie in the midst of the wrappers, all glowing and pretty. She didn't look pathetic or like a victim. I came close to praying that everything would work out for her.

Then we brought out the main present, a crib. She cried. The party broke up. It was about nine-thirty, and most of the people went on to work.

Annie had already said her good-byes to the Musicland and wanted to stay for the last half of the evening.

I asked Adriana, what she thought of Annie staying.

"I don't think it will hurt. Séances aren't especially bad for pregnancy unless she freaks." Adriana gave Annie an appraising look.

My friend looked so happy, and the most contented I'd ever seen. I had a feeling that it would take a lot more than a whiff of Linda's rotten perfume to make her freak.

Teji interrupted. "There's the possession thing. There's always the possibility of attracting an undesirable disincarnate spirit."

"I want to get this over with." Greek Helen had already cleared the table, and set the chairs in a circle. "I don't mind this little game, but it is getting late, and I have other things to think about."

"My, my," I said. "Don't get your undies in a twist. What about those disincarnate whatchamacallits, Adriana?" I wanted to know.

"We'll do the circle of light. Not to worry."

She smiled and Teji shook his head and groaned.

"Well, we are just about ready, I just want to stack the rest of these dishes in the dishwasher." Bev was helping with the tidying up. She never struck me as the domestic type before, but you never know. Right?

"You sure had a lot of dip, Frankie. What do you want to do with what's left over?"

"We'll teleport it to Mars. Get over here, or you guys can get on with it without me." Helen's patience, always slender, was obviously worn thinner, maybe at the breaking point.

"Come and sit down." I motioned everybody to the table. Then, I went around turning out the lights. We were in a similar arrangement as the first time. Adriana began with her little prayer for protection. She surrounded us in light. I could hear Choug's rosary.

Again, we were holding hands in a circle. It had only been a few weeks since the first séance and now we were repeating that strange experience. This time Annie sat next to me. I squeezed her hand and got squeezed back.

Teji began to breathe in, and out with a hiss like a tire losing air. We were surprised by the male voice.

"Good evening, ladies." The smell of a cigar, a good cigar filled the room. I knew who it was. "I told you I would let you know, Frankie. Goodbye." He was gone and Teji was breathing evenly.

Then the woman's voice spoke while his lips moved.

"Thanks, Frankie. Tony can't hurt anyone else now. Some of the others are with me."

"Which others?" I blurted it out before I realized what I was saying.

"Val is here and Alicia. They want to thank you too. We are all here."

Adriana spoke, "Can you see the light, Linda? Tell me if you can see the light."

We all paused waiting for the response.

"I can, in the distance. I don't want to go. I don't have to, do I?"

"Yes," Adriana was firm. "Yes, you must all turn to the light."

"I'm not ready." It was definitely not Teji's voice. "I like baseball." The voice giggled.

"Go to the light. Is everyone turning to the light, Linda?" Adriana refused to let Linda ruffle her. "Go with our love. We all want you to go. Tell the others. Are they going?"

The voice sounded farther away than across the table. "Yes," she said, "yes, we are all going." The perfume that had been such a presence in the room faded in intensity, and then disappeared.

It was over.

The lights came on, we said a small prayer together for all of them, the victims that no one knew about, and those whose lives had touched ours. Then people began leaving. Annie and her sister, who looked like a younger version of Annie. Greek Helen with a new man. She hadn't told anyone about him. He looked older and had a great looking bald head.

Adriana and Teji said they were heading for Height Ashbury, someplace in San Francisco. They invited me to come and visit.

I said maybe next summer.

They wanted to tell me about where they were staying. They had a loft that they were going to share with some other people. It was going to be a very hip gathering. They were planning some Love-Ins. They said that people were starting to call this summer, the summer of love. They wanted to do more about protesting the Viet Nam war. Teji had burned his draft card.

I wished them well. Then they were gone.

Big Bev had something she wanted to tell me. "I know about Brian. He's being hauled in front of a Grand Jury. I think that they have him on perjury, and about a dozen other charges. I know he was somehow involved, the police questioned me, but I didn't know anything before. He never let me know. He just wanted to be around in case something came out. He thought I would tell him." She looked down at her feet. "I'm sorry that I wasn't paying better attention. Maybe I could have saved some . . ."

She couldn't finish. It wasn't her fault.

"You did nothing wrong. I danced with George, and he was part of it. Neither one of us would have had anything to do with those jerks if we'd known anything at all." I put my hand on her shoulder. "Are we still buds?"

She smiled. "We shall rise above it."

I walked her out to the front where a guy on a motorcycle was waiting for her. "Brian is not getting away with it whatever his part was. There's an on-going investigation and he may not know how much they know."

I said good-by and waved them off.

Before I turned off the lights and went to bed, I took a good look at my little house. Can you believe that was the only party that I had ever thrown there? I was moving out at the end of the month.

For lots of reasons.

I would no longer be over the hill from Dodger Stadium, and Chavez Ravine. I won't say that being haunted by the ghost of a murdered dancehall companion didn't have something to do with it, but I was ready for all the changes that were taking place.

There were a couple of things I wanted to mention. For one thing, Lonesome George disappeared. I don't think he has ever been found. I don't like to imagine that he might turn up one day, so I'm glad to hear that it is an ongoing investigation. So many of the people I'd known were gone.

I went to Real Estate School and got my license. I sold my first listing, a large one, to, of all people, Little Louie, who took over Henry's stable, and ended up with a couple of elderly ladies of the night that he didn't know what to do with. I guess he really intends to keep them as part of the family. Anyway, it was a very good first sale, and the commission plus the sale of some of my trinkets, including the diamond, means that I could invest in something for myself. I have an offer pending on a four unit building in Silverlake by the reservoir. I'm still working at Musicland for a while. Commissions are not to be counted on, at least, in the beginning.

None of the romances worked out. Maybe that's why I had the dream the other night. I keep thinking about it. Now that I'm getting closer to leaving Musicland, as soon as I'm successful at Real Estate, maybe it is nostalgia.

Also, I've had a small speaking part in a movie recently. Small, but now I have a real credit. So, about the dream . . .

I dreamed that I was a very old woman, old and bent, leaning on a cane. I was dressed up, in a silver satin and lace dress, very formal. Someone was guiding me down a reception line with their hand on my elbow. I looked down the line, and I could see men in tuxedos on both sides of me. As I came toward them, they shook my hand and some of them kissed my hand, and others kissed my cheek. They said things to me like, "I always remembered, I never forgot you," or I've always loved you," or "I loved you then, and I love you now. Just the same." I noticed that they were old too, but they were all men that I had cared about, men that I had shared something with. They were not all lovers, a few of them were, but most of them were men that I had danced with, or had a brief crush on, and some I'd admired, but never even talked very much with. Some were old friends, like Sam.

I was touched and very happy because they were all the men I've ever loved. Many were people like Sam that I never had anything romantic with, just people that had touched my life in some way, and that I had been touched by.

There was James who danced with me and turned me on. There was Narin, who spoke to me for two hours, and carried the fantasy with him.

I went down the line remembering the moments of my life. These moments that were important because they were the sum, the total of my experience of love and I understood.

Well, wouldn't you know that it would take a dance hall girl to figure out the meaning of life? I think the dream was saying that all the moments of our life are what counts. Nothing else matters as much as the minute by minute, process of loving. I will never forget 1967 and the Summer of Love. It was the summer of love and murder. We learned some things about the way people judge other people. It was a good lesson.

What's important are those times that we touch, the connections we have with each other. Here we are checked in and sitting on the line in the great dancehall of life. We keep expecting something wonderful to happen, while we are clocked in for all those little bits of the real thing.

I lay there in the dark savoring this wonderful dream, and I realized what a great gift it was.

Now I know that love is never wasted.

Never.

I still believe in love and the power it has in our lives.

As a woman who has counted tickets so many times and totaled up the minutes, I know and will never forget, that all the minutes count.

www.ingramcontent.com/pod-product-compliance
Lightning Source LLC
Chambersburg PA
CBHW050025040726
47599CB00015B/1535